Beneath the Glass

Glass

A Novel

by

A L Manley

Ink-Twenty

BENEATH THE GLASS

This is a work of fiction. Names, characters, places, and incidents are products of the author's imagination or are used fictitiously. Any resemblance to actual persons, living or dead, is purely coincidental.

Ink-Twenty

ISBN: 9798993554457

Nous ne voyons pas les choses comme elles sont,

nous les voyons comme nous sommes.

— Anaïs Nin

(We don't see things as they are, we see them as we are.)

🜁 Air – Intellect, communication, breath, and liberation

▽ Water – Emotion, fluidity, intuition, and healing

△ Fire – Passion, transformation, energy, and desire

▽ Earth – Stability, grounding, sensuality, and physicality

Addison frequented her coffee shop, **The Gilded Bean,** not necessarily to manage it, but because it was a place to work outside the house. Always at the same table, with her laptop, headphones, and favorite caffeine fix. Some days she sat for hours, working intently, barely noticing anyone coming or going—just the faint sounds of people moving about, coffee grinding, and the occasional clink of ceramic cups. Other days she lingered just long enough to finish what she was working on, more attuned to her surroundings. On those days, she people-watched, pretending to be oblivious to everything around her.

It was the end of September—a typical autumn day with a cool, welcoming breeze after a sweltering summer that had seemed endless. On this particular day, as she settled in for her caffeine fix, she noticed an attractive woman of medium height, short dark hair, and stylish glasses reading a book without its dust cover. The woman would read a bit, turn a page, take a sip of coffee. Whatever she was reading must have been riveting; she flipped through the pages at an impressive speed.

It made Addison curious. Without the dust cover, she couldn't read the title on the book's spine. Now overly intrigued, she wondered what to do. Sitting there, sipping coffee that had long since gone lukewarm, she had an idea: she would get up, order another coffee, and casually wander close enough to catch a glimpse of the book's binder while waiting for her drink.

Pushing back her chair, she formulated her plan. As she strolled to the counter and placed her order, the barista reminded her that refills were free. Lost in thought, she had completely forgotten.

The barista's comment must have been loud enough to catch the book reader's attention, because for the first time she paused and looked up. Their eyes met. Addison smiled. The woman returned the gesture.

Now standing there, feeling suddenly awkward, Addison hesitated. Should she say something—try to strike up a casual conversation in hopes the woman might reveal the book's title or subject?

All the while, a voice in her head nagged, *Why does this even matter so damn much?*
Without waiting for an answer, she blurted, "Hi, that looks like a very interesting book."

"Oh, it's a great page-turner," the book lady replied.

Thinking of herself as a ditz sometimes, Addison let a pregnant pause hang between them, missing the chance to ask the title. She glanced down as the woman laid the book open, pages down—and saw a familiar name: *Nin*.

"I hope you're reading my favorite," said Addison.

The woman looked down at the book, then back at her. "Are you familiar with the author?"

"I am."

"Have you read other books by her?" she asked.

Addison replied, "Other books as well as a film adaptation of one of them."

"A movie?"

"Yes—a nicely crafted cinematic film made in Paris," Addison responded, suddenly feeling warm and tingling.

She sat silent, as if trying to formulate a sentence. Her pause stretched long enough that Addison felt she needed to rescue her.

"Wait—let me get my phone. I'll show it to you."

Just as Addison turned to walk away, the barista called her name.

"Addison, your cappuccino."

"Thanks, Emily," she said, turning to retrieve her drink.

Walking back to the table, she closed her laptop, set down her drink, and grabbed her phone. As she headed toward the woman's table, Addison noticed she was already walking over, drink in hand. She sat opposite, and Addison resumed her seat. Pulling up the page on her phone, she handed it across. The woman's eyes glistened; her grin was ear to ear.

"Oh my, this is the book I'm reading. Wow!"

"Yes, it's a great read—with all the details the film only implies. Not explicit, but after reading and then watching, the implications are quite clear—and carnal," Addison said.

"You don't say," replied the book lady, clearly preoccupied with the information on the phone.

"If you like, I can text the site to you."

"Yes, that would be marvelous!" she said, extending her hand to return Addison's phone.

Taking it, Addison quickly moved to text mode. "What's your number?"

She called the number out slowly and precisely. The text came through immediately.

"Yes, there it is! Oh—by the way, my name is Barbara Ann. Everyone calls me B.A."

While typing her name into the contact info, Addison said her own name, but B.A. interrupted, repeating what she'd heard the barista say. "Addison."

"Yes, that's correct."

"What a lovely name. Is it Irish?"

"No, it's English. My grandmother used to spell it with a *y* —I prefer the *i*. My father, her son, is Adam." She spoke quickly, thinking no one cared what her dad's name was.

She took a few sips of coffee while B.A. was engrossed with the site. Watching people come and go, Addison noticed B.A. was no longer looking at the phone but at her —specifically, at her blouse. Addison looked down to discover that a strategic button had popped loose, exposing a deep line of cleavage and lace. She didn't flinch or attempt to fix it. Addison liked the view—and B.A. was undoubtedly enjoying it.

B.A. continued her unvarnished glances. "Addison, are you married?"

"No. I'm divorced—and more recently widowed," she replied.

"Oh no, I'm so sorry," B.A. said quickly.

"Which one—the divorce or the passing?" Addison retorted.

B.A. was solemn for a moment, then smiled. "You've got jokes!"

They both laughed, the bonding between them easy and natural. There was no need to ask if she were married—the rock on her left hand said it all.

"I'm glad we're sitting away from the window."

"Why's that?" B.A. asked.

"That rock—with all that glitter—is blinding."

She seemed subdued by the mention of her wedding ring, which Addison later learned was a full three carats. Not sure how to bring the moment back to life, Addison decided to change the subject.

"B.A., are you from here? Or would I be correct in presuming you're from someplace else?"

"Yes, you are correct, Addie—I'm not from here."

"North?" Addison asked.

"Yes, from up north. And so is my husband. He's Monty, by the way. I certainly hope you'll consider meeting him."

And somehow, that actually felt like a natural thing to take place.

The two ladies indulged in conversation for another hour. When Addison realized how time had slipped by, she needed to get back for a conference call. They embraced as they said their goodbyes, promising to have lunch soon—within the week, they each vowed.

⁂

Over the next several weeks, B.A. met Addison regularly at the coffee shop. They sat at the same table, ordered their usuals, and talked about everything. As time went on, their conversations began to center more around carnal erotica. Addison held back on some topics, not wanting B.A. to get the wrong impression. They talked about blowjobs, men's erogenous zones, and how each liked to turn their men on and tease them before coitus. Some days, it was as if they lived in their own cozy world. Secrets were shared by both —trials, tribulations, and happy memories.

During one of their earlier meetings, B.A. had shared a photo of Monty. He was a dashing man, dressed in what appeared to be a tailor-made suit, clean-shaven with mixed gray hair. B.A. explained that he was older by ten years, which by Addison's calculations made Monty about three years older than she. Addison hadn't given him much thought since her focus was on her new friend—someone she liked and, admiringly, wanted to be closer to. Closer as in kissing her, sucking her nice-sized breasts, and parting her vulva to lick her nub to ecstasy. And a few other things she would think about doing to B.A. while she masturbated before going to sleep.

One thing was certain: Addison was sleeping better after her nightly orgasms—awakening refreshed and rested. During her daydreams of B.A., she often wondered how to open the door without offending her.

One day, B.A. showed up wearing a turtleneck sweater that showcased the ampleness of her breasts. The white sweater was made of thin material, and her bra had no padding, allowing a hint of nipple and the hue of her areola to show. It was a challenge for Addison not to stare. It threw her timing off so much that she had trouble finishing a thought. B.A. did most of the talking that day.

To Addison's surprise, her friend didn't seem to notice her distraction. B.A. was on a roll, revealing much about Monty. Addison expected her to pop the question at any moment about having dinner with them. She noticed B.A. checking her phone frequently but thought nothing of it. They had been at the shop for almost thirty minutes when B.A.'s phone buzzed. She read the text and smiled, then immediately went back to talking about her husband and the things he enjoyed in his spare time.

B.A. sat with her back to the door. The shop was unusually busy that day. As she continued describing how great Monty was, Addison noticed through the glass door a striking, mature man approaching. He walked in, looking around, paused, and then joined the line forming at the counter. Addison didn't give it much thought and turned her attention back to B.A., who was still talking about her husband's success as an engineer.

Engrossed in her friend's story, she forgot about the attractive man who had entered. When she glanced back toward the counter, he was gone. Switching her focus back to the table, Addison suddenly realized that the striking man was now pulling out the empty chair beside her, leaning in to kiss B.A. on the lips.

B.A. chuckled with delight, greeting her husband. Introductions were made—polite, civilized—but beneath it, Addison sensed an undercurrent swelling fast. She extended her hand as she was introduced. Monty graciously took it, holding it as he leaned in to kiss her cheeks in European fashion. She remained composed and continental on the exterior, but her insides were at a boil.

Was she being premature in her assessment? Her instincts were rarely off. She knew this man would, at some point in the future, have his hard cock inside her. Which also meant B.A.'s beautiful breasts would be in her mouth before it was all said and done.

Addison forced herself to think of abstract, meaningless things about her work as an editor to keep her pheromones in check. If she was wrong in her assumption, this could go very wrong. She decided to be acquiescent until intentions were clear—and even then, maybe a little submissive. She absolutely felt that vibe. Her senses told her it would all be carnally delicious and quite civilized. He had that kind of sexual magnetism—his voice, the way he carried himself.

They sat and became better acquainted. No discussion of sex or erotica—just harmless conversation about the lives of three people who shared many experiences.

*⁎⁎

Dinner, after much discussion and texting back and forth between the three, was settled upon at the home of Monty and B.A. Then came the meshing of schedules that went on for several days, each trying to get a date sooner than two weeks away. After much consternation on Monty's part—he was the one with business commitments—a date two weeks out was finally set, after a week and a half had already passed.

B.A., having mixed emotions, was ready to blurt out to Addie how excited she'd become about her—about the three of them. Yet she was happy for the time to critique the house, order fresh flowers, schedule grocery deliveries, and prepare for the big weekend. She made a note to find the perfect wine, an after-dinner apéritif, and to discuss with Monty what he wanted to cook.

Monty, as usual, was impatient. He liked what B.A. had found—the perfect person. She fit exactly as they had fantasized during lovemaking. It couldn't have been more perfect for him: a wife who enjoyed sharing sex, visiting nude clubs when she traveled with him on business, taking trips to Vegas, and choosing their companions for the evening. To his surprise, she would often choose women, though once in a while he wanted her to select a man.

They had never invited anyone to the country house before. It had been their haven from the city, where they spent weekends unwinding. When B.A. suggested the country house, Monty was overjoyed. Her asking made it even more exciting, the endless possibilities spinning through his mind. With the house a little over an hour away, he told her he'd worry about Addison's return trip after dark—and wanted her to be able to enjoy at least a glass of wine with dinner.

During a three-way call one evening to finalize dinner plans, B.A., at the country house, without hesitation—and more instructing than asking—told Addison she should bring some things and plan to sleep in one of the three guest rooms. "More than enough room," she gushed. Monty eagerly agreed from his office desk while wrapping up a hectic day.

*
**

When the call ended, Monty's excitement got the best of him. The thought of her sleeping in their home—her bronzed body between the sheets or her presence in one of the showers—made him ache with desire. When Addie agreed that it was a good idea, the sensation intensified. With B.A. at the country house and himself in the city for the next couple of nights, he got up, locked his office door, turned off the overhead lights, left the desk lamp on, and loosened his clothes.

His imagination took over. He pictured her with them, his wife watching as the intimacy unfolded. He could hear her soft sounds of pleasure, feel her responding, see her offering herself without hesitation. The closeness, the heat, the shared breath of the moment pulled him deeper into the fantasy. He breathed heavily, lost in it, wanting to taste her, to feel her respond completely.

The tension built, his thoughts narrowing to sensation alone. He focused on the image of her surrender, the moment cresting beyond restraint. When release finally came, it was overwhelming, leaving him momentarily unmoored.

When it subsided, Monty looked down—evidence of his distraction scattered on his trousers, his chair, the floor. He hadn't lost himself like that since college.

He wondered if Addison could actually be that erotic in real life. He found her strikingly beautiful—elegant, poised— the day he met her at The Gilded Bean. He'd been pleasantly surprised to learn she was the owner of the famous coffee shop. Monty felt mesmerized by this woman his wife had brought into their lives. Sharing a meal and then sharing himself would be something special. He wanted to make it a weekend worthy of her time.

Finding a dry-cleaning bag in his closet along with a fresh shirt, Monty cleaned up in his private bathroom. Once dressed, he picked up his cell and sent a text to an old friend and business colleague. Grabbing his case and keys, turning off the desk lamp, Monty walked to his Benz wagon, deep in thought about the possibilities of the weekend at the country house.

His phone buzzed—an incoming text. He opened it before putting the car in drive.

A resounding *yes* was the response.

✲✲

Addie was a ball of excitement. During the texting and phone calls with Monty and B.A., she could feel her body responding. One evening, when a message from Monty popped up, she closed her laptop, pushed her work aside, and let herself drift—touching herself, following the familiar rhythm of desire, her breath quickening as sensation took over.

Where she usually thought about B.A., this time her thoughts stayed with Monty. She imagined him with a physical presence that felt undeniable, intimate, consuming. In her mind she explored him slowly, deliberately, lingering in the details, letting the fantasy deepen until it filled her completely.

The intensity built. She loved the power of arousal, the way anticipation alone could make her ache, the way desire sharpened when she gave herself over to it. Wanting to be taken, to be claimed, she moved to her bedroom, bent over the edge of the bed, and surrendered to the feeling she was chasing—pushing herself harder, faster, exactly as she wanted him to do.

She imagined his hands on her, guiding her movements, urging her on. The sensation mounted until it overtook her completely, her body tightening, her voice breaking as release tore through her. She collapsed onto the bed, breathless, spent, her body still trembling in the aftermath.

She wanted both of them—wanted to bring B.A. pleasure, wanted Monty with her while B.A. watched. The image lingered: shared desire, unspoken permission, a charged intimacy that left nothing neutral.

If they were all on the same page, the weekend at the country house would be one to remember.

△ ▽ ▽ △

The Saturday drive from the city took Addie over a span bridge with a toll on the other side of the water. Her Benz cruised smoothly through traffic. She had no music playing as she talked aloud to herself.

Her first admission was that she was nervous. Her anxiety then turned to her outfit. *Jeans? What was I thinking?* A crew-neck two-piece sweater set in soft beige. Do I look too prim and proper to be heading to someone's estate to cross a few very deliberate lines with a woman and her sexy husband?

Her hair was in an up-do, held together with a tortoiseshell bear claw. Peeking in the rearview mirror, she impulsively snatched it out, letting her hair cascade down her back and over one shoulder. Panicking for no apparent reason, she reached blindly over the console into her brown leather tote for a brush. Brushing only made it worse.

Balancing her attention between the bridge highway and the mirror made her want to turn around and go home. Her thoughts were all over the place. Was she ready for what would come next? Could she handle not being first string? After all, B.A. would always be first—as the wife. *Right?*

But the excitement took over. She'd spent a small fortune on matching thong panties and bra, a nightgown she probably wouldn't wear—or maybe just to get coffee in the morning. *Morning!* Hell, this could all go wrong and she'd be heading back across this bridge in a couple of hours. Either one of them could back out—she was certainly thinking about it. But what if... what if this was exactly what she'd sensed at the coffee shop?

Her first impression of Monty—so much swag, confidence. How would she handle B.A. if she and Monty connected during those moments? She'd read about couples who experimented then found what they thought was the perfect match—until it all went sideways because one of the spouses fell in love.

"Oh, good grief!" she yelled at seemingly nothing on the hood of her car.

As she emerged from the second tunnel and rose onto the final bridge—more than halfway across to Shore East—she could see the tall pines in the distance, the leaves changing color, the highway slithering between them like an endless serpent.

Traffic was heavier than she anticipated. She settled in, engaged cruise control for the remaining hour-and-fifty-minute drive. Still no music; her mind wandered over the possibilities of what could—or could not—happen. She knew if this was all in her imagination, she'd have to hightail it out if things went south.

Emerged in thought, her GPS began to prompt her for an exit. Snapping to alert, she followed the directions past a national-chain grocer, through a quaint town, then a small strip shopping center. The road became a two-lane highway. On the left stood a road marked by an elaborate sign:

Private Property — Cameras in Use.

The sign wasn't painted but embossed in brass with a black background and a floodlight, she assumed, to illuminate it at night. *This is the sign B.A. spoke of.*

She turned onto the road, driving slowly for about a quarter mile until she reached tall wrought-iron gates anchored by two large brick pillars, fencing stretching outward as far as the eye could see.

As she slowed to a stop, she noticed a black pedestal with a speaker box level with her window. Pressing the red button, she heard a familiar voice sing out:

"Addie, you made it!"

The tall wrought-iron gates began to swing inward. She waited for them to fully open before proceeding. About a quarter mile in, Addison followed the winding road until she saw a large brick house with smaller buildings off to the left and, to the right, a cove with a dock jutting over a marsh and a boathouse at the end.

She continued on the asphalt drive to the front of the house, which was graveled. As she approached the large brick Georgian with its boxy shape and endless rows of windows, she saw B.A. standing beneath a portico, waiting to greet her.

When she pulled up, B.A. motioned for her to follow the path to the left side of the house toward the garage and parking. She drove around as instructed to a multi-car garage, parked, and got out. Opening the trunk, she pulled out her duffel. As she turned, she was met by Monty, who took her bag and gave her a quick embrace.

"Welcome to our humble abode," he said.

"Thanks for having me. I've been looking forward to it."

Right away, Addie noticed how immaculate the grounds were. *They must have a dedicated grounds crew,* she thought. Through the garage windows she could see B.A.'s red two-seater, Monty's full-size SUV, and the rear of a white car she didn't recognize. Two bays were empty.

The gravel turned into a brick pathway lined with ligustrums and low hedges. Beyond the hedges were small ornamental trees, their leaves turning from green to orange. The contrast of the fallen leaves against the grass painted a perfect autumn picture.

The sun hung low, casting long shadows from the roofline and chimneys. The sight slowed Addie's pace until Monty asked if she was all right. Snapping out of her nature trance, she smiled and assured him she was fine, complimenting the house and the grounds.

They walked up the steps and entered through a mudroom. Stainless-steel, front-load washer and dryer units sat on a long surface with drawers beneath. One wall had hooks for coats; beneath it was a long bench for sitting while removing shoes. The house had a *no-shoes* rule, clearly stated on a custom-mounted mat and framed picture. She sat, and Monty sat beside her as they slipped off their shoes. An awkward silence fell between them—until suddenly, B.A. burst into the room, making a beeline for

Addie, her arms open wide. She embraced Addie, who was still seated.

Addison greeted her warmly. Monty donned an apron and went to finish the meal while B.A. began a tour of the house.

Moving through the kitchen, Addison noticed the stonework where the recessed multi-burner range top looked familiar. The countertops were thick and lustrous, the double ovens and French-door refrigerator recessed neatly into the walls. The island was the main focal point, with triple sinks and massive counter space opposite the range. On the other side were six leather-upholstered seats perched on tall wooden legs with footrests. *Chairs on stilts,* she thought.

In the far corner sat a bistro set made of white wood with red gingham covers. The walls were lined with warm-toned cabinets that pulled gold and red flecks from the granite. Overhead lights hung from wooden beams that blended effortlessly with the cabinetry and hardwood floors. The windows were bare—large, bright, and welcoming—letting ample light fill the room.

In another corner, a three-pillow upholstered sofa in gold sat beside a high-back chair covered in red gingham, both facing a fireplace. The cozy corner included two wooden end tables with matching red lamps and cream-colored shades, adding warmth to the granite and high ceilings.

Moving on, they passed a wide doorway leading to a formal dining room. Three sections of glass-paned doors fronted a china cabinet that sat on a multi-drawer buffet. The glass gleamed, reflecting the polished dishes behind it. The table held a long, low floral centerpiece stretching across the eight-seater table. Everything was wood—except for a glass-and-brass, two-tier serving table on wheels.

A floor-to-ceiling window, bare of curtains, allowed sunlight to sparkle through the chandelier. The effect gave the room an open, almost airy elegance. As they walked through, the thick dining room rug gave way to hardwood, stepping down slightly into the living room at the front of the house.

The spaces were separated by a wide foyer with a massive round table centered beneath a carved wooden statue. On one side stood the formal living area—a traditional sofa with four matching upholstered chairs, glass-and-wood end tables, and a massive coffee table anchoring the room. A raised fireplace and mantel created a stately focal point.

The room itself was painted a bright yellow, with two floor-to-ceiling windows dressed in balloon valances that matched the furniture's cream and navy hues. A patterned area rug centered the grouping of sofa and chairs.

Across the foyer stood a baby grand piano, gleaming black with its lid half-open. The room held two yellow settees trimmed in navy piping and three high-back chairs patterned with musical notes.

"Oh my, who's the pianist?" Addison asked.

"I am," B.A. replied. "I've played since I was nine. I used to hate piano practice, but once I got older, it helped me relax."

"You'll have to play something before I go. Would you?"

"Yes, of course. We're hoping you'll stay through Sunday, if that works for your schedule?"

"Sunday?"

"Yes—we're taking the boat out tomorrow, and we hope you'll join us…"

Before B.A. could finish, Monty popped his head in, wearing a red bibbed apron. From the hallway beside the stairs, he called out, "Addison, do you like Brussels sprouts? B.A. isn't a fan, but I didn't want to grill too many if it's just me eating them."

"Yes, Monty, I'm a fan of Brussels sprouts. Grill away!" she laughed.

Once Monty disappeared back down the hall, B.A. led Addison down a corridor opposite the staircase. A door opened into another large room with wood-paneled walls. One wall—opposite a large window—held a recessed bookcase. Both window and bookcase were floor-to-ceiling.

The room was unmistakably Monty's. A large wooden desk with dual monitors, keyboard, and a familiar Apple laptop sat beside a gooseneck lamp. Near the massive window was a drafting table with a swing-arm lamp and tall wooden drawers topped with T-squares and rulers of every size.

The room's rug anchored a four-pillow leather sofa and two leather wingback chairs with brass tacking. Beyond the sitting area was a private door. B.A. noted that this room had its own commode, shower, and small refrigerator.

As they ascended the front staircase, Monty appeared again at the bottom, calling up, "Dinner in twenty! I'll not add the black truffles until I see your beautiful faces. And Addison, I put your duffel at the top of the rear stairs. B.A.—let Addison choose her room!"

With that, he vanished again.

At the top of the stairs, a wide landing opened into a great square space. The rear stairs began at the opposite end. A large round rug—though the area itself was square—left a border of hardwood showing, like lace trim, giving the space a cozy elegance.

Sconces lined the walls, sending light upward toward the high ceiling, while recessed lights above cast a gentle glow downward. Medium-sized oil paintings of various subjects hung along the hallway.

B.A. opened doors as she described the themes of the four ensuite bedrooms. At the rear, nearest the back stairs, a set of double doors marked what Addison assumed was the primary suite.

There was the *Hunt Room*, with a hunter-green motif and hound-dog prints, plaid comforter, and matching drapes. The bath carried the same green-and-white palette, with a separate water closet, twin basins, and a shower fitted with both rain and handheld heads.

Another bedroom followed the same color scheme—hunter green, but no hounds. Then came the *Gingham Room*, red and white, with a matching bath. Finally, across from the double doors, was a room done in *French Blue Toile*. The soft white walls and large double windows were dressed with valances and blackout drapes that matched the bedding: European shams, neck rolls, and square pillows in assorted sizes.

The high four-poster bed stood proudly at the center. The bath offered a larger shower with a stone seat, two basins on a long counter, and towel shelves stacked neatly with

French-blue linens. The water closet was tucked separately behind its own door.

"This," Addison said to B.A., "is the room."

B.A. smiled. "Perfect choice."

She left Addison to unpack and get settled. Addie unpacked a little—not wanting to unpack too much, just in case. She decided to leave her toiletries in the bag.

She headed downstairs to the kitchen, where she found Monty and B.A., both with wine glasses in hand. An empty glass sat on the counter, waiting. As Addison entered, B.A. raised the bottle, eyebrows lifted in question. Addison nodded yes.

B.A. poured generously. Addie reminded herself to sip slowly, even though she wanted to drink as freely as the pour invited.

Monty announced the food was ready. The counter had been set for dinner.

"Addison, you're in the middle," he said with a grin.

She smiled back and took her seat in one of the comfortable tall chairs.

Pivoting from the stovetop to the counter, Monty began his presentation.
"Seared scallops, baked salmon with Brussels sprouts—French string beans for B.A.—risotto, and shaved black truffles."

"Smells wonderful," said Addison.

"Monty is an excellent cook," B.A. added proudly.

"Thank you, my love. I can always count on you," Monty replied with a wink.

The trio began their meal; a silence hung for several minutes before Monty broke it.

"Addison, do you cook?"

"Yes, but not as often as I used to. With it just being me, I've gotten away from cooking."

Addison, feeling a little more comfortable, sipped her wine, throwing caution to the wind. Sitting in a row at the bar, they took turns sharing likes and dislikes about foods as they came up. As it turned out, Monty and Addison had the same likes as well as the same dislikes. This became obvious, though no one said it aloud. B.A. noticed but made no mention.

Monty stood, circled the counter to clear the dinner plates, and moved to present dessert. The ladies, in unison, said they would wait. B.A. began loading the dishwasher. Addison offered to help, but B.A. insisted she head over to the fireplace—and topped off Addison's almost-empty glass. B.A. poured the remainder of the bottle into Monty's glass.

Monty and Addison headed to the fireplace area—Monty taking an oversized ottoman and Addison the sofa set catty-corner from him. Monty began to drink Addison in. Her features were soft, her brown eyes those of a woman of certainty. He liked that she wore jeans and a simple crew-neck sweater—nothing revealing, no outward signals of what he'd been fantasizing about for the past few weeks.

*
**

One night, late, after he'd returned from a three-day business trip, he showered and slipped into bed. B.A. acknowledged him; he tested the temperature and found a *yes*. In the dark, he imagined he was touching Addison, not his wife. The intensity surprised him, the sense that he wouldn't have enough time before the moment overtook him. Only when B.A. interrupted him — as she often did — did he register that it wasn't Addison he was with.

B.A. handed him the lubricant, whispering in his ear, urging him on. She kissed and teased him as he followed her instruction, his focus narrowing as sensation quickly built. He lost control sooner than expected, catching them both off guard.

B.A. reacted with delight, rolling onto her back as Monty followed her lead, his attention shifting to her. He kept the motion steady, intentional, while she responded, guiding herself closer to release. When it finally came, her body tightened and then softened, spent.

Monty cleaned himself up and returned with a warm cloth for B.A., the moment settling into something quieter once it was over.

Returning to reality, Monty poured another glass of wine from a bottle on the side table. After a moment of silence, he took a sip and spoke just as B.A. came to sit at the end of the sofa opposite Addison.

"Addison, thanks for coming. May I speak candidly?"

"Sure," she replied.

Monty continued. "It has been a fantasy of ours to bring a woman into our world—not for a one-night stand, but someone we'd consider a part of us. To travel with us, enjoy the arts, fine dining, and our bed—with both of us, and, when it happens, with either of us. I don't mind telling you we actively searched for a while with no results. We hesitated with some we thought might be a good match, so we didn't. We gave up. We stopped looking—but we kept fantasizing, which only heightened our libidos.

"Addison, hear me when I say: you are more than we could have fantasized about. You're our hopes and dreams ten times over. I want to be with you. B.A. wants to be with you. We want to share you, and we want you to share us. Is that something you might be interested in?"

The kitchen lights were off; only the hood light glowed above the range, and a few ceiling lights barely illuminated their faces as they watched and waited for her response. Her mind raced; her heart thumped hard. She looked at Monty, then turned to B.A., sitting one cushion away. She leaned sideways and reached to set her wineglass on the far side table. She set it down, sat up, and in one smooth movement slid closer to B.A., brushing her lips against hers until the kiss deepened, unhurried and unmistakable.

Addie moved nearer, her hand traveling over B.A.'s body, coaxing her closer, drawing a response that made B.A. relax back into the sofa. Addie lifted B.A.'s blouse, exposing her skin, her mouth tracing a slow path that made B.A.'s breath hitch. B.A. sank deeper into the cushions, breathing harder now, her body responding without restraint. Monty watched, transfixed, feeling himself react as he took in the way this woman made his wife tremble.

They kissed again, more insistently this time. Addie bit B.A.'s lip, her hand sliding lower, drawing a sharp sound from B.A. The warmth, the closeness, the unmistakable intimacy pulled all three of them deeper into the moment. Monty was fully aroused now, unable to look away as Addie explored his wife with deliberate confidence.

Addie leaned in and whispered to B.A., her voice low and certain, telling her what she wanted next.

B.A. responded immediately, her body tightening at the words. She stepped toward Monty, kissed him, then turned back to Addie as clothing was shed without ceremony. Addie watched B.A. move, admiring her, then joined her, their bodies fitting together easily, instinctively. They kissed and touched, drawing pleasure from each other while Monty watched, overwhelmed by the intimacy unfolding in front of him.

Monty reached for Addie, but she gently redirected him, kissing his hand before turning her attention back to B.A., who now lay open and receptive on the sofa. Addie leaned over her, her mouth and hands moving with intention, drawing rising sounds from B.A. Addie paused only to whisper again, her voice promising exactly what she intended to do.

Monty stood, unable to remain still. The sight of his wife being pleasured so openly fueled the moment, pushing Addie to intensify her attention. B.A.'s movements became urgent, her body responding fully, her voice breaking as the tension mounted.

"I'm going to lose control," B.A. cried.

"Let it happen," Monty murmured.

He hovered close, breathing her in, watching, feeling the charge between all three of them without interfering. Addie sensed the moment cresting and guided B.A. through it, staying with her as the release overtook her completely. B.A.'s body arched, then collapsed back into the cushions, spent and boneless.

Monty took it all in, stunned.

Addie turned to him. His arousal was unmistakable. She leaned in, teasing him just enough to make him groan, then pressed him back, taking control. She positioned herself with practiced ease, her own desire evident, her body already responding. She moved slowly at first, watching his reactions, drawing him out, until his restraint began to fracture.

She stayed in control, guiding the rhythm, letting him feel everything before finally closing the distance between them. He responded instinctively, hands gripping her, pulling her closer as they moved together with an urgency that felt inevitable. Their breaths mingled, their sounds overlapping, until they both surrendered to the moment.

They stayed like that for a beat afterward, pressed together, the intensity still humming between them.

From behind them, B.A.'s voice, warm and satisfied:

"That was incredible to watch."

Addie smiled, breathless, unrepentant.

"You can have him anytime. I want to share him with you. Does that mean… yes, you'll be part of our Throuple Entente?"

"Yes, B.A.—I'll be part of your Throuple Entente."

"I second that motion—Throuple Entente," said Monty.

In that moment, sophisticated serenity wrapped itself around Addison like fine cashmere—memories, pleasure, control. All things familiar.

The morning brought bright autumn sunshine to Addison's sleeping quarters. She had forgotten to draw the drapes. Reaching for her phone on the nightstand, she saw it was just 6:15. *Ugh,* she moaned, feeling a slight headache from last night's wine. Addison wasn't much of a drinker, but the wine had given her a boost to enjoy herself without hesitation.

She rose—naked, as she liked to sleep—walked to the bathroom, turned on the rain shower head, and stepped in before the hot water kicked in. Something she liked to do when she'd had one too many drinks the night before. The cold water raised goosebumps, cleared her head, and heightened her senses. As the water turned tepid and then warm, she stepped out to retrieve her cloth and body gel.

For this trip, she'd chosen to bring Oud Bergamot and her signature Lime Basil Mandarin. The bergamot filled her nostrils, waking her fully. Hair wet, she shaved her legs, rinsed off, and turned off the water, now steamy and fogging the bathroom. She wrapped herself in a bath towel and used another to press out the excess water from her hair. The bathroom smelled of bergamot; soon the entire room wafted with it.

She slipped on silk two-piece shortie pajamas—long sleeves, black—and donned the matching long robe, then headed downstairs to figure out the coffee.

In the kitchen, last night's glasses sat hand-washed and upside down on a cloth by the sink. Next to them were three mugs and a note: *If the coffee hasn't started to brew, push the red button.* She turned toward the range top— there sat the double brew machine, carafe and single-serve. The red button glowed as if calling *hit me*—and she did.

As the machine cranked up, she opened the refrigerator and found a small glass container with milk; deeper in, a carton of half-and-half. *Perfect,* she thought. She set the glass container by the mugs and waited for the carafe to half fill, then poured coffee into a mug she'd already splashed with half-and-half. The mix was perfect. Two perfects, she thought. No—three. The shower had done the trick; no remnants of a hangover.

Mug filled and steamy, Addison pulled one of the tall "chairs on stilts" from the counter and sat. Sipping, her thoughts fell to Monty—how he felt inside her, his eyes piercing hers when he came. She sensed he was overwhelmed with pleasure. She wasn't sure, but there was definitely something different about his orgasm.

She carried her coffee to the window overlooking the side of the house by the portico and garage. Was the garage attached or separate? Where was the door? She crossed to the full-glass doors of the mudroom—two doors with a bench between, both with upper panes. One pane showed the sun rising; the other was dark. *The garage,* she decided.

She had just returned to the counter when Monty walked in, hair wet, wearing a terrycloth button-front shirt and matching terrycloth pants, both loose.

She smiled. "Good morning, Monty."

"Good morning, Addison. How'd you sleep?"

"I slept well. Forgot to close the drapes—sun woke me and I couldn't go back to sleep."

Monty, back to her, poured coffee. He spotted the milk and tipped some into his cup. Without looking up, he asked, "I hope I was okay last night. You had me revved up—I didn't last as long as I wanted."

Addison saw his face flush. She assured him he was perfect —nothing to worry about. "First times are tricky," she said, steadying him. Quick to change the subject, she asked about B.A. He told her B.A. was the late sleeper in the family. Addison noticed how his blue eyes sparkled as he spoke. She was intrigued by the way his eyes did that when he talked about his wife. And yet—there was something. She shifted to neutral ground: the farm.

Monty moved around the counter and sat beside her, explaining how his mother's youngest brother had married an older woman who owned the farm, inherited from her father. She had hired migrant workers to tend the acreage for years, then fell in love with his uncle; they married and worked it together with locals and a few migrant workers. "When he took ill—as they say in these parts—she put it on the market, all thirty acres. The house was over fifty years old. The outbuildings were decent, the barns in good condition. I bought it when I thought my life was taking another path. I tore down the original house and built this one, the dock and boathouse, renovated the outbuildings, improved the roads to them and the barns, added cart paths for easier access. I'm working on a putting green beyond the pool and, eventually, a driving range facing the cove."

As he talked, a calm settled in his eyes, something tranquil in his voice and breathing. Addison felt there was something tragic in Monty's life, but she wouldn't pry. As he continued, she laid a hand on his. His eyes locked on hers with an intense focus. He knew she heard him, felt his pride—and wondered if she could sense his pain. Addison felt a bond forming; her pain and his, combined, might somehow make them better.

"El—" Monty began to say.

B.A. swept in with her usual bold entry. Both drew their hands back. B.A. noticed but said nothing. The moment was lost. Monty and Addison shared a glance, then turned to B.A., who naturally commanded the room.

"What time is the boat outing?" Addison asked.

"We expect Caldwell around ten-ish."

"Caldwell?" Addison repeated, puzzled.

"B.A., I asked you last night if you'd told Addison about Caldwell coming today, and you said you had!" Monty said.

B.A. looked stumped. She could have sworn she'd told her about the boat *and* Caldwell's visit. Clearly Addie knew about the boat—she'd brought it up. B.A. was confused. She'd been looking forward to seeing Caldwell. The last time, they'd had a moment in the restaurant hallway— bumping into each other leaving the bathrooms. With a couple of glasses of wine in her, she'd teased that he probably hadn't had a good kinky lay in his life. Caldwell —never shy—pulled her into an alcove by the giant ice machine, rubbed his cock against her butt, and slid a hand lightly around her neck. B.A. got so caught up, her nipples went rock hard; she pressed her butt firmer into his crotch and covered his hand with hers, encouraging a slightly tighter hold. Quick—but it left an impression. She hoped it had on him, too.

"Well, B.A.? What gives?" Monty asked, firm.

Sensing the tension, Addison stepped in. "Maybe she told me, and with so much swirling around us last evening, I could have forgotten…"

B.A., not wanting to seem ungrateful for what Addie was clearly doing, made light of the moment by asking what was for breakfast.

Monty, still visibly annoyed, told them they'd be going into town for breakfast—and meeting Caldwell there.

The room fell silent. B.A. poured another cup of coffee while Addison excused herself to get dressed, having already had two cups.

As she rose to leave, Monty told her they'd head to town in about thirty to forty minutes.

***

Monty and Addison sat in the rockers on the back porch, waiting for B.A. to come down. She announced her readiness by opening the center door to the garage and backing out her Jaguar SUV.

Monty muttered something under his breath as he stood, closing the mudroom door behind him. He offered Addison his hand to help her down the steps and across the stone path to the front passenger door. Addison hesitated—she preferred the back seat—but Monty insisted. She got in, and he closed the door for her.

As they pulled out, Addison noticed B.A. in the driver's seat, looking calm and composed. She was her usual chatty self, though her topics bounced all over the place— unfocused, unlike her. Addison thought so too. Monty occasionally chimed in with a few short sentences. B.A., glancing into the rearview mirror, seemed to enjoy the light banter between them, trying to pull Addison into the conversation. Addison merely nodded and smiled, quietly thinking this *Perry* must be someone special. She had the sense they were both vying for his attention.

The ride took about twenty minutes, along roads Addison had traveled the day before. This time, as a passenger, she could take in the scenery—the houses, cars, and quiet rhythm of Evanston. When B.A. began to slow, Addison saw the signage for the diner.

B.A. pulled into the lot, circled slowly for a parking space, and settled into one near the middle row. They got out and started toward the entrance when a voice called from behind:

"Montague Langford! How the hell are you, old boy?"

The three turned in unison. Monty stepped forward to greet his old business friend, extending a hand.

"How the hell are you, Caldwell, old man?"

B.A.'s voice lifted, delighted. "Caldwell Marchand! You made it! I'm so happy to see you!"

Monty, still gripping Caldwell's right hand, placed his left on the man's shoulder. B.A. slipped between them, wrapping her arms around Caldwell and planting a kiss square on his lips. Monty released his friend's hand to make room for his wife—accustomed to her sometimes laid-back, sometimes overly affectionate exuberance. It was part of what he loved about her—her unfiltered zeal.

Addison, meanwhile, stood a few feet away, caught between shock and fascination. She hadn't imagined the couple knew anyone familiar. Then recognition dawned.

"Perry Marchand?" she said, incredulous. "Oh my, I can't believe it's you! How are you?"

The tall, tanned man with the salt-and-gray hair released B.A. and walked past Monty to stand before Addison—an arm's length away, stunned. *Someone who knows me by my first name,* he thought.

"Lady Addison Hollace!" he said softly. "Oh my... you look as stunning as ever." He reached out and drew her into a proper embrace.

"Well," B.A. said, half-laughing as she stepped beside Monty, "looks like introductions aren't necessary. You two know one another?"

Addison stepped back as Perry kissed her cheeks, then took his hand, holding it deliberately as she began to speak. She took control of the moment, shaping the narrative the way she wanted it told—past, husband, and all. Perry, always the gentleman, let her lead.

"Perry and my late husband, Thayer, were on the golf team together at Colgate," Addison explained smoothly. "Later they played a number of charity tournaments—Palm Gardens, Sawgrass, a few others. We met during one of those gala events."

As they began walking toward the diner's entrance, Addison continued praising *Perry Caldwell Marchand*, reinforcing her framing.

Perry, realizing her direction, joined in with his own recollections—mentioning the South Hamptons, Westchester, Carmel, South Florida. "The list is endless," he said with an easy smile.

B.A. and Monty exchanged a look. They hadn't realized how connected Addison was. B.A. wasn't intimidated—just surprised. Monty felt only confirmation: his instincts about Addison had been right. She was extraordinary.

The hostess led them to a booth by the front window. Addison slid in first, Perry beside her, leaving B.A. and Monty opposite. They ordered, confessing they were starving.

"So, what have you all been up to?" Perry asked lightly— an innocent question that made Monty tense.

He answered evenly, "Addison drove over yesterday for dinner. B.A. convinced her to stay and join us on the boat today." Then, taking quiet control of the moment, he added, "Once we're back, the guys will pick up an eclectic spread for dinner. We'll play Monopoly afterward."

Breakfast arrived, and conversation flowed easily— hopping across topics, laughter blending with the clink of coffee cups. They shared bites, passed syrup, and traded stories.

When B.A. announced she needed the ladies' room, Monty stood automatically to let her slide out. "I'm heading to the men's room too," he said. B.A. asked Addison if she wanted to come along, but Addie waved her off. "I'm fine, thanks."

That left Addison and Perry alone—much to B.A.'s irritation and, quietly, Monty's dismay.

As the couple disappeared toward the restrooms, Perry leaned in. "How are you?"

"I'm doing well," Addison said softly. "Things have settled since the lawsuit. The NDAs finally forced the media to back the hell off. I've grown into a new lifestyle—one Thayer would approve of. And I'm having fun."

He smiled. "You look fantastic. You always had that sense of elegance—never threatening, never entitled. I'm over the moon to spend this unexpected time with you."

"So you've known the Langfords a while?"

"Mostly Monty," Perry said. "We've crossed paths over contracts and legal matters for developers he's designed for. I also knew his first wife, Ellen."

Addison looked up. "First wife? I wasn't aware. Divorced?"

"No," he said quietly. "Widowed. She died under... odd circumstances. Some said an accident. Others said it wasn't."

"Killed?" Addison whispered. "As in murdered? Perry, what are you saying? Monty's wife was *murdered*?"

Before he could answer, Addison glanced up—Monty was walking toward them. "Don't look," she said under her breath. "Monty's coming back. Whatever happens tonight, come to my room after. We may not have another chance before tomorrow."

Perry gave a faint nod just as Monty slid back into the booth.

"Are we ready to head back to the house?" Monty asked evenly.

⁎

Perry dropped his weekender on spinner wheels in the hunter green guest room—the one without the hound prints. It was closest to the room Addison occupied.

They made their way down to the dock, where *The Best Tide*—a Hatteras M75 with twin MTU diesel inboards—rumbled softly, waiting. Monty's captain and mate stood ready as the trio boarded.

Once they were underway, the vessel eased from the cove into the open bay, the hum of the engines blending with the rhythm of the water. Monty gave a tour as they cruised: a full upscale galley with a Sub-Zero refrigerator, a cozy salon, and four staterooms—master ensuite aft, another queen ensuite, a smaller yet elegant cabin with its own bath, and the crew quarters nearest the engine room.

"She's tranquility on the water," Monty said, as he often did when describing his indulgence.

B.A., not much for deep-sea fishing or deep water, rarely joined these trips when Monty took potential clients out for a weekend of R&R.

Perry was impressed, and so was Addison. She agreed wholeheartedly when Perry suggested Monty should cruise the Intracoastal and dock at Quay Island—spend a few days that winter enjoying warm weather and a few rounds of golf at the Grand Hotel's course. "Their slips are top-notch," Perry said.

Monty seemed intrigued by the idea.

They sat together on the stern in cushioned lounge chairs, watching the foamy wake trail behind them. B.A. also liked the thought of Florida in winter. "Where do you stay down there, Perry?" she asked, hoping he'd say *the island*.

Addison, ever poised, interjected lightly. "Perry's a snowbird on Orchid."

Monty smiled. "Then that settles it. We'll make the trip—if Addison can make herself available for the voyage down."

Addison laughed softly. "At the very least, I can go down and fly back."

The laughter faded, and conversation turned to lighter chatter, but Addison's mind drifted. She couldn't shake what Perry had told her that morning at the diner—about Ellen, Monty's first wife.

She stood barefoot at the stern rail, the wind teasing her hair, eyes fixed on the swirling wake of the propellers as they churned the bay.

Monty watched her from a distance. He sensed something was off but knew better than to ask—not yet, not in front of the others. He'd wait until they were back at the farmhouse.

The sun had begun its early dip in the west, painting the water gold as *The Best Tide* turned toward home.

⁎⁎⁎

Once the captain and his mate had dropped the foursome off at the dock, the men headed out in Perry's rental to pick up the to-go orders B.A. had placed around town.

Remembering they were out of beer, B.A. called across the pool to Monty, telling him to add it to the list. He and Perry were deep in conversation; Monty simply raised his hand in acknowledgment without turning around. Addison, walking beside her, glanced for a reaction—but B.A. gave none.

Inside the house, Addison decided to rinse off the salt air and change into something more comfortable. B.A., washing her hands at the kitchen sink, agreed she would do the same after setting everything up. The women parted.

B.A. moved through her quiet ritual—setting out wine glasses, beer glasses, plates, utensils, napkins, serving bowls, spoons, and tongs. She removed the centerpiece from the coffee table in the kitchen's sitting area and sank onto the sofa—the same spot where, the night before, Addison had given her the orgasm of a lifetime.

Her nipples tightened at the memory of Addison's command to *take off your panties*. A soft flush spread through her chest. She slipped into a red negligee, added patent red heels, and fastened her black leather collar with its silver D-ring. Her hair, loose in a high ponytail, brushed her shoulders.

Running a hand over her breast, she felt her pulse quicken. A soft sound escaped her as she slid her hand down her jeans, aware of how strongly her body was responding. She lifted her fingers to her mouth, tasting the evidence of her desire, the memory of Addison still vivid. The sensation emboldened her. She stood, stripped off the rest of her clothes, and headed upstairs toward Addison's room.

She could hear the shower running.

Without hesitation, B.A. walked into the steamy bathroom and stepped inside.

Addison was using the handheld spray, careful not to soak her hair. Eyes closed, she guided the warm water over herself, following familiar paths, lost in sensation. She didn't hear B.A. enter.

Hands slid over her hips — B.A.'s hands — slow, deliberate, moving lower with each pass. B.A.'s body pressed against her back, the heat unmistakable, their closeness charged. Addison inhaled sharply, her body reacting instantly.

When Addison tried to turn, B.A. stopped her, guiding her wider, holding her steady. The warm water cascaded between them. B.A. adjusted the spray, changing its rhythm, directing it with intention. Addison braced her hands against the wall, opening herself to the sensation. A deeper sound tore from her throat.

With her free hand, B.A. explored further, circling, teasing, pushing just enough to draw a stronger response. Addison moaned louder, pressing back, her movements quickening as she matched the rhythm B.A. set.

Then, abruptly, B.A. stopped.

Addison gasped.

Without a word, B.A. stepped out of the shower.

Addison steadied herself, still trembling, the need sharp and insistent, preparing to finish on her own — until B.A. returned, holding something soft in her hand along with a small bottle of lubricant.

Addison met her gaze and gave a faint, knowing smile.

B.A. coated the object, and Addison added a few drops to her own fingers. Facing one another in the steam, Addison reached for B.A., her hand sliding lower as B.A. guided the sensation back to her. They pressed closer, thighs tangling, their movements syncing as the intensity built.

Water streamed over their bodies. Their breathing grew ragged. They moved together without hesitation, without restraint, until release overtook them both — loud, unguarded, complete.

When it was over, they stayed close for a moment, breathing in the steam and the aftermath.

Then B.A. stepped back, leaving the object behind on the shower floor.

She returned to her room, showered, dressed, and composed herself.

Addison washed again, wrapped herself in a robe, and lay across the bed for a few minutes, replaying everything. B.A. had been different this time — more controlled, more deliberate.

Finally, Addison rose, returned to the bathroom, cleaned and dried what they'd used, wrapped it neatly in a towel, and left it on the counter. Then she dressed and headed downstairs.

The guys hadn't returned yet, and Addison was famished— and thirsty. Orgasms had a way of doing that.

Opening the fridge, she spotted a bunch of grapes. She grabbed a stalk, a paper towel, and a bottle of water, then slipped through the mudroom, slid on her shoes, and stepped outside. The air was still warm from the day, with the faint scent of salt clinging to the breeze. Settling into an Adirondack rocker on the porch, she sipped her water and plucked grapes one by one from the stem.

After a few quiet minutes, she heard the crunch of tires on gravel winding up the drive.

Monty was driving Perry's rental. He pulled up in front of the porch, and Addison stood, offering to help with the haul. The men got out and opened the rear hatch of the Jeep Cherokee. The smell of warm food rolled toward her—fried wings, seafood, fries. Monty laughed as he hoisted a large bag.

"Expecting guests I don't know about?" Addison teased.

Monty grinned. "No guests. Just provisions. Once B.A. and everyone head out tomorrow, I've got a project to finish before flying to Texas on Tuesday."

Perry added, "And don't forget our tee time Friday—in Jacksonville."

The three each grabbed a bag. Monty carried the beer, calling over his shoulder that he'd throw a few bottles in the freezer to chill fast. Inside the mudroom, Addison and Perry stopped to remove their shoes; Monty, juggling two bags and the beer, kicked off his with a practiced motion.

B.A. appeared just in time to rescue her husband, taking the bags from his hands. Everyone moved to the counter, unpacking food containers. Addison grabbed a few fries, eyeing the wings.

Watching B.A. and Monty on the other side of the counter, setting out plates and utensils, Addison wondered if B.A. would tell Monty about what had happened between them upstairs. Then another thought struck—would tonight's game turn into something more adult? Would Perry play along? And did she even want him to see her in that light, knowing he had been Thayer's friend?

She munched the last fry and slid onto one of the tall chairs, finishing her water just as Monty joined her, sitting beside her. B.A. placed a drink in front of the stool next to Perry, who took his seat beside Monty. The women sat on opposite ends, the men in the middle.

"Dig in," Monty announced. "Just leave me enough for tomorrow and Monday."

They ate, laughed, and talked about nothing serious. It was an easy evening—takeout food, casual banter, no pretenses. When they finished, Monty and Addison loaded the dishwasher while B.A. handed out beers to Perry and herself. Perry settled on the sofa, looking over the Monopoly board.

Monty joined him, beer in hand, and began reading out the rules in his own modified version.

"Get out of jail costs a hundred. That goes under Free Parking. Pass Go, you get three-fifty. Roll doubles, you get another turn *and* twenty from the bank. Community Chest —twenty from each player to the bank goes to Free Parking. Boardwalk or Park Place? Double rent, hotels or not. Houses and hotels only after your turn. Mortgaged properties can be sold or traded, but the original owner gets first offer."

It was clear Monty had played—and played to win.

B.A. rolled first, a three. Perry rolled a six. Addison rolled a nine. Monty rolled a seven. The game began in high spirits.

By eight o'clock, B.A. declared bankruptcy, laughing as she slid her remaining property—Kentucky Avenue— across to Monty. He'd built a small empire: St. James, New York, Tennessee, Kentucky, Indiana, Illinois, the cheap purples, and both utilities. He had houses on the oranges and hotels on the reds and dark purples.

Perry held Oriental, Vermont, Connecticut, and the yellow trio—Atlantic, Ventnor, Marvin Gardens—with houses on each. Addison, however, was the quiet powerhouse. She owned the entire upper stretch—Pacific, North Carolina, Pennsylvania, Park, and Boardwalk—with hotels on all but two, plus all four railroads and a healthy pile of cash she'd won landing on a jackpot Free Parking.

When Perry finally folded, the night turned into a showdown between Addison and Monty. He seemed to relish it—the challenge, the tension, the playful competition.

Perry grabbed two beers from the fridge, handed one to Monty, and headed outside to join B.A., who was already on the porch sipping wine.

"You too?" she said when he appeared, lifting her glass.

He chuckled. "Those two are serious players."

He sat in the rocker beside her, still. She didn't rock either, just stared out toward the trees. He watched her profile—strong, dark-haired, her expression unreadable.

"Let's take a walk down to the pool," she said suddenly.

She stood, lifted her half-empty wineglass, and without looking back, started down the steps.

Perry hesitated for a moment, then rose and followed. She didn't slow or look back. The night air was cooler now, carrying the soft hum of crickets and the faint clink of pool water lapping against tile.

When he caught up, they walked side by side in silence. She had a presence—a charge that pulled at him. Then she took his hand, fingers interlacing with his. Her touch was warm, almost soothing. He didn't pull away, though his mind whispered: *she's my friend's wife*.

At the gate, she unlatched it and pushed it open. The lights around the pool shimmered across the surface, mist rising in the chill. It looked ethereal, provocative.

B.A. walked to the far corner, to a cushioned settee half hidden in shadow. Perry sat catty-corner from her. She slid to the edge, crossing one leg, then letting it fall open.

In the muted light, he could see only her eyes clearly—the rest of her face and body half obscured. Her voice was low, controlled. She spoke of wanting something she shouldn't have. Of wanting it so badly it ached.

He wanted to ask *what*, but she kept talking—telling him she had fantasized about him, touched herself thinking of him, that being near him made her nipples hard. Her words were measured, almost clinical, but her tone was velvet.

"I know it's wrong," she whispered, "and I feel guilty for it."

"Don't," he said quietly. "There's nothing wrong with fantasy. It's human. Everyone does it."

Her mouth curved in a faint smile.
"Look at me, Perry."

She shifted, her posture opening just enough to be unmistakable.

He swallowed, pulse drumming.

Before he could speak, she said in a slow, deliberate hush, "I don't want you. I want you to do this while I watch. Can you do that for me, Perry?"

He couldn't find words. He only nodded.

"Good," she murmured.

She reached into her dress pocket and produced a small clear container, holding it out without breaking eye contact. He leaned forward to take it. When he settled back, he noticed the towel folded beneath him—the same color as the cushion, deliberately unobtrusive.

When he looked up again, she had unbuttoned her dress. One side slipped open, revealing skin; the other remained half concealed. Her legs shifted, widening slightly.

"Whatever you do," she said softly, "don't close your eyes. Don't look away from me. Do you understand?"

He nodded.

The space between them tightened. She watched him closely, her breathing slow and measured. His body responded without permission.

Without prompting, he began to undo himself, each movement deliberate. She held his gaze the entire time.

"Feel it," she said. "But don't rush."

He obeyed, breath growing uneven.

"Now," she said, lower, firmer, "do exactly what I tell you."

He hesitated—his eyes flickered downward—and she corrected him instantly.
"Eyes on me."

He complied.

"Sit back," she said. "Use it."

He opened the container and followed her instruction, the cool sensation sharpening everything. She moved in quiet rhythm, watching him, never looking away.

"Now," she whispered, "the way you do when you're alone."

He obeyed, slowly at first, then with growing urgency, his breath breaking.

"Stop."

He froze.

"I'm not ready for you yet."

He nodded, gripping the towel beneath him, tension coiled tight.

"Now," she said again, her voice unmistakable, "like you're with me."

He followed her command, gaze locked to hers. When release finally overtook him, it was sudden and overwhelming—his body shuddering, a sharp sound escaping as everything spilled over at once, uncontrolled.

He blinked.

She was gone.

For a moment, he wondered if it had been a dream, until the cool night air met the stickiness on his skin. He leaned back, dazed, reaching behind him and finding a chilled bottle of water tucked in the cushions. He used it to rinse off, wiping with a clean corner of the towel.

Standing, unsteady, he looked toward the path. No sign of her.

Her flip-flops sat in the mudroom corner when he returned, along with the blanket she'd wrapped around herself earlier. *Did she plan this?* he wondered.

Shaking his head, still unsure what to make of it, he grabbed another cold bottle of water from the fridge and headed upstairs to his room to shower.

When he reached the second floor, he saw Addison's light on and her door ajar. He knocked softly and waited for permission to open it farther. When she said yes, he peeked in and told her he was going to take a quick rinse and would be back in a jiffy. He noticed she was still dressed. Not entirely sure, after his encounter with B.A., he asked if she still wanted to catch up. She affirmed, and they agreed on twenty minutes.

Perry showered and thought about the intensity of his orgasm—the control B.A. had taken and the way she seduced him without touching him. He hardened again. He tried to put it out of his mind and focus on catching up with the wife of a dear friend who was gone. The last time he'd seen Addison was at Thayer's services in the Hudson Valley village of Millbrook, where they had both grown up. Perry attended Catholic school; Thayer went to a nearby co-ed boarding and day school. The boys ran into each other at equestrian events, competing in eventing when they were young and later on the same polo team. They'd moved in different circles because of their schools, but when they both showed up at Colgate, they were inseparable.

After college, their paths diverged. Perry went into property development with his father and brothers as their CFO in Illinois. Thayer entered the world of finance on Wall Street and ultimately became a successful hedge fund manager. During a summer in the Hamptons, Perry saw Thayer again —both men successful and married. Perry had a daughter and a stepdaughter. Thayer had no children by his first wife; his second—drop-dead gorgeous—wasn't drinking because they were trying to conceive. Tall and slim, long brunette hair, piercing gray eyes, and bronze skin that lent her an exotic air. Perry remembered his first encounter with Addison—her smile, captivating—and the way she looked up at Thayer, making everyone around them twinge with envy. They were a power couple: he confident and successful; she an editor at a major New York publishing house. They golfed together often and genuinely enjoyed each other's company.

That Hamptons summer, Perry spent a lot of time with the Hollaces. His second marriage was crashing; his wife decamped to the Vineyard to be with family. He was happy to have Thayer on the weekends in from the city. He and Thayer played golf on Thursdays while Addison was still in Manhattan. Some weekends Addison went to North Carolina to see her elderly aunts—the "spinsters," she called them—old-fashioned Southern ladies, one a teacher, the other a nurse, each married once, with no children. Perry found the couple fascinating. Later, Thayer's mother and Perry's mother ended up in the same senior residence outside Westchester. Both fathers had died years before; both families old wealth. Perry's parents had separated when he was young; his mother's second husband was a successful real estate mogul in the Northeast. One day up in Montauk, over golf, Thayer mentioned his father had died when he was six and his sisters were eight and ten.

That summer was like their Colgate days—inseparable. Sometimes they dined just the two of them; other times with Addison or another couple from the club. Addison always reassured Perry to think of himself as their friend enjoying the poshness of Suffolk County. She made no secret that she preferred East Hampton to their Upper East Side townhouse. Thayer would wrap an arm around her and say, "One day soon, my lovely," and kiss her forehead. Perry fell in love with Addison as a sister. She clearly made Thayer a happy man.

He threw on pajamas and a matching robe, grabbed two bottles of water from the kitchen, and headed back to Addison's open door. He stepped in. She was seated *sukhasana* at the head of the bed, hair bundled on top of her head, long legs extending from her shortie PJs. She looked up from her tablet and greeted him as warmly as she had earlier in the diner parking lot.

"Come on in, Caldwell," she teased.

"Why thank you so much, darlin'. Don't mind if I do," he said, in a comically bad Southern accent.

Addison snorted with laughter. He was always trying to sound Southern. He grinned at the snort, claimed his accent was improving—at least he thought so—and then his grin softened. He sat at the foot of the bed, content to see she could still find lighthearted moments.

"You seem content, my friend," he said. "I'm happy to see that—but surprised to see you with the Langfords, especially out here." His face turned serious.

"I like to think of myself as at the end of my transition," she said. "From happiest wife to saddest widow, drowning in sorrow—throwing back any semblance of the happy life I thought would last 'til death do us part. Then one day I had to face that that's exactly what happened. Death parted us. And I decided to explore a life I'd thought about—and somewhat experimented with in high school and college."

"Oh? And what life is that—if I'm not prying?"

"For the sake of conversation, let's just say *erotic freedom*."

"Oh," he said, an eyebrow lifting.

"Come on, Mr. Caldwell—I've seen how you look at B.A. Don't try to play Edwardian," she scolded, smiling.

"No, not stuffy," he said. "I suppose—as much as I hate to admit it—I always saw you as a sister. Until this morning in the parking lot. There's a different look about you—still you: beautiful, poised, elegant... with something added. Something alluring. Exotic."

"Now, Caldwell, you and I are like brother and sister—you just said so yourself."

"Yes, yes," he agreed. "But I'm still a man, and I know a sexy woman when I see one—sister, friend, or otherwise."

He took a sip of water. They sat in companionable silence for a moment—like siblings, letting the moment breathe. Then he spoke in a hush.

"I've seen how Monty looks at you—my God—especially when you're not looking. He's a man about to fall head over heels for a vibrant, exciting, affable woman who's very sexy to boot."

Addison didn't comment. She'd noticed it, sensed it—especially last night when she straddled him, facing him, as he stroked in and out of her. Their rhythm had been undeniable, and just before he came he'd given her a quizzical look—as if unsure he should explode inside her. When he did, eyes closed, she felt him flood her. When he finished, he opened his eyes and mouthed *thank you*. She wondered if she and Perry were close enough to discuss it. Before she could speak—

"He's undeniably into you, Lady A," Perry said. "Be careful if you decide to sleep with him—especially if you don't want to break up a marriage."

Lady A. She hadn't heard that in ages—not since the Hampton summers.

"Well, Mr. Caldwell, before I give you the 411, tell me about this first marriage Monty had."

Addison listened as Perry told Ellen Langford's story—how she and Monty met while she was in college. It was a wonderful love story, until he described Ellen herself—her soft quietness, her devotion to Monty, and his to her. They'd moved from the city and bought a house in Evanston, north of Chicago, while Ellen worked on her PhD at Northwestern. Monty often commuted by car. The area was perfect—shops, restaurants, trails for biking and walking. Ellen became a neighborhood figure, walking to campus and almost everywhere else.

Perry described the vibe between them: he'd sat with them at a banquet and had the best time. It was a company event; awards were being presented. Monty had just finished a mixed-use development Perry's company and he had worked on together—magnificent—glass and steel with exposed brick. He'd poured his soul into it as lead structural engineer and received a Citation of Merit from the City of Chicago for urban development and public safety standards. A standing ovation. Monty spoke; Ellen's pride was palpable. Their staff sat at the table behind. It was a great night all around. Monty and Ellen left early—something about wine spilled on his tux trousers. That would be the last time Perry ever saw Ellen.

"What? Why? What happened?" Addison slid closer, legs dangling off the side of the bed.

Perry explained: Monty was beginning another project and decided to stay overnight in the city for a late meeting. Afterward, he tried calling several times—no answer. He called again early the next morning—still no answer. He phoned a neighbor—woke her. He could be that way when he cared. The neighbor was an older woman whose husband had died; her sons lived in California. Ellen had "adopted" her—sister, mother, something close. They each had keys to the other's house.

The neighbor, in a robe, walked over, rang the bell, waited, then used her key. Inside, sofa pillows were scattered. She called Ellen's name and headed down the hall. In the kitchen, Ellen lay on the floor, blood on her shirt, eyes fixed. The neighbor dialed 911—Evanston police.

"My God, Perry—what the fuck!" Addison exclaimed, pacing.

"Yes, I know, Lady A." Perry sat up, arms around his knees.

He went on. Someone had killed Ellen. Stabbed multiple times. The autopsy put the time around 6 p.m. the prior evening. No sign of forced entry. She still wore her three-carat engagement ring, diamond pendant, and watch—all from Monty.

Perry paused. Addison edged closer, almost touching. "What, Perry?"

He drew a breath. "Some strange things were missing. We only noticed once I was allowed back in with Monty."

Addison's eyes widened. "Again—what the fuck? What?"

"They took Monty's pillowcase off the bed, a shirt he'd left hanging on his valet, a hairbrush, and his terrycloth spa towel wrap," he said softly.

"What a sick fuck," Addison whispered.

"No joke, Lady A." Perry stood, pacing now. The police concluded it was someone she knew—she must have opened the door. Maybe they argued—sofa pillows tossed, dishes broken on the kitchen floor, a knife missing from its sleeve on the block. The items taken made the police speculate about a scorned lover—or a stalker. Chicago PD put an unmarked patrol on Monty for a few weeks; he couldn't stay in the house. He moved back to the city, took a couple of weeks to handle arrangements, and hired an auctioneer. Everything remaining—Ellen's clothes, her psychology books—was donated to nonprofits in Chicago and around Northwestern.

"That is awful, Perry."

"Weirdest thing. He refused to wear anything from that house again. Went out and bought new everything. A few weeks after the funeral in her hometown, Woodbury, Minnesota, he bought a condo in one of the high-rises my brothers and I had just completed. Perfect for him—fresh start, lake views, gym, secure parking, twenty-four-hour doorman. We slept better knowing some creep couldn't get to him."

Perry told how Monty became a workaholic—and a recluse.

"He was grieving, Perry," Addison said gently.

"Yeah, maybe. But it was tough to watch. He grew a beard, let his hair go long, wore jackets and slacks that made him look like a college professor. Not Monty—the sharp, tailored dresser with Italian shoes, clean-shaven, hair never out of place," Perry said, standing and stretching with a wide yawn.

They sat again at the foot of the bed. Perry's eyes were red, and Addison's messy bun had loosened, strands falling over her shoulders. Perry eyed the clip; she pulled the claw and let her hair fall like a curtain.

Tired from the long day, they agreed to pick up tomorrow. Addison gave him a wide-eyed look.

"What?" he asked.

"Damn—there's more? WTF, Perry!"

"Not much more—just a few nuances you may want to hear."

"Are you leaving?" she asked.

"I thought you were ready to curl up. It's getting late."

She protested enough that he agreed to sleep there: his head at the foot, on top of the sheet but under the comforter. He ducked out to take a leak, grab his phone and a pillow, and returned. He heard the bathroom water running. He settled in. The water stopped; the door opened; the bathroom light clicked off. The bedside lamp glowed low and dim. Addison slid in under the covers and pressed her foot playfully against his knee.

As she reached to switch off the lamp, Addison said, "Look here, friend—if you need to masturbate during the night, just don't shake the bed, please."

Perry chuckled. "Oh, don't worry—your friend took care of that earlier."

She shot upright in silhouette.

"No, I'm not talking," he said lightly. "A gentleman never tells. Go to sleep, Lady A. Good night."

They fell asleep facing each other.

*
**

Across the hall, Monty got up to use the bathroom. B.A. slept with her back to the room, the bathroom door, and the double doors. What she'd revealed to him just before drifting off had left him restless. Work tugged at him, but Addison now occupied his thoughts completely.

B.A. had told him she'd had an explosive release in the shower, something she knew would affect him. Certain intimacies with her had always intensified his responses. On more than one occasion, at private invite-only parties on Saint-Martin, she had even encouraged him to engage with another husband who was openly bisexual. He always brushed it off, insisting he wasn't interested, but he watched. What turned him on most was the dynamic — two men and a woman, all three involved.

He told himself it was the woman's presence that made it work for him.

Still, memory complicated that explanation. He recalled sitting at a pool bar, watching one husband attend to another while their wives were occupied elsewhere. He remembered how strongly it had affected him.

He had to admit that certain acts appealed to him, even if his wife didn't fully share that interest. That same night, she had repeatedly urged him to explore further, then disappeared for several hours, leaving him alone at the pool bar. Women drifted toward him, confident and unembarrassed, taking turns with him while the night unfolded around them.

When he felt he couldn't hold out any longer, the last woman — older, short white hair, striking breasts, long legs — led him behind a curtained lounge where a small gathering was already underway. He settled back among pillows as she took control. Another woman from the group joined them, positioning herself close, facing the woman with him. A small crowd formed as the scene drew attention, the atmosphere thick with permission and heat.

He gave himself over to the moment, hands and mouth moving instinctively as the women responded. When release finally came, it was fierce and overwhelming, leaving him momentarily disoriented.

When he opened his eyes, they were gone.

Only a server remained, offering a warm towel with practiced discretion.

Returning to the present, standing at the sink and feeling himself firm, he grabbed his robe from the hook, took his phone from the nightstand, and eased toward the double doors into the hall. As the door opened, B.A.'s eyes flicked open, though she didn't move. Monty slipped out, holding the latch so the click wouldn't sound as it shut.

He saw Perry's door open and stepped over to check—
empty bed, untouched. Looking down the hall, he noticed
Addison's door ajar and walked toward it, purposeful. He
nudged it wider: Perry's back under the comforter,
Addison's head the opposite way on the bed. In surprise
and confusion, Monty didn't register that Perry wasn't
under the sheet—only the comforter. He stood there,
wanting to wake them and confront them, but decided to
handle it differently. Tomorrow, knowing Addison rose
early and Perry didn't, he'd speak to her alone and let her
explain. He tried to convince himself he wasn't jealous—
she was free to do as she pleased—but he'd thought they
had agreed to be a throuple. *Just them*. His head spun. He
closed the door quietly and headed downstairs. He
wouldn't sleep until he'd talked to Addison.

Monty dozed off on the sofa in the kitchen's sitting area,
where they'd played Monopoly the night before. Before
lying down, he'd piddled with the coffee maker, filling it
with *The Gilded Bean* grounds Addison brought. He filled
the creamer with fresh half-and-half and placed raw sugar
in the bowl. Two mugs sat ready. He set the timer for 6:15
a.m.

When the timer triggered and the brew began, the smell of coffee woke him. No Addison. No sounds from upstairs. Disappointed, he walked to his office, used the bathroom, and splashed water on his face. In the mirror, he looked conflicted. Had he misread Addison's attention? Why would B.A. tell him about their anal play if she thought Addison wasn't attracted to him? And Perry—had Addison and Perry been intimate? Should he include Perry to keep Addison close? Why would B.A. encourage bringing Addison in if she thought Addison wasn't attracted to him, only to her?

He turned off the bathroom light, crossed his office, and glanced at the project work he needed to finish before Texas. He scolded himself for losing focus—the one constant he'd learned to depend on. He opened the custom Roman shade with the remote and looked out over the pool, dock, and cove. Then he headed back to the kitchen.

At the counter stood Perry, and at the coffee maker, Addison. Both were dressed: Perry in jeans and loafers, a polo, his jacket hanging on the back of a barstool; Addison in jeans, navy tennis shoes, an oversized striped shirt over a T-shirt, hair in a ponytail. Her sunglasses lay on the counter. Two duffels sat by the mudroom door. Monty's heart sank. He was still in his robe, hair mussed from the sofa; they were fresh and ready to hit the road—he north, she south.

"Good morning, you two," Monty said, chipper, masking his disappointment.

"Monty—we hope we didn't wake you," Perry replied.

Relief flickered across Monty's face; they didn't realize he'd slept downstairs. He clapped Perry's shoulder and smiled broadly.

"Good morning, Monty," Addison chimed.

"Good morning, my dear. I trust you had another peaceful night?"

"Yes, Monty. I slept well. You've been a charming host. I've enjoyed the entire weekend getaway."

"We must do it again soon," Monty said.

"Of course we will," she answered, giving him a warm, satisfied look.

It helped, but disappointment lingered. He needed a reason to delay her—just long enough for a walk around the grounds and a real talk. He wanted her in their lives—not hit-or-miss, but as a throuple, exclusively.

He poured himself coffee, and the three sat at the island, chatting, when B.A. appeared descending the stairs. All three turned, puzzled: she was fully dressed with a carry-on over her shoulder. Monty's shoulders slumped. If B.A. was leaving too, there was no chance Addison would linger.

"Good morning, my love," Monty said. "Are you leaving this morning, too?"

Before B.A. could answer, Perry and Addison offered their good mornings.

"Well—everyone's up and ready, I see. Good morning," B.A. replied.

Dressed in a denim shirtdress, flats, and a sage sweater tied at her waist, B.A. grabbed a mug, poured coffee, and added her fixings. She pulled fruit, yogurt, forks, spoons, small plates, napkins—and leftover chicken—from the fridge, arranging everything within reach. Quietly, she emptied the coffee grounds into a compost container, rinsed it, placed a fresh filter, refilled with coffee, and started another brew.

Silence, she figured, would let them think through the weekend. She replayed her own reel: teasing Monty to a full erection Friday before Addie arrived—him begging her to stop so he could save himself; watching Addie suck her breasts and nearly command her to take off her panties; the thrill of Monty watching as Addie licked her close while B.A. held herself from tipping over until she chose to; watching Addie blow Monty and then ride him while he suckled her breasts—B.A. wide-legged, pinching her clit to orgasm unseen; and last night with Perry, the controlled theater of making him masturbate and come. *A very good weekend,* she thought. And she was right—the others were each in their heads as she brewed and set out food.

Monty broke the quiet. "I'm going to run up, shower, and change quickly. No one has permission to leave before I get back."

They nodded, filled bowls with fruit, opened yogurts. Monty dashed upstairs.

They ate and kept it light—no heavy topics. Monty returned as B.A. rose to load more dishes into the nearly full dishwasher from the night before. He poured coffee, put a few cold chicken tenders on a plate with some fruit, and ate. They all kept talking about nothing in particular— each with unspoken conversations on the tip of the tongue.

Monty, most disappointed of all, resigned himself: he and Addison wouldn't have their final talk before she left.

He finished, added his plate to the washer, cleaned the carafe, wiped the counter. The others gathered their things and headed toward the parking area, B.A. out the mudroom to the garage. As Monty stepped onto the porch, the garage door rose. B.A. started her car, pulled out next to Addison's SUV, and got out again. Engines idled.

They came together—hugs, thank-you, the easy chorus of farewell. Monty saved Addison for last. He hugged his wife; she climbed into her sporty two-seater Jag and rolled toward the drive. Perry had already said his goodbyes to Monty, B.A., and Addison, and now idled in his rental behind B.A.

Monty held Addison's door as she got in, closing it gently. She surprised him by lowering the window just as she started to roll forward. Perry crept along, as if waiting for her to catch up.

She slid off her sunglasses and held them with the hand on the wheel. "Monty, would it be okay if I called you on my drive back across the bay?"

His face answered before he spoke. She took it as a yes.

"Great. Let me make a couple of calls, and I'll ring you shortly."

Before Monty could say anything more, Addison rolled up the window and accelerated down the drive, gravel skittering in her wake. Monty stood and watched, happy now—excited. Then he turned and walked back to the porch.

‎⁂

△ ▽ ⩢ ⩢

As she rolled down the Langfords' driveway, she could see
Perry's rental turning onto the highway. B.A.'s car was
nowhere in sight when Addison reached the road, making
the left and following into the small town of Centerville.
Her first call was to her handyman and gardener, D.J., to let
him know she would be home to give the guys a long walk.
She needed it herself. There was so much to digest. This
couple who seemed to have everything might be missing a
few things after all. The fact that Monty was married, B.A.
being his second wife, and his first having made him a
widower—and how that came about—was mortifying. But
if anyone understood overcoming grief, it was her.

Her second call was a message to her housekeeper,
Celestine—who had weekends off—letting her know not to
worry about the grocery-list pickup tomorrow because
Addison had placed an online order to grab on her way
home. She would tell them both, in person, of her plan to
sequester for about eight days—not just to catch up on
work, but to give herself time to digest the past three days
and consider her life moving forward.

She hadn't opened her laptop since she'd left home, but now reality set in. Her third and fourth communications were messages to her associate, Simone, and her assistant, Marcus, both in New York, along with Pilar, her editorial assistant. Marcus was her mini-me; even though he didn't look like her, he was her mainstay for fact-checking and manuscript prep. She would take the next couple of days to meet with each person on her staff via FaceTime and hold a group Zoom by Wednesday. Fall was always busy—books being readied for the holiday giving season and for winter reading as snowbirds soaked up the warm weather down south, lazy pool time with a book. The goal was to avoid any inquiries from Brian Crudup, assistant to Bill Sodder, her Executive Editor. Bill—a burly man with thick-rimmed tortoiseshell glasses—was a nice guy until you missed a deadline or came unprepared to a meeting. She placed her calls as she turned onto the interstate on-ramp.

Her final call, about ten miles from the bridge-tunnel, was to Monty. He picked up on the first ring. She was a little nervous at first, but as the conversation progressed her jitteriness subsided. Monty, she thought as he spoke, was an easy man to talk to. She felt his awkwardness was largely due to B.A.'s often stern demeanor. He praised the weekend as a success and said how wonderful he thought she was on Friday and all weekend. Ruefully, he admitted he'd hoped more would have happened—and realized that B.A. had invited Caldwell, announcing it literally as Addison was arriving Friday. She assured him she enjoyed the weekend and was especially looking forward to sharing more time together. Not wanting to assume, he asked flat out if she meant time with him and B.A. She chuckled and scolded him for being unsure—she meant the three of them as a couple—then corrected herself mid-sentence to *throuple*.

Monty broke into a huge smile hearing her say *throuple*. It was their word, and he was pleased that she thought of them that way. Her instincts told her to mention Perry — Caldwell's overnight stay in her room. She had no idea he had seen them. When she mentioned that she and Perry had hung out and fallen asleep on her bed, Monty's breath caught; he felt his groin release and again felt a stir for this woman on the phone.

When Monty asked the age-old question she figured was around the bend — *when would they see her again* — his phrasing was, "…when will I…?" She took a breath before she purposely embellished a family commitment, saying she would be out of town for several days — her way of giving herself space and time to get serious work done. He sounded disappointed, but not for long; he began offering her his jet and arranging car pickups at the airport. She assured him she could manage and not to worry — she would call them as soon as she returned.

As she approached the highway sign — *Bridge-Tunnel 5 miles* — she told him that Perry had told her about Ellen. Before he could respond, she continued, telling him she had had a similar experience with her husband. That seemed to quiet Monty for a few seconds. He was stunned that they would have such tragedy in common. They offered equal condolences and promised to have a quiet moment to share what they had in common. They disconnected saying *see you soon* rather than *good-bye*, and *looking forward to the next time*.

Addison was reflective as she passed through the toll gate, entering into the eighth wonder of the world, which had gone through a couple of metamorphoses since its inception. She could not imagine driving on a narrow two-lane, each direction, bridge — let alone a tube that took you under the water to the floor of the bay. As it was, two lanes in the same direction wasn't that great either, but better than the ferry boats that littered the Northeast.

✲
✲✲

She worked remotely from her home nestled on the river, in the palatial, upscale, gated community of Windermere Grove. The grounds were home to an exclusive country club featuring golf, tennis, racquetball, squash, pickleball, and Addison's new obsession—paddle. It gave her the unparalleled serenity she coveted. Deer, foxes, and birds of prey were plentiful along the riverbanks, and the view across the narrows revealed the vast sweep of the National State Park.

Leaving the grocery pickup, she decided to swing by *The Gilded Bean* for some fresh coffee beans. She loved mixing blends to create her own private, one-of-a-kind brews. As she exited the car, the smell of fresh-baked bread from the bakery a few doors down tempted her to visit there first. She bought a loaf of her favorite multigrain and a half-dozen brioche rolls.

Slipping into the coffee shop, she hoped no one would recognize her or stop to chat about how wonderful the café was. She also hoped her general manager would be too busy to notice her on a mid-Sunday morning. She tentatively opened the glass door, peering to see who was behind the counter—no one she recognized, which meant she could slip in unnoticed.

Her timing was impeccable; there was no line. She walked up to the young man behind the counter, his crisp new Oxford shirt and apron neatly pressed. His name tag read **Walter**. She smiled and called him by name as she ordered a mix of beans. He stepped away to fill the bags from the coffee silos in the barista-only area. The aroma of fresh beans filled the air around the twelve digital dispensers, branded *Coffee Silo by The Gilded Bean*.

When he returned, the bags were custom-labeled. He presented them to her for approval, smiling now—someone in the back had clearly told him who she was. She nodded her approval, and Walter began to bag the beans. She handed him her personal *Gilded Bean* employee card, which he swiped through the tablet mounted on its sleek pedestal. Her total was zero. Addison had adopted this method to track employee consumption while still allowing them ample free items throughout the store. Some had taken to collecting cups and travel mugs—an unintentional marketing strategy that enhanced the customer experience.

She thanked him and headed quickly for the door. Safely back in her SUV, she drove toward the Grove, making one more quick stop at the *Dawg-Gone Wild Bakery*. The gang deserved a treat. Back on the road, a few miles later, she turned into the divided entrance of Windermere Grove, using the far-right lane marked **Residents Only**. As she approached the closed gate, she pressed the button just above the windshield, and the gate slowly opened. The light turned green, and she drove through. Sundays were always busy at the Grove—residents returning from church, from trips, or heading out for brunch away from the club.

*
**

Her home was her sanctuary—stone and glass nestled behind manicured hedges and gardens bursting with perennials in golds, lavenders, reds, and whites. Little Gem magnolias shaded the entrance to the driveway. The side-load garage gave the one-story structure a grander presence, and the ten- and fifteen-foot ceilings made the black roofline feel even more expansive. The stone façade —soft beiges, pinks, and golds—paired with the solid mahogany double doors lent the home a quiet diplomatic elegance. Three evergreen magnolias stood sentinel across the front.

Addison had worked with one of Perry's architectural engineers on the finishing details. The original design had been Thayer's—a two-story Georgian—but Addison wanted her life contained on one floor. Her redesign required a double lot to accommodate an attached three-car garage, a pool, and separate utility housing for the HVAC, water system, and generator, tucked behind the garage but accessible from the circular drive. During construction, she added a carriage-style structure for D.J.—complete with a full kitchen, living room, one-and-a-half baths, and a

bedroom with a private entrance beyond the gate. Screened by its own hedges, the cottage wasn't visible from the street. Where stone gave way, soft gray Hardie plank siding complemented the manicured ligustrums, boxwoods, and golf-course-green lawn. A custom yard sign at the foot of the driveway read:
Klaus, Margo, and Scout—Do Not Disturb.

Pulling into the garage and closing the door behind her, she could already hear Scout howling—something he always did when overly excited. That set Klaus and Margo off in alternating barks. It was the kind of welcome that never got old. As she stepped into their space, she was surrounded by moans and whines that said *missed you* and *where's my treat?*

One by one they flipped through the doggie door into the house. She waited for Klaus to enter, then opened the door to her light-filled home. Large windows lined the rooms, fitted with white Levolor shutters. At the rear, double French doors stood bare, framing a panoramic view of the river and the covered patio with its outdoor kitchen and stone fireplace.

Inside, walls were papered or painted in soft tones with custom moldings throughout. The great room featured floor-to-ceiling bookshelves filled with titles on gardening, fiction, nonfiction, and psychology—signed editions of books she had edited for her publishing house, and a few of Thayer's old finance texts.

During her years at UNC Greensboro and graduate school at Duke, she'd been fascinated by what motivated creative minds.

"The psychology of an author is the cornerstone of every book," she would say when asked. "To understand the author is to understand how best to serve them."

Across from the shelves, a massive flat screen rested on a glass-topped table with arched teak legs. Pocket lighting and sconces dotted the foyer, hallways, and great room. It felt like breathing fresh air again—her space, her world.

She made several trips back to the SUV for groceries, leaving the door open so the pups could follow. Each trip brought fresh whining—pleas she knew translated to *where's my treat?*

The kitchen, bright and open, featured its own double French doors to the screened patio. White marble floors, pale gray granite counters with black-and-white swirls, and textured wallpaper met crisp chair rail molding. She put away pantry items, leaving refrigerated goods on the round glass table surrounded by upholstered black chairs.

Every time she came home, she marveled at the perfection of this dream kitchen with its Gaggenau glass-front refrigerator, hidden drawer freezer, and La Cornue *Château* range with twin side-opening ovens. She had scoured the internet to find every exact fit—determined to make it perfect.

In the corner by the garage door sat the feeding station: three raised bowls, two silver water buckets, and a laminate screen covering the wall. She'd saved the *Dawg-Gone Wild* bag for last. Scout had already figured it out. He sat handsomely, his brown eyes locked on the bag—a model sitter.

Margo circled him like an impatient sister, as if saying, *get your butt in the kitchen, the bags are already here*. Klaus, ever the sentry, stood at the open door guarding against any escape attempt.

They were her bright lights. Klaus, the Giant Schnauzer she'd raised with Gerta—her late female Schnauzer—had been her constant through grief. Gerta passed six months after Thayer's accident. In the chaos of widowhood—deciding whether to sell the Hamptons house, sorting his finances—Addison had known instinctively that Kellum County, Virginia, would be her next chapter.

Before listing the New York townhouse, she and Klaus took a drive up the Hudson Valley to visit a Bernedoodle breeder she'd read about. Klaus, ever the road snob, insisted on the front seat. When they arrived, he immediately chose his companion—a tri-colored puffball who followed him everywhere. Addison named her Margo, *Klaus's pearl*.

The moment Addison slid the *Dawg-Gone Wild* bag from the SUV, Scout barked, signaling the others. All three circled her as she walked toward the kitchen. Not one broke formation until she said the magic word:

"Sit."

Like a well-trained platoon, they dropped in unison—yawning, squealing, ears back, eyes fixed on the bag. She placed a treat in each bowl, crossed to the refrigerator for a bottle of water, and glanced back. They hadn't moved.

"Okay, good guys."

That was all it took. They were at their bowls in a frenzy of crunching peanut-butter biscuits. Scout glanced back as she

left the kitchen, duffle in hand, heading toward the rear of
the house.

***

Her bedroom reflected a woman of sophistication and
elegance. The windows, with custom coverings that could
let in light or block it completely, matched the wall
treatments. In one corner of the room sat three framed
photos of her and her husband. Addison could still recall
the valet's hand shaking as he approached her at a business
dinner, handing her the phone—it felt like yesterday. The
voice on the other end belonged to a stranger who identified
himself as a trauma surgeon at New York–Presbyterian
Lower Manhattan Hospital.

"Mrs. Hollace, your husband has been seriously injured.
Please make your way here—we need to rush him into
surgery."

Oh my God. Addison's mind was screaming as she dropped
the phone and bolted toward the restaurant entrance. The
maître d', who had taken the call, informed her that a car
service was waiting. Her instinct was to hail a cab, but he
insisted she take the car. Confused and desperate not to lose
another second, she jumped in, and the driver sped off
toward the hospital's emergency entrance. As she opened

the car door, she tried to hand the driver a bill. His refusal to accept it began to irritate her.

"Mrs. Hollace, I've been instructed to wait for you."

"Oh, don't be silly. My husband's been rushed into emergency surgery—it could take hours," she said, pushing the money over the seat.

"No, ma'am. I'm a friend of D.J.'s. He called the restaurant —and me. My orders are to wait and take you wherever you need to go."

"This is ridiculous," she muttered, exasperated.

But there was no time to argue. She got out of the car and ran through the emergency doors, tears already spilling down her face.

Inside, she collided with the nurses' station, so hard she winced. Breathless, she identified herself and mentioned the surgeon's name. The nurse confirmed he was in surgery with her husband and would speak to her afterward. She gave Addison directions to the trauma surgical suites.

Scrambling through her purse as she waited for the elevator, Addison found one of Thayer's handkerchiefs—a keepsake she didn't remember placing there. She blew her nose just as the elevator doors chimed open. It was empty —thank God. She pressed the floor number and rode in silence, gripping the handkerchief like a lifeline.

When the doors opened again, she stepped into a dimly lit hallway lined with small waiting rooms. A vending machine hummed beside a coffee dispenser. She found an empty room and sat. She didn't want to call his mother or business partners yet. She would wait until he was in a room—until she knew his prognosis. Her mind flickered to her work schedule, to how she could rearrange the living room for his recovery.

She pulled out her phone to make notes, but before she could type a word, D.J. walked in—with Thayer's business partner, Greg, right behind him, and Celeste trailing with a duffel bag and a change of clothes. Addison fought back fresh tears. She didn't even remember calling them. How had they gotten here so quickly?

She stood to hug Greg and explained that she hadn't heard anything yet—the surgeon she'd spoken to was still operating. Celeste gently suggested she change into jeans, a T-shirt, and tennis shoes, pointing toward a small restroom in the corner. Still in shock, Addison obeyed, returning a few minutes later with her dress and heels tucked into the duffel. Celeste took the bag as D.J. stepped forward and wrapped an arm around her shoulders. Addison broke down in sobs against his chest.

When she finally pulled away, she dabbed at her nose and eyes and remembered the conversation with the driver.

"Did you hire a car service for me?" she asked.

D.J., guiding her to a chair, answered evenly, "Yes. Under the circumstances, a car will be your transportation from now on."

"D.J.," she scolded through tears.

"No, Lady A. This isn't up for debate."

Celeste knelt in front of her, handing her a fresh handkerchief. Addison wiped her eyes, trying to steady herself, but their concern only made her feel more scattered. She wished the doctor would hurry—and immediately regretted the thought, scolding herself for wanting answers that might destroy her.

Unable to sit still, she stood abruptly and fled to the restroom. She sat on the closed toilet lid, rocking, blowing her nose, wanting to call someone—anyone—but not the people waiting outside. They were managing her, containing her, and she hated it.

She stopped rocking, stood, and opened the door. All three turned toward her.

"What am I missing, D.J.?" she asked, her voice sharp.

"Come sit, and I'll tell you," he said gently.

She walked over and sat, crossing her legs, eyes swollen and red. Before D.J. could speak, three men entered—two in jackets, one in uniform. The older of the two detectives introduced them and asked for Mrs. Hollace. Celeste, D.J., and Greg all turned toward Addison.

D.J. sat beside her, Celeste on the other side, holding her hand as the detective began explaining what had happened.

A city taxi had struck her husband and fled the scene. Thayer had hit his head on the concrete, losing consciousness. There was a tremendous amount of blood. An officer nearby had arrived within seconds. Several witnesses described the vehicle as a city cab, though none could identify the driver. The officer managed to get a partial plate before running to Thayer's side.

The detective's voice was steady, clinical. Thayer had been crossing in the crosswalk, the pedestrian signal lit. The cab came out of nowhere, clipped him, and sped off.

Paramedics arrived within minutes and transported him here.

Addison heard the words as if from underwater—muffled, distant, unreal. She closed her eyes, trying to make sense of them, when D.J.'s voice pierced the fog.

"Addison."

She opened her eyes to see another man standing before her in green scrubs—the voice from the phone.

He introduced himself again and apologized softly.

"Mrs. Hollace... I'm so sorry. Your husband didn't survive the surgery."

Addison's head shook before her mind could process the words. *No.* Her lips moved, but no sound came out. She was saying the word, but her voice was gone. Everything slowed.

"That's not possible," she whispered hoarsely. "He had a last-minute meeting—just three blocks from our townhouse. He should be home by now. Where's my phone? I'll prove it. Let me call him."

She tried to stand, reaching for her pocket, but dizziness washed over her. The detectives caught her as she slumped forward, and D.J. helped ease her back into the chair. Her head dropped, and the sobs came in violent waves. Each one a reminder—he was gone.

Thayer Hollace was gone.

And Addison knew, with hollow certainty, that her life would never be the same.

In the beginning, during the height of her grief, she was angry with Thayer. If he had turned down that meeting, his driver would have taken him home. He wouldn't have been crossing that street. He would have been home — waiting for her. She had placed these photos in a drawer after having them framed, unable to bear seeing them. Once the house was finished and she began unpacking, she set them out on the table. As the months passed, her anger softened into grief, and as she settled into her new life, she began to heal.

Passing the table with the photos, she entered her closet and dropped the duffel onto an upholstered bench to unpack. The walls of the room were lined with glass doors revealing neatly arranged clothing — blouses, shirts, tops, slacks, jeans, suits, and dresses, all color-coordinated. Her shoes were displayed behind double glass doors on floor-to-ceiling shelves, and beside them, another set of doors revealed a fine collection of handbags — Chanel, Judith Leiber, Louis Vuitton, and a Birkin. Pocket lighting illuminated everything, with a crystal chandelier centered above the space.

An overstuffed chair sat near a clear glass end table topped with a whimsical MacKenzie-Childs lamp. In the opposite corner, a wall of drawers rose eight high. She opened one and pulled out sweatpants and a sweatshirt. Kicking off her shoes, she removed her jeans and shirt. As she pulled up her sweats, the gang arrived, circling her with excitement.

Margo carried a battered tennis shoe—her signal that it was time for a walk. She dropped it at Addison's feet and looked up expectantly. Addison smiled, picked up the shoe, and sat on the bench to slip it on. The three dogs began pacing in and out of the closet, anticipation in every movement.

She emptied the duffel, placing most items into a wicker hamper except for two sweaters, which she hung neatly on a hook. Retrieving the matching shoe confirmed to the trio that the walk was indeed happening. Their pacing grew more animated, claws clicking on the hardwood as they moved from the bedroom to the hall.

Addison left the closet and sat on her four-poster bed, its drapes and comforter coordinated in muted elegance. The silk Asian rug covered most of the pine floor, and the pillows echoed the patterns from the settee and bedskirt. From the bedroom, she could hear the dogs' rhythmic tapping as they patrolled the hall and other rooms—their way of urging her to hurry.

Her office overlooked the river, with two high-backed brown upholstered chairs and a rattan-and-glass desk without drawers. A tall beige leather chair stood behind it, and a short mahogany credenza held her office printer. She checked the paper tray before noticing Scout giving a low growl, as if affirming her every move. Klaus and Margo sat at the doorway, patient but alert.

She smiled. "Just a minute more," she said aloud.

Her three companions—a Giant Schnauzer, a Bernedoodle, and the rescued mix of Lab and Shepherd—were her constants. Unlike Klaus and Margo, Scout was relentless in proving his worth, ever watchful and protective. In some ways, he reminded her of her late brother, Chris, who'd died in Afghanistan.

Celeste, her housekeeper, allowed Addison privacy while ensuring quiet company when needed. D.J., her handyman and groundskeeper, was the hawk always circling— trimming, tending, maintaining perfection. Both had been part of Thayer's life before they became hers.

Celeste, tall with ash-blonde hair usually twisted into a bun, was a French-Canadian trained in estate management at a private arts academy in Quebec. She had come to the U.S. as a young woman to work in private homes. Thayer, friends with a Canadian diplomat returning home, had hired her to oversee his Manhattan penthouse before he and Addison met. Her skill in calligraphy won Addison over when she handwrote two hundred invitations for their Millbrook wedding. There had never been any question that she would follow Addison to Kellum County—she understood Addison's rhythms and her need for solitude.

Darnell "D.J." Jefferson was her sentry. A fifteen-year Army veteran with multiple tours as an engineer, he was tall, clean-shaven, and spoke with quiet authority. He'd been doing handyman work in the Hamptons after his divorce when Thayer hired him to build a pergola at their summer home. He soon became the house sitter and groundskeeper. Like Celeste, he followed Addison to her new life in Belhaven, Virginia.

Time lost its edges. She filled her days walking the dogs, swimming in the pool, cycling, and practicing yoga. She worked late into the night, catching up on manuscripts, answering messages only in the early evening to appear as if she were two time zones away—limiting unnecessary chatter. The solitude restored her.

B.A. left voice messages—brief at first, then longer, ending with *talk soon*. Nothing from Monty. A few texts from Perry, which she answered politely, and a couple she sent to B.A. out of courtesy.

Nearing the end of her self-imposed retreat, Addison woke one morning restless—and unmistakably aroused. She skipped her workout and decided to take the dogs for a walk along the river path behind the golf course. Klaus found a sizable stick, and she threw it again and again, laughing as all three chased it. Sometimes she'd sprint ahead, letting them catch her—tails wagging, lungs burning, heart light.

 Back home, after water and naps, she stepped into a long, hot shower. Steam wrapped around her as she let the heat settle into her muscles and reached for something familiar, adding a generous amount of glide and giving her imagination room to move.

The water streamed over her chest, and she pictured Monty's hands there—cupping, teasing—until her breath changed and her body answered. She let more glide trace the curve of her back, the warmth echoing the sensation she was thinking of, her reaction immediate and unguarded. A low sound escaped her as she brought the sensation closer, letting it build, imagining him with her—steady, deliberate, fully present.

The rhythm intensified as water continued to pour over her, slick and insistent. She followed the feeling lower, circling, lingering, letting the pressure deepen. In her mind, Monty's hands were firm on her hips, guiding her, holding her as the movement became more consuming. Her breathing quickened. The sensations merged, layered and relentless.

When release finally came, it was sharp and overwhelming, taking her without warning.

Her knees softened and she sank to the shower floor, the object slipping away as water streamed over her face and chest. She stayed there a moment, heart racing, letting the intensity ebb until her breathing steadied again.

Finally, she stood, rinsed off, and slipped into sweats.

As she walked toward the kitchen, her thoughts returned to Monty—wondering if this would please him, or if he and B.A. had ever shared that kind of intimacy. For the next few days, that question lingered in her mind.

Midday on the final day of her seclusion, Addison called B.A. and reached voicemail. She left a brief message. An hour later, Monty texted, asking her to call his private office number.

She dialed; it rang once before he answered. He sounded exhilarated, calling her *Sweetie*—several times. Addison, never fond of pet names, felt her stomach tighten. *This could be a problem,* she thought.

Monty, talking fast, told her she was on speaker and that B.A. was with him. He asked where she was, whether she needed a ride from the airport, offering to call a driver— without taking a breath.
Yes, Monty was definitely excited about something.

When he finally paused, Addison jumped in.

"Hi, B.A. Yes, no worries on time. I'm en route. Thank you, Monty—it won't be necessary."

B.A., perched on the edge of her husband's desk, could feel his near-giddy energy. As he stopped to listen, she placed a hand over his. He looked up at her; she smiled and began speaking to Addison.

"We're so happy you're coming back. I know you haven't had a chance to catch your breath, and I hope everything went well with your family. But, Addie, we have some exciting news—or at least, we *hope* it'll be exciting for you. As you can tell, Monty's beside himself."

"I miss—I mean, *we* missed you, Sweetie!" Monty added.

Addison cringed again at the word but answered politely.

"I've missed you all, too."

B.A. raised an eyebrow. *Sweetie* wasn't a word she'd ever heard her husband use before, and she made a mental note to address it later. Addie didn't strike her as a woman who'd appreciate that kind of familiarity.

Still, she didn't want to cool Monty's enthusiasm. She kept talking, her voice bright and warm.

"Addie, I don't want to overwhelm you. I'm sure you've got work to catch up on—house things, the dogs. Can I help with any of it?"

Addison smiled faintly. Truthfully, she'd enjoy the company after days of solitude, but she needed time to protect her little white lie about "family matters."

"How about tomorrow? Late lunch, early dinner?" she suggested.

It would give her time to order takeout from her favorite deli and drop Klaus, Margo, and Scout at daycare for a morning play session—ensuring a quiet afternoon when B.A. arrived.

"No worries about my list, B.A. Let's say three-ish? Now—what's this exciting news?"

"Perfect," B.A. replied. "Monty has a dinner meeting tomorrow evening. I'll leave your place and head to the farmhouse afterward."

"As for our news," Monty interjected.

"Yes?" Addison prompted.

"Oh, no—you said I could tell her!" B.A. exclaimed.

"Then *tell her*, B.A.!" Monty said, laughing as he sank into his chair.

"What's the news, guys?" Addison asked.

"Well, go on," Monty said again, clearly impatient.

"Addie," B.A. finally announced, "we're going to Atlanta! Strictly for fun—shopping, lunch, dinner, and an adult club!"

"Adult as in nude dancers?" Addison asked, half amused.

"No!" B.A. burst out laughing. "Adult as in *adult club*, Addie—lots of naked people acting like adults!"

"Ohhh," Addison said, drawing out the word, smiling despite herself.

"Monty has it all set up, based on the dates we talked about last month," B.A. added, looking over at her husband with that playful sparkle he hadn't seen in years.

"Well, in that case, I'd better start shopping. Are we talking a weekend?"

B.A. nearly squealed as she listed the itinerary—the days, the flights, the restaurant reservations, every detail rehearsed.

"We can go over it all tomorrow," she said. "Are you sure I can't bring anything?"

"No, I'll have everything ready by the time you arrive," Addison replied.

Monty sat back in his leather chair, quietly observing. He hadn't seen his wife this animated in years. In that moment, he was more convinced than ever that Addison's presence was good for them—for the marriage, for the energy between them. The revived intimacy, the excitement, the anticipation—it all felt new again.

Lately, B.A. had been more receptive, less controlled. Their sex life had long been defined by her dominance—her finishing herself, orchestrating every move. But now she seemed open again, warmer.

Still, as Monty listened to the two women's voices over the speaker, his arousal deepened. Nothing—not even his wife's rediscovered enthusiasm—could compare to the heat that surged when he imagined Addison's mouth on him. He could feel himself harden, his pulse quickening, just listening to her speak.

And as the call ended, he sat for a moment in silence, his mind racing with thoughts he couldn't quite push away.

Monty had been at the top of his class in engineering school. Success came early, helped along by his brother's introduction to a prestigious firm in Illinois. He met his first wife, Ellen, while she was still in college, working part-time for an upscale catering company. Monty knew the first time he laid eyes on her that she would be his wife. He set out to win her—completely.

As Ellen later told it, *"I couldn't figure out why a man with a promising career wanted to hang out with a bunch of broke-ass college students. My roommate told me, 'Hold on to that nerd. He's totally into you. That's why he's always hanging around. It ain't got nothing to do with the pot.'"*

During graduation festivities, Monty proposed. By then, they were inseparable—he busy with projects and travel, she planning a modest wedding and preparing for graduate school. When she moved from her cramped off-campus apartment into the house they'd found near Northwestern, Monty had already remodeled it for her—complete with a study so she could pursue her degree in psychology.

They built a comfortable rhythm: work, classes, and weekends with friends—potlucks, winter ski trips, summer camping by the lake.

Life was good. Ellen buried herself in her studies, Monty represented his firm at client meetings and dinners. At one such dinner, he met Russell Tierney—his age, strikingly handsome, fit, and polished. Russell's steel-gray eyes and red curls gave him an intensity that drew attention.

They quickly discovered they both played squash. Each belonged to a different club, so they began alternating locations. After several months and countless matches, they became friends, and Monty introduced Ellen to Russell.

Russell, however, wanted more than friendship. The time spent showering in separate stalls after their matches had stirred something in him. He was captivated by Monty and wanted time with him—without the wife. Ellen, unaware, took to calling him "Russ," despite his correction. She meant no harm, but to Russell it felt like a dismissal.

One evening, the three attended a formal dinner together. During the clearing of plates, a waitress accidentally spilled au jus onto Monty's lap. She was mortified, but Monty accepted her apology graciously. Russell, visibly irritated, took control.

"Let me help," he insisted, snatching a bottle of club soda from a waiter.

Ellen asked for another bottle and followed the men to the restroom door, perching on a bench across the hall while they went inside. Monty looked back and smiled at her before the door swung shut.

Inside, Russell grabbed a burgundy cloth napkin from the counter, soaked one end with the soda, and knelt in front of Monty.
"Hold still," he said. "Just trying to save your tux."

The stain was close to Monty's groin, just above the line of his briefs. Russell dabbed gently, then let the cloth linger, moving it in slow, deliberate strokes. The motion lasted too long to be accidental. Monty's body reacted before his mind caught up.

Russell's pulse quickened. He moved his hand higher, pressing the napkin more firmly against the warmth beneath the fabric. When he murmured, "Let me dry the other side," his voice dropped, unmistakably suggestive.

Monty didn't stop him. Caught between alcohol and confusion, he let Russell's hand slip lower, the touch growing more insistent. The rhythm changed—steadier now, more certain. Monty's head tipped back, his breath catching, the shock of it scrambling his thoughts. The closeness, the heat, the sudden loss of control left him suspended between reaction and recognition.

Then Ellen's voice came through the door.

"Is the stain coming out, honey?"

Monty snapped to attention, fumbling to zip up.

"Yes, honey, we'll be out in a sec."

Russell, flushed and aroused, wanted him to stay—to finish what he'd started. Monty looked at him once, adjusted his trousers, and walked out without a word.

By the time Russell rejoined them, the couple was already seated again, laughing softly over dessert. Russell's jaw tightened. He wanted acknowledgment, something—but Monty didn't look up. The red blotches rising along Russell's neck didn't go unnoticed by Donna, the office manager's assistant, seated nearby. She knew his temper.

Months earlier, she'd seen it firsthand.

One afternoon, at a corner drugstore near the office, Russell had argued loudly with his partner—a well-dressed man in a gray pinstripe suit and pale pink tie. The man's diamond stud caught the fluorescent light as he tried to reason with Russell, who was seething.

Donna had caught only fragments—"condo" or maybe "condom"—but the tone was unmistakable. Russell was furious. His voice rose, and before storming out, he shouted, "We're done!" The other man stood frozen, humiliated in the middle of the aisle.

When the stranger finally composed himself, he set a small box back on the shelf, rubbed his temples, and left empty-handed. Donna wandered past a few minutes later, confirming her guess. The aisle was lined with condoms. *Well, I'll be damned,* she thought.

Later that afternoon, on her way to the mailroom with an armful of architectural tubes, she saw Monty and one of the firm's partners boarding the elevator. They greeted her warmly before the doors slid shut. Seconds later, Russell appeared, nearly breathless.

"Was that Montaque Langford getting on the elevator?"

"Yes," Donna said, noting his navy sport coat and lavender polo—his eyes, strikingly gray against the fabric.

"Did he happen to mention if he'd be returning?"

She blinked. *Why would a senior associate tell me his comings and goings?* Before she could answer, he waved a hand.

"Never mind. Pay me no mind, Miss Donna. This new contract's got us all in a tizzy."

He smiled tightly, tapped her shoulder, and strode down the hall toward his design office. She watched him go, wondering if he'd patched things up with his lover after the drugstore scene.

Monty and Russell continued to work together on major projects—Russell always maneuvering to be assigned wherever Monty was. After work, they played squash, trading jabs and confidences. In the locker room afterward, their banter often drifted toward office gossip and sex.

One night, the conversation turned to two colleagues—one a woman in Project Management, the other a man in Records.

"Think the guy's gay?" Monty asked casually.

Russell smirked. "If he ain't now, I'll turn him."

Monty laughed. "I don't doubt it. A straight man wouldn't stand a chance with you, Russell."

The air thickened. Separated by a waist-high tile partition, Monty could feel his body react again, unbidden. Russell, already aroused, began to lather himself with soap, stroking deliberately. Quietly, he unlatched the partition gate and stepped closer.

But before he could move in, the door swung open. Three men entered, talking loudly, taking the empty stalls. Monty turned off his shower, grabbed a towel, and left without looking back.

"Good night, Russell," he called over his shoulder.

Russell stood motionless beneath the spray, the lather rinsing away, frustration simmering under his skin.

△ ▽ ⩔ ⩑

"Atlanta Approach, Citation N987AB, level at one-zero thousand, inbound to Charlie Brown Field, information Bravo."

"Citation N987AB, radar contact. Expect visual approach Runway Two-Six. Fly heading two-one-zero, vectors for sequence. Descend and maintain five thousand."

"Heading two-one-zero, down to five thousand, Citation N987AB."

"Citation N987AB, turn right heading one-five-zero, descend and maintain three thousand. You'll be west of the field for right base to Runway Two-Six."

"Right turn one-five-zero, three thousand, Citation N987AB."

As the jet banked right, the blue of the sky was mesmerizing. Addie couldn't recall ever seeing such a flawless shade of blue, despite her countless flights. She felt the charge of excitement rising within her—the electricity of the city already humming from the skyline now in perfect view. *This is going to be an epic getaway,* she thought.

"Citation N987AB, turn right heading two-five-zero, maintain three thousand until established. Cleared for visual approach Runway Two-Six. Contact Fulton County Tower one-two-three-point-seven-five."

"Right to two-five-zero, cleared for the visual Two-Six, switching to Tower, Citation N987AB."

"Fulton County Tower, Citation N987AB, visual Two-Six, five miles out."

"Citation N987AB, Fulton County Tower, winds two-seven-zero at six, Runway Two-Six cleared to land."

"Cleared to land Runway Two-Six, Citation N987AB."

The jolt as the wheels kissed the runway brought B.A. from her nap. She'd been up since four a.m., catching up on a few important listings. Leaving the showings to her assistant, she told herself, would be good experience. Especially if this trip opened doors for the private project she'd been nurturing for months.

This getaway had been her idea—born from the need to reassert herself, to make a statement. She felt good about it. The risk was real, but the rewards were closer than ever.

"Citation N987AB, exit left at Taxiway Bravo, contact Ground on one-two-one-point-nine."

"Exit left at Taxi Bravo, switching to Ground on one-two-one-point-nine, Citation N987AB."

"Citation N987AB, Fulton County Ground, taxi to Signature Flight Support via Taxiway Bravo and Alpha."

"Taxi to Signature via Bravo and Alpha, Citation N987AB."

As the Citation X rolled to a stop, several men approached the aircraft—three in flight jumpsuits with headsets, two in matching polo shirts and khakis, and one in a black polo, black slacks, and polished shoes. Behind him gleamed a Cadillac Escalade ESV, its chrome trim catching the late-afternoon sun like a prism. At the rear passenger door, another man stood with a tray of hot towels, chilled water, and champagne flutes.

Monty was more than pleased. Every detail of his request had been executed to perfection.

"Ladies," he said, grinning, "our ride awaits—and welcome to Atlanta."

The co-pilot unlatched the cabin door as the ground crew began unloading luggage from the jet's belly. A who's who of designer brands: Monty's **TUMI Alpha Garment Bag** and 24-inch **Spinner**; B.A.'s **Briggs & Riley 25-inch Spinner** in olive with her **Guyana Triple-Zip Duffel** in stone, both monogrammed *BAL*; and Addie's **Louis Vuitton Horizon 70** and **Bandoulière**, elegantly embossed *AGH*.

The throuple entente, assisted by the pilot and co-pilot, descended the stairs of the Citation X.
The driver of the Escalade was already approaching, offering a polished welcome to Atlanta before motioning toward the waiting tray of hot towels and champagne. The trio accepted the gesture with quiet appreciation, slipping into the cool leather of the rear cabin while the ground crew carefully loaded their curated luggage into the SUV's cargo bay.

Once everything was secured, the hatch lowered with a soft thud, and the Escalade eased away from the tarmac through an electronic gate marked **EXIT ONLY**. The driver rolled his window halfway to acknowledge the guard, received a nod in return, and merged smoothly onto the access road.

The drive to the **St. Regis Atlanta** was long and deliberate. Evening traffic had reached its crescendo, a familiar Atlanta ballet of brake lights and impatience. I-85 was clogged in both directions; SR-400 offered only marginal relief. Still, inside the car, conversation flowed easily—plans for the next four days, beginning with dinner that night at **Atlas**, the hotel's Michelin-starred jewel.

Monty had handled all the arrangements, though the trip had been B.A.'s inspiration. Her research into Atlanta's hidden world of adult entertainment had been meticulous, leading her to the city's most exclusive erotic club— **Cirque Écarlate**—tucked within the industrial southwest district.

As was his habit, Monty had done his own reconnaissance. Several weeks earlier, on a business trip out west, he'd diverted his route south. His pilot landed at Fulton County, where Monty rented a nondescript car and made a quiet visit to the club just as the night's energy began to rise.

He paid the steep single-male entrance fee and stepped into a world of pulsing light and curated decadence. A hostess in a backless tuxedo and opera-length pearls greeted him with an expert smile. Her shorts barely covered her toned backside, her composure unwavering.

"Good evening, sir. May I help you find a room, a friend — or help you *make* a friend?"

Monty, never one to shrink from curiosity, met her gaze.

"Perhaps just a few questions," he said.

She smiled knowingly, took his elbow, and led him through double frosted-glass doors framed in red velvet drapes. To the right, she opened an indiscreet door with a gold handle and motioned him inside. The sound of the DJ and dance floor faded instantly.

"Please, sit," she said, taking a seat on the coffee table across from him with a leather-bound notebook and pen in hand. "What can I make special for you, sir?"

Monty hesitated, then decided to be direct.

"There will be three of us," he said. "We're a throuple entente, if that's a word. I want the evening to be unforgettable. Perhaps a fourth person — someone to add a little heat. I'm not sure yet whether that means a man or a woman, but I want everyone vetted properly. Health, discretion, background — you understand."

The hostess nodded approvingly.

"We handle requests of all kinds. Discretion and safety are part of our brand. Some guests prefer voyeurs, others like to perform. We can arrange men or women comfortable with either, or both."

It was exactly what Monty wanted. He reached into his jacket and pulled out a roll of hundreds. The hostess lifted one finger delicately—wait.

"Oh no, sir," she said quickly, smiling. "Quite the contrary —I'm pleased you're well prepared. But we include gratuity in our fee. I simply need to record your specifics to ensure everything meets your expectations."

"I see," Monty replied. "Then note that this will take place in a few weeks. We'll be in town for four days, and I want everything arranged before we arrive."

"Even better," she said, her tone brightening. "Time to plan means time for perfection. Give me a moment to write this up. Coffee while you wait?"

"If it's available, yes—cream only."

She nodded and spoke softly into her phone. Within seconds, another woman appeared carrying a silver tray with a porcelain cup and saucer, a small pitcher of cream, and a spoon. She set it on the table with practiced grace.

"Thank you," Monty said.

The coffee was excellent—strong, dark, and smooth. He took a sip just as the hostess returned, her leather notebook closed around a slim digital tablet.

"Mr. Langford, everything is arranged. Just your signature here, and I'll forward confirmation to your membership contact."

Monty reviewed the digital form—details, fees, all precise—and signed with the stylus. As he handed it back, his phone vibrated with a confirmation message.

"You're all set, Mr. Langford," she said warmly. "Feel free to reach out with any adjustments or special requests."

He stood, extended his hand, and she accepted it firmly before speaking softly into her phone again. A young attendant in a red jacket appeared to escort him to the exit.

The night air outside was cool and sharp, carrying the faint scent of magnolia and rain. The attendant opened the door of his rental car with a courteous nod.

Monty slipped him a ten, slid behind the wheel, and drove toward the street that had led him there. He felt a deep satisfaction settle in his chest. *B.A. will be thrilled,* he thought. *And Addison... even more so.*

By the time his jet leveled on its westbound course later that night, Monty had fallen fast asleep—pleased with his own secret planning.

As the Escalade pulled up to the gate, the ladies noticed Monty had been preoccupied.

"Are you okay, Montague?" B.A. asked.

"Yes, love. I'm relaxed—and excited for you ladies to enjoy every part of this weekend."

The driver spoke into the call box, and the gate opened with quiet ceremony. They weren't just staying at the St. Regis —they were guests at The Residences at St. Regis. The SUV glided up to the glass entrance doors where a stately man greeted them. He opened the rear door, and Monty stepped out, giving his name. The man welcomed him warmly.

On the opposite side, the driver opened the door for B.A. and Addison, who emerged looking effortlessly elegant and chic. B.A., dressed in fitted slacks and a knit sweater top cut low enough to show a teasing hint of cleavage, wore sleek flats. Her cropped hair was slicked back, catching light in strands of gold and amber woven through her dark tresses.

Addison was striking in a flowing midi skirt with a pronounced slit that revealed her toned legs as she moved. The soft breeze from the automated doors lifted the fabric, offering a flash of thigh that made one wonder if she wore anything beneath. Her matching blouse, sleeves rolled just below the elbow, was unbuttoned enough to reveal a glimpse of lace—muted periwinkle, the same shade as the subtle stripe in her shirt and skirt. Her strappy heels elongated her legs, and her hair, pinned in a loose updo with a large claw clip, shimmered under the lights. Diamond hoops completed the look, sparkling with each turn of her head.

Monty, now at the concierge desk, had removed his jacket and rolled his sleeves, speaking easily with the suited gentleman behind the counter. He was handed two sets of keys. A valet gathered their luggage onto a gold trolley and followed the trio into the elevator up to the twenty-third floor.

The elevator opened to the private foyer of an expansive three-bedroom, three-and-a-half-bath residence. The windows framed a sweeping view of the Buckhead skyline. White-trimmed walls, soft taupe floors, and matching roman shades created a quiet sophistication.

A large taupe sectional, piled with deep-red and brown throw pillows, anchored the living room. A long rattan-and-glass console supported a pair of jade lamps with cream silk shades, while two overstuffed chairs flanked a porcelain-patterned lamp in red and black toile. Along the hallway stood a high-boy curio cabinet displaying Asian statues and delicate Baccarat figurines that caught the afternoon light.

In the open kitchen, a private chef was already preparing dinner. The adjacent dining room, awash in natural light, featured a dark-wood table set for three. Beyond the main living area, the hallway led to four doors—the guest bath in white accented with bold greens and blues, the primary suite at the end, and two guest rooms across from each other, each with its own en suite.

"How are we doing this?" B.A. asked.

"Doesn't matter to me," Addie replied.

"Well, ladies," Monty said, "both guest rooms are well appointed. I thought each of you would take one, and I'll take the primary."

Before Addison could answer, B.A. had already agreed. The bellman was instructed where to place each bag. Monty tipped him generously as the women disappeared into their respective rooms. On his way back down the hall, he conferred with the chef, then tapped on both doors, letting them know dinner would be in an hour and a half. Both answered in agreement through closed doors.

Monty retreated to the primary suite—a spacious room with a California king bed, marble floors, and a glass shower large enough for four, fitted with both a rain and handheld showerhead. He stripped, showered, and dressed for dinner.

The women emerged before he did, both wearing sundresses with bare shoulders and sweeping hems. B.A.'s was white and gauzy; Addison's, a pale olive that hugged her figure. Monty appeared last, in navy slacks and a dark-green polo, barefoot as usual.

A server prepared their drinks: a dry martini for B.A., a perfectly chilled glass of Sauvignon Blanc for Addie, and a poured-to-perfection Duvel in its signature glass for Monty.

Addie, wine in hand, moved to the window. Below, Peachtree Road shimmered with headlights, the Buckhead skyline reflecting the red afterglow of the setting sun. The sight filled her with warmth and anticipation. She was ready—for tonight, and for what tomorrow might bring.

From behind her, the recessed lights cast a soft glow over B.A., who had been uncharacteristically quiet since they'd landed. Gone was her signature sparkle of diamonds. In its place, a white-gold ring with a small diamond on her right forefinger and a white-gold pinky ring on her left hand—an ouroboros with a ruby for its eye.

"It's a gift from an old friend," B.A. said, catching Addison's glance. "I don't wear it often anymore, but this trip felt like the right time. A symbol of our... free, erotic selves."

Addie smiled. "It does have presence. I came across it once in my post-graduate work—the psyche and its need to evolve."

"I think we're evolving," Monty said as he stepped beside her.

Addie turned toward him, amused by his relaxed posture—barefoot in his "haughty-taughty Hamptons polo," as she called it.

"Monty! You're a country boy at heart, dressed to impress in your Hamptons best and bare feet!"

He grinned. "It's the Hamptons look, my dear lady. Warm night, dinner done, you lose the jacket, roll up your pants, kick off your shoes, and take a walk along the shore. Maybe make out a bit."

B.A. laughed softly. "Oh, trust me—the sea breeze, the water lapping the shore—it makes for a *great* orgasm, doesn't it, Monty?"

He winked, and the three of them dissolved into easy laughter.

Moments later, the chef reappeared to announce that dinner was served.

The meal was exquisite. The wine flowed, the conversation turned playful, and laughter came easily. When dessert arrived—a delicate soufflé served with decaf from a heated carafe—the chef and his staff cleared the kitchen quietly.

For the first time since their journey began, the three were finally alone.

***

Anxious to be with her, Monty poured himself another glass of wine. He walked around the table and topped off each glass. B.A. nibbled at her dessert while Addie got up, disappeared down the hall, and returned with a neatly rolled joint and a lighter. The three, glasses in hand, moved down the hall to the primary suite. They ended up in the large bathroom—marble and glass gleaming under soft light, the shower easily big enough to hold the three of them.

B.A. sat on the edge of the soaking tub. Monty and Addie sat on a towel on the marble floor. They sipped their wine and passed the joint among them. When it was just a nub, Monty stood, walked to the commode, and flushed it. When he turned back, he saw Addison unbuttoning her dress—revealing smooth skin beneath her bra, unmistakably bare beneath the fabric. The way she stood, open and unapologetic, made Monty's pulse jump.

B.A., still perched on the tub, leaned back and exposed herself further, her body responding instantly. Monty reached for her, his hands moving with familiarity, drawing a soft sound from her as her breath quickened. Addison moved closer, kneeling between them, her hands sliding along B.A.'s thighs and gently encouraging her to open. When B.A. yielded, Addison leaned in, slow and deliberate, making B.A.'s voice break.

The sounds were encouragement enough. Monty felt the reaction under his hands as Addison's attention stayed steady and unhurried. He stepped free of restraint, standing over Addison as B.A. drew him in. The closeness, the shared heat, made him groan despite himself.

B.A. lost herself quickly, Addison knowing exactly how to keep her balanced on the edge—drawing it out, not letting her fall too soon. When B.A. shifted to reposition, Addison had no choice but to pull back. She watched instead, her own desire undeniable, her body responding openly as she leaned against the glass, breath uneven.

Their eyes met. Monty saw the tension in Addison's posture, the way she arched, trembling. He wanted her— wanted that connection again, the one that had marked them from the beginning. Addison never looked away. Her breathing told him she was close.

Monty moved first. He drew back from B.A., motioning toward the bed. Addison followed last. B.A. climbed onto the mattress, pulling back the covers, waiting. Monty reached for Addison's hand, and when their fingers touched, the charge between them was immediate. He didn't want to let go.

Still holding her hand, he led her into the bedroom. B.A., already positioned, watched as Monty settled back and drew Addison over him. He adjusted himself, then guided B.A. closer, positioning her above him, facing Addison.

Before she could settle, he pulled Addison in, kissing her deeply, tasting his wife on her lips. His hands moved over her, possessive and sure, drawing a moan from her before he leaned back again.

B.A. took her place, and Addison eased down onto Monty, teasing him, making him wait before closing the distance completely. When she finally did, she lifted her gaze to B.A., their eyes locking as Addison began to move.

Addison reached for B.A., touching her, kissing her, their mouths meeting as their bodies answered one another. Monty's movements grew more urgent beneath Addison as B.A. responded above him. The sound and sight of it pushed Addison higher, her body taut with want.

The intensity built until it could no longer be held. B.A. was the first to break, crying out as she collapsed back onto the bed, spent. Monty rolled Addison onto her back and followed her down.

Braced over her, he looked into her face—hair loose, eyes heavy—and brushed it back before kissing her softly. She wrapped her legs around him as they found their rhythm together, breath and movement filling the room.

Addison cried out as release tore through her, Monty following, their bodies tightening and then giving way together. He stayed with her, close enough to feel her heartbeat slow beneath him.

They turned their heads. B.A. lay beside them, still flushed, an object resting forgotten against her skin. Monty rolled to the opposite side, Addison between them, the air thick and quiet.

B.A., her thoughts still spinning, drifted back to a darker fantasy, the marks she'd imagined leaving behind. Addison lay glowing in the aftermath, Monty beside her, that familiar electric connection still humming. He remembered B.A. telling him that Addie liked it rough — that she wanted it right there.

They drifted off together — B.A. on his left, her back against him, Addison on his right, her spine pressed to his chest.

The morning arrived, the bedroom darkened by heavy blackout drapes. Monty stirred to find himself alone in the king-size bed, tangled in the sheets, his head throbbing from the wine he'd drunk the night before. His mind raced to recall the aftermath of the evening's events. He didn't remember either lady leaving the room. Listening for sound beyond the door, he heard nothing. Maybe they were still asleep.

He got up and headed to the bathroom — no clothes, no wine glasses. The towels they'd used were in a heap in the corner. He turned on the shower, made it extra hot, and activated the overhead rain shower. Breathing in the steam to clear his head, he scrubbed down, rinsed, stepped out, wrapped a fresh towel around his waist, and shaved.

With sweats on, he opened the bedroom door to a blast of bright sunlight and the smell of coffee and something baking. Adjusting his eyes to the light, he walked barefoot down the hall. Addison's door was ajar; B.A.'s was closed. As he rounded the corner to the kitchen, he found Addison removing pre-made dishes from the oven, the microwave humming, and the coffee maker finishing its brew cycle.

She looked elegant—without an ounce of hangover. Her hair was piled high on the crown of her head, and she wore a short dress in a wild floral pattern with deep patch pockets at the hips, barefoot and glowing. She turned when she heard him clear his throat.

"Good morning, Montaque. I trust you slept well."

"Yes, I slept well, thank you. Bright, sunny morning to you, Addison."

They stood looking at one another. In the brief silence, he knew she was happy with the night's culmination. She smiled, turned back to the oven, and busied herself with the dishes. He walked to the counter, grabbed a mug she'd set out, and poured himself coffee. A steeping mug sat by the window. He took his cup, pulled out a chair, and sipped quietly, not wanting to interrupt her rhythm.

As she removed two dishes from the oven, the microwave chimed. She pulled out a covered bowl and set it beside the others. From the refrigerator, she retrieved a pitcher of orange juice and proudly displayed a container marked *Martinelli's Apple Juice*—her favorite. Bringing both to the table, she smiled at him.

"What?" he asked.

"Montaque Langford, you've thought of everything — my juice, quiche, and not just any quiche, but my favorite: spinach."

"Why, little lady, you ain't seen nothin' yet," he replied in a mock Western drawl.

Addison laughed. He did that — made her laugh. She liked it. But she was still guarded. The *throuple entente* was a pack, but in reality Monty and B.A. were husband and wife. She didn't want to become attached to him, yet this trip had melted her defenses. Last night, he'd lit a fuse in her she hadn't felt in years. She could still feel the connection while they made love —
No, she told herself. *You can't go there*.

She continued transferring dishes to the table. Monty sat gazing at her, wondering what she was thinking. He resisted asking, just kept watching — the strong jawline, her glowing skin, tendrils of hair falling around her face and neck. Then he heard a buzzing sound.

Addison stopped, set down her mug, and pulled her phone from her pocket. She looked at it, then slipped it back. Monty stayed silent, still watching as she brought juice glasses to the table and sat. He finally noticed the full spread — three place settings, juice glasses, and a carafe of coffee on a warming plate.

"It smells delicious. Let's eat!" Monty said.

"Should we wake B.A.?" Addison asked.

"No, let her sleep. I've got you all to myself, and I want to be selfish — if only for a moment."

He smiled at her, and she returned a shy grin. They ate in silence for a bit, then Monty began detailing the day's itinerary: shopping at Phipps—"Maybe get yourself something for tonight. Lacey, thin, and revealing." Lenox Square after that. "They've got your favorite store. Then lunch at Houston's on Parkside, to wind down from our retail adventure. Back here to rest before dinner and dressing for Cirque Écarlate."

He explained that the driver would pick them up at 9:30 since the club was across town and traffic was always heavy. He'd even arranged for an extra guest at the club—to make the evening more exciting, more adventurous.

Addison sipped her coffee, taking small bites as he spoke. The fact that he'd thought of everything—planned it all—aroused her. She hoped he'd enjoy himself too; he always seemed to take care of everyone else. That made her smile as he continued talking. She returned to the conversation when she heard him say, "The club also has a breakfast bar after 1 a.m."

"Wait, what?"

"A breakfast bar," he repeated.

He took a sip of coffee and continued explaining. "This club is like no other. The atmosphere's electric and first-class—from the drive to the bar, the dance floor, the private rooms. There's a couples-only area, threesomes, women-only, men-only, open space for all—and in the back, a room called *Crimson Key*."

"What's that?" Addison asked.

"Not fully sure. The hostess said it's a specialty area."

"That sounds ominous."

"Yeah, it's bold. Double red doors guarded by two male hosts. There's a rear entrance from the dressing area with showers—also guarded."

Addison chewed in thought, recalling the ring B.A. had worn the night before and what she knew of its symbol. She wondered, then denied the connection, but the thought lingered. Monty kept talking, describing his reconnaissance visit to the club while she'd been "away with family." The mention made her cringe—she'd been less than truthful about her absence. She wanted to confess, but he looked so happy, so relaxed. She couldn't ruin the moment.

And yet she wondered *why* she wanted to tell him the truth. Why *him* and not *them*? The thought unsettled her. Was she actually falling for this man? Losing control of her emotions? She'd promised herself never to get attached again. But with Monty, something felt different.

Her turmoil must have shown on her face. Monty looked at her quizzically. As he raised his cup, his eyes met hers over the rim.

"What?" she asked.

"You seem lost in thought. Everything alright? Are the plans too much? I can change them—change everything if it doesn't appeal to you. I'll make tonight whatever you—"

"Montaque." She interrupted softly, reaching across the table to lay her hands over his.

"Yes, my love?" He flipped his hand, taking hers in his.

"Tonight is perfect. You've made me feel special, and I wouldn't change a thing."

They sat for a quiet moment, his hand still holding hers. Then they heard a door open and footsteps approaching. Addison withdrew her hand, grabbed the carafe, and refilled her cup as B.A. entered the kitchen, fully dressed.

"Good morning, you two," she chimed, grabbing a mug and pouring coffee.

They greeted her in unison, watching her—dressed for business. Before they could ask, she began explaining: a client wanted her to look at a property while she was in Atlanta. Before Monty could protest, she reminded him of his own board meetings that had taken him away more than once. It wasn't an apology—it was a statement.

They bantered about the day's plans. Monty mentioned he'd arranged some jewelry showings for her, but he no longer looked relaxed or pleased. He pressed for her timeframe; she offered none. Monty stood, visibly frustrated, and moved away from the table while B.A. sat, tearing a croissant and spreading strawberry preserves on it —a deliberate way to end the conversation.

Addison, still seated, freshened her coffee, added a dollop of cream, and quietly moved to the sunlit living room to give them space.

A few minutes later, B.A. approached and announced she'd see Addison at lunch and to enjoy shopping. She was a vision of power—black suit, white blouse, red pumps, hair sleek, makeup flawless, *Birkin* in hand. As she leaned in to kiss Addison on the lips, Addison noticed the pinky ring again—the ruby eye, the "O" ring. She wanted to ask but thought better of it.

B.A. left. Addison turned to see Monty sitting at the table, forehead in his hands. She waited before approaching. When she finally began clearing dishes, he spoke.

"Addison, no need to worry about the kitchen. Housekeeping will handle it. And I apologize for my wife's rude behavior."

"Monty, it's fine. We all have business that pulls us away. B.A. said she'll meet us for lunch. We'll enjoy the day—and I'll torture you at Neiman's by trying on at least a hundred dresses."

He looked up. She stood there smiling, radiant—the promise of a good day. He stood, hugged her, and they parted to dress. As she reached her door, she called out,

"Jeans, Montaque!"

He replied as he closed his door, "Yes, Lady A."

She smiled, pleased he remembered the nickname Perry had given her.

Dressed in jeans and a pullover layered over a T-shirt with Italian leather shoes, Monty called out to Addison that the driver had arrived downstairs. Addison rushed out of her room, still tossing items into her brown quilted, double gold-chained Chanel bag, her hair pulled into a low knot. She wore jeans with block heels, a dress shirt, and a plaid jacket.

Monty noticed she smelled delicious. As she reached the door, she smiled up at him, and he kissed her forehead before they headed down the hall to the elevator. He wanted to clasp her hand as they walked but thought better of it. There was an electricity between them.

The elevator already had three people aboard when the doors opened. Monty stepped in first, Addison following behind, standing directly in front of him as the car descended past the lower floors of the hotel, giving the ride an express-elevator feel. He looked down at her; her diamond studs caught the light, sparkling. He adored her. He knew what he was feeling wasn't fair—putting her in that awkward position as the third in the *throuple entente*. He didn't want to jeopardize what they had.

The doors chimed open to a lobby bathed in light and refinement. Monty lightly took Addison's elbow, guiding her toward the door, where an attendant opened it for her. As they stepped into the fall breeze of Georgia, he knew today would be special, even if his wife chose to work. The driver opened the rear door of the Escalade; Addison got in first, then Monty.

The day was bright and sunny, a light breeze signaling fall's approach to the metropolis. Monty's phone buzzed as the driver headed north on West Paces Ferry Road. Addison admired the oak-lined street and its Georgian mansions. She loved Kellum County but also longed for the high-end shopping of New York. She'd resisted making any kind of list—wanting instead to meander and enjoy the luxury that awaited.

Monty kept texting. She leaned toward the window, taking in the view of this southern megacity as they passed the Buckhead MARTA station adjacent to the financial center. The skyline of glass towers signaled their descent into the polished bustle of Buckhead's business district. People scurried about with purpose. Turning onto Peachtree, Lenox Square came into view—massive and gleaming. The *Neiman Marcus* signage was impossible to miss.

No list, she thought. *Just laid-back shopping.*

Glancing to her left, Monty was still engrossed in his phone. She nudged him. He looked up just as the valet walked toward the rear door to greet them. The driver reminded Monty to text when they were ready to be picked up and where to meet him.

Monty stepped out first, turned, and offered Addison his hand.

"We've arrived, my dear. Let's go get some retail therapy."

They passed the large planters of greenery and walked directly into the store. Addison felt her pulse quicken—not because she was entering her favorite store, but because Monty had taken her hand. She couldn't tell whether it was habit from being with his wife or whether he simply wanted to touch her. She looked up at him as they walked farther inside.

"Where would you like to start?" he asked, eyes scanning the store.

"Shoes," she answered without hesitation.

They circled the entire *Neiman's*—from shoes to suits for him, to evening dresses, to casual attire for both. She was caught up in his gentleness, the way he spoke into her ear. It was as if they were the quintessential couple, meandering through the store without a care.

Back on the main level, passing the cosmetic counters, they stepped into the mall. They walked slowly, chatting as Monty carried their shopping bags. Passing *Burberry, Dior, Tory Burch*—a who's-who of designer luxury—they finally found an empty bench and sat. Monty placed the bags between them.

"Wait here, I'll be right back. Coffee or water?" he asked, standing.

"I'd love a regular coffee, but I should hydrate. Coffee," she said, smiling.

He gave her a warm look and walked off toward the escalator. Addison sat people-watching, her thoughts drifting to B.A. She hadn't really thought about her until this moment. She tussled with whether to have a word with her about skipping the shopping trip. They'd discussed her role before—her intimacy with Monty, her comfort with the arrangement. They'd agreed Monty seemed fine with it, even labeling it their *throuple entente*. Both women had promised to keep communication open.

But Addison couldn't shake the feeling that B.A.'s "client appointment" wasn't real. Something about it didn't ring true. She decided she'd talk with her before they went to the club that night.

Lost in thought, Addison looked up to see Monty handing her a coffee—just how she liked it: a small amount in a larger cup, with cream. She accepted it and took the water bottle he offered as he sat beside her.

"I thought we could share the water if you don't mind. If you do, I can grab another—"

"It's fine," she interrupted. "Yes, we can share."

They sat sipping coffee, the water bottle between them, both lost in thought—both thinking about the same subject: B.A.'s disappearance. He wondered what he'd done wrong. She'd become unpredictable lately. He decided he'd have his own talk with her.

He glanced at Addison, still watching people, and thought about her—the night before, the way she'd felt, the sound of his name on her lips.

"Montaque Langford?" a voice came from behind him.

As the man walked around the bench, Monty looked up to see Russell Tierney, with another man behind him—dressed in denim, fancy sneakers, a white T-shirt, and a half-zipped hoodie.

"Russell!" Monty exclaimed, carefully setting his coffee down beside the water bottle.

Addison, now holding both cups, stayed seated as Monty made introductions. Russell cut him off almost immediately, exclaiming that she must be Monty's wife and going on about how lovely she was. Monty raised a hand to stop him mid-sentence.

"No, she's not my wife. She's a family friend. Addison—this is Russell," he said firmly.

Russell's smile faded, chastened by Monty's tone. He bit his lip, extending a hand toward Addison, who was still holding both cups and unable to shake it. *Oh thank God,* she thought. Something about him—and the young man beside him—made her uneasy. *Is he even of legal age?*

The encounter lingered awkwardly. Only a few minutes had passed, but it felt longer. Monty invited them to join him and Addison for lunch. Addison forced a polite smile as Russell accepted, his eyes locked on her. She stood, two heads taller than the red-haired man, and decided she didn't trust him. Still, lunch would be her chance to learn more.

She carried the cups to the trash, holding up Monty's as if to ask whether she should toss his too. He nodded, still talking to Russell, who had his back turned. She raised her shopping bag and mimed *call me*. He nodded again. She smiled and slipped into the crowd of shoppers.

She wandered into the *Louis Vuitton* boutique, greeted by a finely dressed doorman who held the door open.

"Good afternoon, madame. Welcome to our boutique. May I help you find something special today?" said an older gentleman in a tailored suit.

Addison wasn't much of a mall shopper—online purchases and personal stylists were more her speed—but she'd planned this one indulgence for the Atlanta trip. She and the salesman walked to the rear counter, where she requested a monogram canvas Hobo bag. He smiled politely, and she explained she wanted it shipped to her home in Virginia.

He disappeared briefly, then returned carrying a large brown box with the signature *LV* monogram. He opened it, removed the bag, and placed it on the counter for her inspection.

"Yes, this is perfect," she nearly purred.

He smiled and began the purchase process. She signed, thanked him, and left with her bag.

Back in the mall, she spotted *Bvlgari. Why not?* she thought. She paused, hung her shopping bag on her arm, and pulled out her phone to text B.A. The phone buzzed— not B.A., but Monty. His message read simply, *twenty.*

She smiled at his casual brevity—his "trucker talk." She responded with her location. Within seconds, she saw him approaching.

"How much more are you shopping? We've got an appointment to make before lunch with B.A. and Russell at Houston's," he said, taking her bag.

"I'm ready whenever you are," she replied.

They walked back the way they'd come, past the bench where they'd sat earlier, through *Neiman's,* and out to where the Escalade waited. They climbed in and pulled away from Lenox Square.

The drive to the jeweler's was short—just across the street.
Traffic on Peachtree was thick, as always during lunch
hour. The driver stopped in a no-parking zone. Monty and
Addison got out; Monty leaned in to say something to the
driver before he pulled away.

Guiding Addison toward the glass entrance of the building,
Monty said nothing. She was curious but didn't ask. He
liked that about her—she trusted his lead.

At the elevators, he pressed "8." The doors closed; they
were alone.

"What?" she asked, noticing his grin.

He cupped her elbow as the elevator chimed and opened. "I
hope you like it," he said.

Beyond the glass doors stood an attendant in uniform—
armed—who asked Monty's name before opening one
door, which triggered the next. Inside, Addison felt as if
she'd entered a dream. Diamonds of every shape and size
shimmered on raised platforms of burgundy velvet. The
glass cases sparkled under bright white light, making the
jewels appear to float.

A short man in an impeccable navy suit and Princeton tie approached. "Monty!" he greeted warmly, clearly an old acquaintance. They shook hands, and Monty introduced Addison to Mortimer.

"Coffee, champagne, or water?" Mortimer offered.

Addison, curious but composed, declined politely. Monty did the same.

"Well then," Mortimer said, "let me retrieve your purchases. I'll be right back."

Addison drifted around the showroom, drawn to a display marked "DY." David Yurman. In the corner of the case, she spotted a medium chain bracelet—its textured heart surrounded by diamonds. It captivated her.

A petite woman in a navy suit appeared from nowhere, offering to show it to her. Addison nodded. The woman unlocked the case and placed the bracelet on a black velvet pad.

Behind her, Mortimer returned, and Monty's pleased tone suggested everything was in order. Addison turned from the bracelet and joined them.

On a larger velvet pad lay two necklaces—each sparkling under the lights.

"Exquisite," she said.

"I think they're perfect," Monty agreed.

Mortimer straightened. "Each diamond is 0.5 carats, round brilliant cut, matched for exceptional consistency and quality. Flawless clarity, D color, 1.5 carats total, set in 18-

carat white gold. Minimal prongs for maximum light performance and brilliance, suspended on high-polish white-gold cable chains to disappear against the skin—making the stones appear to float. Just as you requested, Monty."

Addison was mesmerized by their sparkle.

"I'll prepare them for you," Mortimer said. "Gift wrap?"

"No, Mort—you've outdone yourself."

"Very good. I'll box them in our traditional presentation." He disappeared again through the walnut door.

As they waited, Monty asked the lady about the bracelet Addison had admired. She brought it over on its black pad and placed it on the counter. Monty immediately noticed the heart, the diamonds. Without looking at Addison, he said, "We'll take this as well. Use my card on file. The lady will take the box, but she's going to wear it now."

Addison took a deep breath, beginning a quiet protest, but he stopped her gently.

"It's done. Which arm?"

No longer resisting, she held out her left wrist, already adorned with a slim tennis bracelet and a Piaget Polo Date 36 mm watch. He fastened the toggle, holding her arm as she admired it.

"Thank you," he said softly.

She looked up at him. "No, Montaque—it's I who should thank you. The necklace is stunning, and the bracelet... well, it's wonderfully personal. Are you sure this is okay?"

"Nonsense. A man's allowed to buy his lady a gift."

Mortimer returned with two bags—the necklaces and the empty *DY* box. Monty and Mortimer shook hands, and the couple departed for the elevator.

Inside, Addison turned to him. "Thank you again," she said, reaching up to kiss him. The moment was warm, tender, personal. Monty wrapped his arms around her waist, returning her kiss.

The elevator chimed. The doors opened. Through the glass, they saw the Escalade idling at the curb.

Once inside the SUV, Monty leaned over, gently touched her chin, and kissed her again. She wrapped her arms around his neck, returning it fully. He murmured how fortunate he was to have her in his life.

It felt like a turning point—no longer *throuple entente,* but something deeper. Monty felt it. Addison felt it. The connection had been building, and now it was electric.

As the SUV pulled into the restaurant parking lot, Monty saw B.A., now wearing jeans, a navy blazer, and heels, her hair in its natural curl. He also spotted Russell, whose red hair blazed in the afternoon sunlight. Monty glanced at Addison, who returned his look, then looked at both B.A. and Russell. It occurred to her that neither B.A. nor Russell knew they'd be sharing a meal together.

The SUV rolled to a stop. Monty got out on the passenger side, and the driver opened the rear door behind the driver for Addison. She deliberately took her time rounding the SUV, giving Monty and B.A. a few moments without her presence. Did she feel remorse for kissing Monty, or was she feeling awkward about the bracelet? She wasn't sure, deciding to forego any guilt. *Guilt? Why should I?* B.A. chose not to accompany them on the planned excursion. Addison looked up to see the driver standing with his door open, eyeing her quizzically.

"Don't mind me—it's a moment of uncertainty," she said to the driver.

Addison walked around the vehicle just in time to hear Monty introducing B.A. to Russell—Russell making a comment about "standing out here waiting for the same person." Addison could feel her eyes roll behind her sunglasses. *What is it about this man I don't care for?* As Addison came into B.A.'s view, B.A. seemed happy to see her, walking over to embrace her—seemingly also not fully charmed by her husband's friend.

"He's having lunch with us. Did you know?" B.A. whispered into Addie's ear as she drew close.

Addison nodded *yes*. B.A., looking over her sunglasses, gave a quizzical grimace. At least they were in agreement about this guy, Addison thought, as she turned B.A. toward the entrance to follow Monty and Russell, who were now headed inside. Russell, last through the door, didn't bother to hold it for the ladies. They exchanged a simultaneous look as B.A. opened it.

Once inside, the group was led to a large booth. Monty slid in first. B.A. stepped up to position herself next to her husband, but Russell slid in directly behind Monty. The two women exchanged another glance. Addison motioned for B.A. to go first so she could sit across from her husband, and Addison slid in after her. It didn't seem to faze Russell that he took B.A.'s place beside Monty. Addison, still wearing her sunglasses, gave him a hard look before removing them. Russell must have felt it; he stared back.

The waitress came for drink orders. Monty indicated the ladies order first, which they did, and he ordered after Russell. The table sat in a moment of silence until Monty broke the ice by asking about the guy Russell and Addison had seen with him at the mall.

"Just an old friend who lives in Atlanta," Russell replied.

"Oh, you don't live here?" Addison asked.

Turning his attention to Addison, Russell said, "No. I live in the D.C. area—Northern Virginia, to be exact."

"Yes, you were saying earlier about the firm you were with. Do you commute from Virginia into the District?" Monty asked.

"Actually, no. I'm in Virginia on the Metro line—commuting is fairly easy. I have a condo—no upkeep, no pets. It's an easy lifestyle, unlike Chicago. I learned my lesson about living outside the city. The commute was a grind."

In a quick beat, Addison chimed in, "I would think you could have moved into the city, or closer, for a better commute."

Russell tried not to glare at Addison, smiled, and said, "You're absolutely right, it would have—or could have—been that simple, but—"

Addison interrupted again, "What's your commute time now, now that you're in D.C.?"

"Are you familiar with the area, Addie?" Russell asked in a snide tone.

B.A., wanting a piece of this guy for herself, said, "Monty talks about the commute grind of Chicago all the time. What did you say your commute time was in Chicago?"

"I didn't say," Russell snapped.

Before Addison could poke again, their waitress—along with another—arrived with drinks and plates of sushi. Beverages were sorted, and the sushi was placed in the center of the table, with small plates passed around. Addison reached for a couple of pieces of tuna and rice. The waitress asked if they needed anything else; Addison asked for a separate bowl of sauce. Monty ordered sashimi; B.A. asked for a traditional salad with vinaigrette; Russell ordered another beer.

They continued to eat in silence, everyone using chopsticks, selecting from Thai Tuna Roll, Salmon Mango Roll, Spicy Tuna Roll, and Rainbow Roll. The portions were generous. When the waitress returned with Addison's sauce, B.A. asked for more tea, saying there was no rush. Russell handed over his empty glass and immediately began sipping from his second beer. Notably, he was the only one drinking alcohol; the *throuple entente* was in sync on no alcohol for lunch with the big night ahead.

They munched in silence until Russell decided to break it.

"Addie, I don't recall you wearing that fabulous bracelet when we met at the mall. Is it new?"

"Yes, as a matter of fact it—"

Addison was interrupted by Monty. "Yes, it is new. Addison acquired it earlier today after we ran into you and your friend. Where is he, Russell? The invitation was for both of you."

Russell looked flustered. "As I said, he's an old friend who lives in the area. He had a previous engagement."

Addison could see his face reddening. She didn't buy the story. The young man, though appearing much younger than Russell, seemed quiet and out of his depth when Russell and Monty were talking at the mall. *Boy toy* came to mind. She'd seen it many times in New York: older gent, younger guy—less polished but apt in other ways. And judging by Russell's attention to Monty, that was really his preference. Russell seemed more accustomed to being the younger filly to older, financially stable suitors.

It hit her: the thing gnawing at her about Russell—he had a thing for Monty. The Chicago connection, the sports club and racquetball, the way he took the seat beside Monty and bumped B.A., the way he addressed the door—*that* was it. She wondered if Monty knew, if they'd had a moment of some sort. How would she even ask him?

Conversation between Monty and Russell continued; Russell was completely immersed. B.A., raising her hand to catch the waitress, finally asked the burning question Addison had wanted to know—and it was perfectly appropriate coming from the wife.

"What kind of relationship did you two have in Chicago?"

Open-ended. It hung for a second or two before Monty took the lead.

"We were club members at the downtown sports club. Racquetball was our thing. We played—"

"We played a couple of times a week sometimes," Russell interjected.

"Yes," Monty agreed.

B.A. continued to probe—clearly probing—while Addison took a back seat, enjoying the last of the tuna roll on her plate.

"You guys ever do anything other than racquetball?"

"Dinner sometimes after our game," Monty replied.

Addison could see Russell becoming bothered by B.A.'s questions.

"Casual dinners, diner dinners, or dining at the sports club after a competitive game?" B.A. inquired.

Russell bit back. "Well, you do know Montaque had a wife at home!"

"Yes, of course I know that, *Rusty*—good to hear you knew," B.A. said evenly.

With the temperature rising at the table, Monty cut in, asking if anyone wanted coffee or dessert. He asked B.A. if they could share a key lime pie. Still nibbling her salad, B.A. declined.

"I'll have a coffee and share a slice with you, Monty," Addison said.

"Great. What about you, Russell? Coffee or dessert?" Monty asked.

Draining his beer, Russell replied, "Coffee, but no dessert."

This time Addison caught the waitress's eye while B.A. continued with her salad. The waitress returned shortly with three coffees, creamer, and spoons. Addison waited for Russell to pour his cream before she poured hers. As she glanced up, Russell poked the bear again.

"Addie, you didn't answer me earlier about your bracelet. It's new—where did you get it, if you don't mind me asking?"

"From a jeweler—not in the mall. My personal jeweler. I had some items to pick up; Addison saw it, liked it, and it's hers," Monty answered, his voice stern.

"What's with the curiosity about my bracelet, *Rusty*?" Addison asked.

"I just noticed it, that's all. No special reason," Russell replied, trying to hold it together.

The ladies had landed two clean blows—calling him *Rusty*. He remembered Monty's first wife, who called him that all the time, even after he'd said he preferred Russell.

The pie arrived—two forks—along with another round of coffee and an additional cup requested by B.A. They finished. Monty paid the check and told Russell to let him out. Monty headed to the men's room, and Russell, of course, followed.

The women exchanged a knowing glance. Addison thought it could be innocent. B.A., out loud, called him "Rusty the mouse." Addison nodded in agreement. As the men returned, B.A. decided to drop another question just as they approached the booth.

"Assuming the dance around the bracelet—Monty purchased it."

There it hung, out loud, with no time for Addison to react or explain. Addison stood; B.A. slid out of the booth, saying she'd meet them out front—she was going to the ladies' room. Addison continued toward the exit, the men behind her.

By the time B.A. appeared, Russell and Monty were saying their goodbyes. Addison stood a few steps away, checking her phone. She'd had enough of Russell. She sensed he'd single-handedly put a crimp in the *throuple entente*.

The ride back to the St. Regis Residences was unusually quiet.

Arriving at the Residence, the driver once again opened the rear door on his side of the vehicle as a valet opened the other. Addison exited on the driver's side, Monty and B.A. on the other. As Addison stepped out, her phone rang. Seeing it was D.J., she let it continue and walked toward Monty and B.A.

"I have a couple of calls to make. I'll be up when I'm finished."

A flat statement—allowing no questions. Addison walked through the door and over to a sitting area in the Residence lobby. B.A. and Monty headed to the elevators, disappearing from sight. Addison sat and took a deep breath. Half not wanting to call. Half hoping it wasn't an emergency—but part of her hoping it was, so she'd have an excuse to head home. *If it is an emergency, how will it look?* she thought. She didn't want to appear rude to Monty, and B.A. clearly had some things on her mind, thanks to Mr. Rusty.

Taking another deep breath, she tapped D.J.'s icon. It rang a few times before he picked up. Caller ID eliminated greetings; he got straight to it.

"Hey, Addison. Hate to bother you, but Scout's been beside himself. I took them out for a walk a bit ago—he decided to jump in the river. He's covered in mud! I can give him a bath, but I wasn't sure if you wanted to take them all to the groomer. I saw on the calendar in the mudroom you've got them scheduled for Monday. Scout can't wait that long, and no sense giving him two baths. I called the groomer—they can take them at three o'clock, but I've got to call her back straight away. They're holding those spots open."

Addison knew better than to interrupt D.J. when he was on a mission, and clearly this was one. She let him finish.

"Sure, if she's got a spot for all three, go for it. Tell her to put it on my account. I'll stop by next week to settle up. And remind them—Margo likes the facial. They'll have an easier time trimming her nails if they give her the facial first."

"Okay, glad you mentioned that. She's a beast when it comes to her nails." He laughed, his deep voice warm through the phone.

"How's everything else going?" Addison asked.

"Everything's going. I just finished a fresh batch of kombucha. Peach!" he said proudly.

"Good to hear. And honestly, D.J.—I can't imagine peach kombucha. It just doesn't sound appetizing." She chuckled. "I'll be home Sunday, most likely around four-ish, maybe earlier."

D.J. knew her too well; something in her voice seemed off.

"You okay, Lady A? Everything alright down there? What can I do?" he asked.

"Everything's fine. And what you can do is get off the phone and head to the groomer's. I'll text The Gilded to let them know you're bringing the guys by after for a non-dairy treat. Remind them—no cones, only the wide-mouth cups, and one serving. Klaus gets one serving, no matter how much he begs."

"Yep, got it. One serving each. You know if you need anything, I'm a call away. I've got contacts in the A-T-L."

"Yes, I'm sure you do. Now go—you don't want to be late."

They disconnected, and Addison sat in her thoughts. She missed her guys. Scout's muddy escapade was his way of acting out because she was gone. That pup had borderline separation anxiety. The thought made her smile. But the present loomed large, and that made her sad. She and B.A. were going to have a long talk to straighten things out before tonight's event. Then she thought about Monty, and her heart warmed again. She couldn't understand—it was B.A.'s doing. The book that started it all. Her befriending Addison, talking candidly about what she and her husband wanted, what they'd been cautiously seeking. Now B.A. seemed preoccupied and distant.

What was today really about? Was she even at a meeting? And that ring... Clearly there was something B.A. wasn't sharing.

Once on the elevator, Addison slipped off her shoes and dropped them into her Neiman Marcus shopping bag. The door chimed open—and there stood Monty in a terrycloth robe and flip-flops. Before she could say a word, he let her step into the foyer as he stepped into the elevator.

"I'm going for a swim. B.A.'s in her room. I've ordered a light dinner to be served around seven-thirty."

With that, he pressed the button; the doors chimed and closed. He was gone. She didn't get to ask if he'd told B.A. about the kiss—or rather, the kisses. The bracelet. The necklaces.

She dropped the bags in her room, removed her blazer, and headed for B.A.'s door, which was ajar. *No time like the present,* she thought as she walked in without knocking.

As she entered, she froze. On B.A.'s bed lay items of black leather, gold chains, patent-leather spiked heels, a black corset, balls attached to leather ties, a pair of fur-lined handcuffs, and more boxes still unopened. B.A. stood with her back to the door, humming as she opened another box. Addison thought of the day before, when B.A. had walked in while she was showering—with a small dildo designed for the butt.

"What the fuck, B.A.?"

B.A. turned, wearing only her bra and panties, stunned by Addison's outburst.

"What the fuck, B.A.? Why did you leave us today? This had all been planned—you told me the damn plan and pleaded with me to accept the invitation. Then you disappear to heaven knows where—or should I say *what,* judging by your bed! It would have been—"

B.A. interrupted, "Would have been what, Addie? Would have been better if I'd been with you and Montaque during your little jewelry shopping spree? Don't 'what the fuck' me, bitch. I saw the bracelet as soon as you sat in the booth. That little shit of a man did you a favor by calling it out."

"Get off your high horse, B.A. You're the reason we were together all day—"

"Oh, so it's *my* fault that you got to spend a few tender moments with my husband?"

"Cut the shit, B.A. You set this whole thing up! You had somewhere to go all along. It was your plan—for me to keep your husband occupied. Don't you dare bullshit me. You know it, and you know I'm on to you."

"Addie, I've given you an opportunity of a—"

"Cut the shit. Just cut it, right now. I see through you."

"Look, Addison, nothing was planned, I swear to you. I had a meeting—"

"Oh yeah? Looks like some kind of meeting, judging by your bed."

"These are tools of my craft. It's not what you think. Please, Addie, let me explain. I can explain all of this—and the meeting—but I need your confidence. I need you to hold it, not repeat it..."

"Not repeat it to Monty?"

"Yes. Especially not to Monty."

"What the fuck, B.A.?"

"Here, let me put these things away and let's talk. I really want to explain. I really do care about us—the *throuple*.Honestly, I do, and I want this to continue. But I need to explain."

B.A. put the items back in the boxes and into the bags, setting them on the far side of the bed as Addison stood watching in silence. B.A., still in her lace bra and panties, made Addison notice her nipples were erect. Strangely enough, it turned her on. She wanted to throw B.A. onto the bed and suck her nipples while B.A. pleasured herself—but she wanted everything out in the open first. The kiss. Had Monty told her? If he hadn't, Addison decided she would reveal both kisses and just let the truth fly.

Even as her arousal built, she kept telling herself what she really needed now was for B.A. to explain.

With everything put away, they sat on the bed, and Addison let B.A. talk.

The Escalade pulled into the circular driveway of the large warehouse building with a black awning covering double oversized wooden burgundy doors. Under the awning were aluminum heaters. On each side stood valet stations staffed by a dozen men in burgundy jackets, opening doors for arriving vehicles and helping finely dressed women who exited and walked through the doors, held open by two more attendants in burgundy-and-black jackets, black formal slacks, and black bow ties. Two additional limos and another SUV were ahead of the throuple entente. Men and women, dressed provocatively in long gowns, short dresses, and high heels, clustered beneath the awning.

From the SUV directly in front, two couples emerged— men in blazers and slacks, women in low-cut dresses displaying ample cleavage. Addison felt electricity travel through her and a tingle between her legs. In a mauve wrap dress—loosely tied—with matching bra and thong panties, patent-leather slingbacks, flowing hair, and a clutch, she looked like a goddess. Men stopped to look as the valet helped her out of the Escalade.

Next came B.A., her hair slicked back, wearing a black halter dress cut low to her navel and slit up the side to her hip. Black heels, red lipstick, clutch bag. And a sparkle at each woman's chest: a pendant of three diamonds, one stacked above two.

Last to exit was Monty—black pleated slacks, a starched white Nehru-collar shirt unbuttoned to his waist, neatly tucked beneath a black double-breasted blazer; Italian loafers, no socks. The men in bow ties greeted them, welcoming them to Cirque Écarlate as they opened the doors.

Inside, a second set of double frosted-glass doors bore *Cirque Écarlate* engraved in the panes. A large round burgundy rug emblazoned with the club's name in gold covered the floor. The walls were a soft yellow, giving the space the feel of a foyer, not a lobby. The thrum of music vibrated through the glass.

To the right stood a large desk where several hostesses greeted guests, printing and attaching bracelets to patrons' wrists. Between the desk and the entrance were five metal detectors; everyone passed through to enter the main area. To the left, at a smaller desk, the throuple entente were greeted by the young woman Monty had met several weeks earlier. She secured a bracelet to each of their wrists—lime green with a gold stripe—and explained: the color granted access to the entire club; the gold signified they were a throuple but could also move about alone; the numbers tied to the bottles Monty had given the other hostess, which would be poured only for them.

She then introduced a well-groomed, fit younger man who'd been standing patiently behind her. "Ken," she said. He, too, was exclusively theirs for the evening. He enjoyed women and men, she was sure to mention. He would check in whenever they asked. Any questions before she continued about the back bar? The throuple had none.

She went on: Once inside the dance floor area, there would be another set of doors. The first room was the changing area. To pass beyond, all street clothes had to be removed. Wrap towels were provided; women could wear undies or nothing; men could only wear wrap towels. To the rear of the changing room were showers—some with glass doors for privacy, two with frosted glass visible from the second-bar lounge, and two open with no doors. The rooms beyond were clearly marked, and the center held the second-bar lounge. Condoms and other items, in all sizes and types, were clearly labeled in glass bowls throughout the rear area. If anything was missing, ask Ken.

As the hostess spoke, Addison felt heat rising within her. After their talk, she better understood B.A., knowing her erotic attraction to Monty wasn't a threat. Addison didn't love the secrecy B.A. had sworn her to, but her desire to be with B.A. heightened. The atmosphere reeked of sexual potential. Looks and glances as people meandered by had her body anticipating their first adventure—hers with B.A. —with the sole purpose of Monty watching, fully aware that others might also watch as they pleased each other. The rest of the night would be a free-for-all, and she was ready.

The throuple decided to skip the dance floor and head to the second-bar area behind the doors. Monty whispered something to Ken, and he disappeared. Monty stripped down and donned the terry wrap; his cock, excited, tented the front, causing the wrap to gap open.

B.A., naked beneath her dress, pulled a laced thong camisole from her clutch. Addison slipped out of her dress, revealing lace panels framing her bra and a delicate triangle beneath. She gathered her hair into a claw clip and stepped forward, kissing B.A. deeply. Their tongues met, their gazes locked. Addison turned, kissed Monty with the same unguarded intent, and felt his response immediately.

When they entered the lounge, Ken sat in a semi-round booth guarding three glasses of wine. He rose to greet them. B.A. kissed him first, her hand slipping behind his wrap, deliberate and intimate. After they clinked glasses and she settled beside Monty, Addison moved to Ken, kissing him just as deeply, her touch unmistakable. She leaned close, drawing a visible reaction that sent a jolt through Monty.

Addison slid in beside B.A., placing her between them. The three clinked glasses again and sipped, watching the scenes unfolding throughout the club.

The lounge was U-shaped, the bar at the open end. Along the inner curve, clearly marked doors led to Men/Men, Women/Women, Couples, Threesomes, Mixed Couples, and a sixth, farthest from the bar—a guarded double door watched by a man in slacks and bow tie and a woman in gold pasties with black tassels, heels, and elbow-length gloves. Both wore black, save the shimmer of the pasties.

Addison glanced toward B.A., who was absorbed in watching a woman moving confidently between two men, fully aware of the attention she commanded. Addison tried to catch her eye, but B.A.'s focus shifted—to a chaise where bodies moved without restraint, the rhythm unmistakable. Wine glasses paused midair as they watched, desire building with every glance.

Monty leaned in and whispered something to Ken. Ken stood, moved behind Addison, reached around her, and began to touch her openly. Addison let her head fall back, breath slow, deliberate. B.A. took her glass and kissed her deeply, their tongues meeting again. Hands explored freely. Ken's touch grew firmer, purposeful.

B.A. and Ken alternated their attention. Addison's desire climbed. She opened her eyes to see Monty watching, his own restraint visibly fraying. She slid her hand to B.A., setting a slow, teasing rhythm.

Ken stepped aside as Addison shifted over B.A., leaving her no choice but to recline and stretch her legs toward Monty. Addison kissed her way down, unhurried, then positioned herself so Monty had a full view. Before continuing, Addison leaned up to kiss Monty, letting him taste exactly what she intended to do while he watched.

Monty took in the sight—Addison flushed, focused, hovering over his wife as Ken's hands kept B.A. open and responsive. B.A.'s voice rose, breathless, encouraging. Addison stayed with her, deliberate, drawing it out.

As B.A.'s movements shifted, Addison paused and watched instead, her own arousal evident as she leaned against the glass, breathing unevenly. Their eyes met. Monty saw the tension in Addison's posture, the way her body trembled.

He wanted her—wanted that connection again, remembered from the farmhouse. Addison didn't look away. She was close.

Monty moved first. He pulled back and gestured toward the alcoves. Addison rose last. B.A. followed moments later. Monty reached for Addison's hand; when their fingers touched, the charge was immediate. He didn't want to let go.

They moved through the crowd. A woman reached for Monty, another lingered close, a third leaned in briefly. Ken paused as one of them opened Monty's wrap and kissed him openly before turning back to her own engagement. Ken and Monty moved on.

At a beaded opening—an alcove without chair or light— Ken lifted the strands and stepped inside. He removed his wrap and knelt. Monty shed his and followed. Ken began slowly, deliberately, drawing Monty deeper into sensation.

Not ready to finish, Monty slowed him and glanced toward the beads. Addison stood just outside. He reached for her; she entered without hesitation, kissed him, traced her tongue along his ear, then moved lower, intensifying the moment. Ken continued until Monty whispered for control.

Monty eased away. Ken paused. Addison moved in front of Monty, breath rapid, eyes dark. Ken quietly asked for a moment. Monty and Addison exchanged a look.

Ken returned with cloths and lubricant. Monty hesitated; Addison nodded—she was ready. Ken wiped Monty carefully, then prepared him. Addison and Monty kissed deeply; she pinched his nipples. He turned her, bent her slightly, and entered her slowly. They moved together—

Addison controlling the pace—then she directed Ken to join, his hands finding her, steady and precise.

The rhythm built. Addison guided Monty, then pulled him free and shifted, taking him again in one smooth motion. The intensity tightened, the moment holding. Monty finished with a groan. Time seemed to pause.

Addison waited, then carefully eased away, her legs unsteady. Ken steadied her, handed her a cloth. The alcove smelled of heat and menthol. Monty wanted to hold her, but Ken murmured that they should clean up. The men left.

Addison eased to the floor, letting sensation settle. Nearby, others continued unabashedly. She was spent—and amazed.

B.A. spotted Monty and Ken heading toward the men's washroom and waited. When they emerged, she indicated she wanted Ken. She seemed to know instinctively that Monty wasn't ready. Ken glanced at Monty; Monty nodded.

They found another alcove. Ken returned with more warm cloths. B.A. removed her lace teddy and knelt, confident and composed. Monty brought over a stool, covered it with a towel, and directed Ken with a quiet word.

Ken followed, touching B.A. as instructed. She responded fully. Ken looked to Monty; Monty gave permission. Ken moved into her as she opened to him, braced at the edge of the stool. Monty watched his wife, feeling himself stir again.

As Ken neared release, B.A. took control, drawing him away at the last moment and finishing on her own terms. She came quickly, decisively.

Monty handed Ken a bag and opened another warm cloth for his wife. She kissed Ken and left the alcove.

On her way to the changing area, B.A. checked the clock—after one in the morning. Around her, the club was still alive with movement and desire. She wanted more—but not yet what she knew would fully satisfy her.

She grabbed a final glass of wine and moved through the second bar to the changing room. At their locker—Addison's dress gone, Monty's clothes still there—she undressed, took a towel and her wine to the private showers. Alone, she rinsed, cleaned herself, turned the water hot, and let it cascade for a long while.

She toweled off, slipped on her dress, slicked her hair back with her fingers, drained the wine, stepped into her heels, and headed back toward the main bar.

The dance floor was nearly empty, music lower now. A buffet was out; some lingered with plates. In a corner, a flash of mauve—Addison, she thought. Approaching, she saw Addison had been through the buffet and was drinking coffee. A bartender set a carafe and creamer at her elbow. Addison thanked him and swiveled to greet B.A.

"Hey. The food is very good," Addison said.

"It *smells* good. I'll get a plate—be right back."

"Don't forget a cup. The coffee is wonderful," Addison called.

B.A. returned and settled beside her. The bartender brought B.A. a cup and saucer; she thanked him and turned to Addie.

"I didn't realize it was after midnight," B.A. said.

"Yeah. Time slips when your libido is raging," Addison said with a grin. "You disappeared after our romp. Did you explore the double doors at the rear of the lounge?"

"No. I couldn't."

"Couldn't? Why not?"

"Addie... what I left out—there's an NDA. I've already shared too much, but only because I know I can trust you, and this *does* affect you. I felt you were entitled to some of it."

"NDA? B.A., what are we talking about here?"

"I've said more than I should. I have to stick to it. But trust that you know the important part. I need to be comfortable that I can trust you."

"Yes. I've given you my solemn word. You *can* trust me— and you can also trust me either way, with the rest of whatever this is."

"I know. But I can't... just can't. Let it go, okay?"

"Okay—gone. But I'm here for whatever you need. Just remember that, will you?"

"I will. And I know."

They swiveled on their stools, eating and talking about the sights they'd seen. Laughter erupted a few times. Soon Monty arrived—jacket over his arm, eyes bloodshot, hair damp—plate in hand. He joined the ladies. They ate, had coffee, and talked about the evening. Monty finally felt all three were in sync, on one accord.

He decided to wait to share the invitation to St. Martin. He and B.A. had gone a couple of times before, when they'd first begun their search for the perfect woman for them. This time, he thought, they had her—Addison—to include in the swaray.

They headed to the main door when Monty's phone chimed: their chariot awaited. Addison, full of breakfast, sexually satisfied, and ready for bed. B.A., hopeful for her future. Monty, pleased with his reconnaissance—and with Ken.

They climbed into the SUV. The driver eased down the drive to I-285, then onto I-85 toward Buckhead.

△ ▽ ⩔ ⩕

B.A.'s office was located on the ground floor of one of the tallest buildings in Bayhaven's downtown financial district —the commercial headquarters for the company. On the other corner of the building sat one of the many banks that serviced Kellum County. The main entrance was accessible through double glass doors and a turnstile set between them. The lobby rose three stories, allowing the ground-floor offices to span the second and third floors within. B.A.'s office was on the third floor, down the hall from the Executive Offices. She and two other top producers shared a pool of clerical support and a private waiting area; each office had floor-to-ceiling windows. B.A.'s office faced another building and offered a view of the downtown intersection.

Clerks used a clear box marked "MAIL" that sat on her credenza. Any mail addressed to her personally was placed unopened on her desk. Messages were displayed on her dual-screen desktop, giving her access to past transactions, messages, and files. This morning she had come in early to prepare for a conference call with a client overseas. Dropping her keys on the desk, the gray envelope caught her eye. She stopped; her breath hitched.

The envelope was fine linen, her name neatly typed in Caslon: **Barbara Ann Roberson Langford**. Her name and address were the only printing on the front besides the imprinted postage seal.

Picking it up, she felt the weight. Turning it over made her knees go weak. She reached for the arm of her executive leather chair and practically fell into it, staring at the return address and the deep burgundy wax seal. In smaller all-caps: **THE MARCHMONT CONSERVATORY BELGRAVIA LONDON**.

This was her answer. Whatever the envelope contained would be her future. She would either stay and be as she was, or the life's itch would be satisfied—the final measure. She broke the seal, flecks of wax crumbling onto the desk. The letterhead, embossed in black, announced its old-world presence.

B.A.'s palms were clammy; her hands shook. Opening the folds, she read the first paragraph aloud:

"...it is our privilege to inform you that you have been granted admission to the Marchmont Conservatory."

B.A. sat erect in her chair, hands resting on the desk, still holding the letter. Her heartbeat elevated. She swiveled toward the window, to the intersection below, the traffic signal facing her window green, cars moving slowly. Her mind raced. So much to do. Monty—how would she tell him? When should she tell him? She second-guessed her process so far. Then Addie—how would she soften the blow? It was the purpose of finding the perfect person. In that moment, B.A. understood: she had handled everything just right. It would be painful for him at first, but he would be left alone—again.

She folded the letter, returned it to the envelope, and tucked it in her purse. There were three pages; she would read the rest after her conference call. Picking up her desk phone, she summoned her appointments clerk. She would reschedule her lunch and her only afternoon appointment for the next day.

In B.A. style, she was all business during the call—almost ninety minutes—giving no second thought to the life-changing informatio

⁎⁎

She needed to relax and think it through. She went to the one place that always brought her peace and comfort: the library. Downtown Belhaven's library was a museum in itself, full of history from before the city converged with six other towns to become Kellum County. It's what had brought her here twelve years ago. Artifacts encased in glass were sprinkled throughout the four-story building of glass, light diffusing across shelves of books, reading tables, and comfortable chairs and settees. The mezzanine was her favorite part—one flight up to quiet reading. She found an empty chair overlooking the park along the river.

B.A. removed the envelope and read all three pages this time. Journal in hand, she began to make notes—the way she always organized her thoughts and how-to-dos. The interview would be held in three weeks at the offices of Rowland, Keats & Morrow LLP at The Battery/Truist Park complex, Cobb County, Georgia. A panel of three and legal attendance. Ten o'clock, Friday, October eighteenth, for two and a half hours.

From her executive handbag, she pulled out her tablet and began searching for adult clubs—high-end adult clubs in the Atlanta region. A plan was formulating. Her mind wandered.

*
**

The youngest of five children—and the only girl—Barbara Ann, "Babbs" as her brothers liked to call her, was her father's *baby girl* and her mother's *Barbara*—or *Barbara Ann* when she was about to be scolded, which was often.

As an adolescent, she was normal—but not in her mother's eyes. B.A. was part tomboy, part dreamer, and endlessly inquisitive about life. Her fourth-grade teacher, who saw her potential, was also the town's music teacher. When her mother balked at the cost of lessons, the teacher offered to teach B.A. in exchange for light chores.

Every Saturday, she'd bike to her teacher's house after finishing her mother's chores to take her lessons, do the work, and stay after to practice. It became her escape—by the time she was thirteen, her sanctuary.

Her mother, worn from caring for four boys and a husband whose only job was at the mill, never received help in the kitchen or laundry. When *baby girl* was born, her father was overheard saying to anyone who'd listen,

"Finally, Mother's got help taking care of us. That's what girls are for—tending to the needs of the family and her husband."

B.A.'s brothers were extensions of their father. The oldest was five years older than she was; the next two were four and three years older, and the youngest boy just fourteen months ahead. There was always someone telling her what to do, when to do it, and plenty of things she wasn't supposed to do.

Her piano teacher found an old upright, persuaded her parents to take it, and they agreed—on the condition it would go in the storage shed out back. The boys built a wooden floor, a makeshift bench, and a door for the opening where the piano was placed. Every day, B.A. finished her chores, carried her books to the shed, finished her homework by lantern light, and played until she was summoned for dinner—and more chores.

In high school, she played for the school chorus and read glossy magazines in the teacher's lounge while waiting for choir practice to begin. That's where she discovered life beyond Kerns Corner—and became fascinated. She took a computer class, which opened her world even more. Research became her second passion.

After graduation, she wanted to attend college in eastern Pennsylvania, but her parents directed her to the community college near the mill where her father and brothers worked. The daily commute saved her from most chores and gave her time to explore the internet while she waited for her family to pick her up each evening. Her mother didn't drive, and her father was adamant that she shouldn't.

"Women ain't got no reason to learn how to drive. That's her man's duty," her father would say.

After community college, she was offered scholarship money to attend a school in Pittsburgh. When her father said it was *too far*, B.A. didn't argue. She worked as many hours as possible—summers and holidays—at the hardware store, where she'd been employed for three years.

Her piano teacher, during one visit to the store, offered B.A. an old laptop. She used it at work since there was no internet at home—researching everything from how to write a résumé to finding apartments in Pittsburgh and Philadelphia. She filled a journal with notes she carried religiously in her school bag—maps, job listings, addresses, possibilities.

One early spring evening, she told Mr. Archer, the store owner, she would close up and promised to lock the doors before dark. B.A. pulled out her laptop, set up her screen, and recorded a video interview for a real estate company in downtown Philadelphia. Logging on, she answered a series of questions, completed a typing exam, and recorded her video—explaining why she was the best choice for their receptionist position. She asked about dress code and apartments in suitable neighborhoods close to the office, giving explicit instructions to reply to her email only.

She clicked *send*, sat a moment, closed her laptop, and made her way through the darkened store toward home.

When graduation came, Barbara Ann Roberson finished at the top of her class, excelling in computer applications including Microsoft Office Suite and Adobe Acrobat 9. Her parents were baffled by her subject choice; her brothers laughed out loud when her Community College Curriculum degree was announced. Everyone in the auditorium applauded except her family, as she crossed the stage to receive her diploma.

"Well, Mother, it may not mean a damn thing, but it could help Baby Girl find herself a decent husband," her father muttered, leaning toward his wife to be heard over the crowd.

B.A.'s mother looked at him in horror but said nothing. She was simply glad the "school foolishness" was over—Barbara Ann could finally come home to help with chores again. None of the older sons had married; all were still living at home.

"It'd be a day sent from heaven if one of them boys would marry and git their own place," she grumbled.

Roberson glared back—a warning not to push.

"Mother, you got a good life. You ain't done no real work since the day I married you and brung you from Bethlehem, Wes Virginny."

There was cake after dinner that night. Her brothers found new ways to mock her accomplishment. When the table was cleared and her parents retired early, B.A. hugged each of her brothers, whispered, "I love you guys," and went to her tiny room. She waited for the house to quiet, gathered her belongings into a large zip bag she'd ordered online and shipped to the hardware store, and tucked her savings on her person.

Shoes in hand, she crept through the house in silence. She had left the back door ajar while doing dishes. Slipping out, she walked through town to the post office–gas station and boarded the 5:00 a.m. bus east. *Last stop: Philadelphia.*

Barbara Ann never looked back.

During her research, she had found several clubs—but none as exclusive as *Cirque Écarlate*. She was exhilarated and decided to finish her research tomorrow. Presenting it to Monty would come then too; once he took hold, he would fine-tune everything—as only he could.

The weekend at the farmhouse had been an enormous success. Adding Perry gave the throuple an edge—or better still, gave Monty the dose of another male's presence around Addie. Him knowing her was the icing the cake needed.

With Addie out of town with family, B.A. knew that as soon as she resurfaced, Monty would pounce—presenting her with the trip, the club, and a throuple-filled weekend.

For the rest of the afternoon, B.A. wanted to bask in her accomplishment: securing a place in one of Europe's most prestigious schools for dominatrix training—The Marchmont Conservatory. Completing that curriculum would give her elite credentials and unheralded privilege in a world she had longed to enter since that night in Philadelphia.

Closing her tablet and dropping it into her bag, she sat back, watching people stroll along the riverfront—some seated on benches, others eating lunch. Her cell phone vibrated: a client. Reading the text, she rose from the mezzanine chair and headed toward the staircase and exit.

It was back to work—before basking.

*
**

The return flight from Atlanta was relaxed for the throuple entente. Monty didn't seem annoyed with B.A. for missing the shopping excursion, and Addison appeared fine with knowing something had happened, though she didn't have all the details. The post-midnight breakfast at *Cirque Écarlate* had broken the tension from earlier that day, and sleeping in their respective beds afterward provided the rest everyone needed. It was back to reality.

When the flight landed at Belhaven's FBO, Monty had an SUV waiting for him and B.A. Addison's SUV had been left by D.J.—she had called him after the tense exchange with B.A. at the St. Regis Residence following lunch, her way of reasserting independence from the couple.

The throuple stood together in the FBO lounge to say goodbye, both women wearing their necklaces. B.A. and Addison embraced, B.A. whispering, "Let's do lunch." Addison nodded in approval. With Monty standing so close, they left it at that. He stepped forward, wrapping his long arms around both women, kissing Addison's forehead and thanking her for joining them and making the weekend so special.

With luggage loaded, the throuple entente parted— promising to meet soon for dinner and a visit to the townhouse.

Addison sat at the wheel of her SUV for a moment before starting it. She yearned to see her guys. She missed them.

"I miss them!" Addison said aloud.

A text from B.A.: *Lunch on Wednesday? Place TBA.* Addison texted back: *Yes. Someplace casual. I'm in edit mode and jeans all week.*

*
**

The first couple of days back, the throuple entente found their groove after a well-planned weekend in Atlanta. Monty's schedule was filled with meetings on his latest project. Addison spent her first day in sweats—walking the dogs before dawn, later hosting video meetings with her staff to begin editing a major client's new book. And B.A. quietly organized her notes, files, and client accounts for the day she'd hand them over to a junior associate.

No one called, messaged, or texted for two days.

On Wednesday morning, B.A. texted Addie: *Lunch at Brad's Deli on River Street okay?* Addison replied: *Yes, perfect. Noon?* *Yes.*

When B.A. arrived at the deli, it was bustling—women in tennis outfits, others in jeans, men in golf shirts. Addison sat at a high-top table, fiddling with her phone, wearing a crew-neck sweater with a bear embroidered on the front, jeans, and mules. Her hair was pulled into a ponytail; she looked radiant with no makeup, something that always baffled B.A., who wore a satin blouse, knit vest, matching slacks, natural curls, and her usual polished makeup.

B.A. slung her executive bag onto the chair beside Addison. Addison looked up, immediately stood, and pulled her into a long hug. B.A. returned it, then leaned back, puzzled.

"What's this?"

"What's what?"

"This."

"Can't a friend be glad to see her friend?"

"Well, yes, but—"

"No *but*, B.A. I'm genuinely happy to see you. We had an interesting weekend—one I hope created a bond, an unusual one, considering we're intimate with the same man. A man who just happens to be your husband."

"Addie, I—"

"It's all good, B.A. I assume we're having lunch—just the two of us—so we can iron out the pages that are about to unfold for us, including Montaque."

"Yes, you're correct. There are some things I need to clear up and explain."

They left the table and went to the counter under the overhead sign *ORDER HERE*. B.A. ordered after Addison,

Page 164

who told the clerk to put both meals together. After a brief back-and-forth, Addison won and paid for both, tossing in a fresh-baked cookie for each.

They gathered their drinks and returned to the table. B.A., not wanting to start before the food arrived, made small talk about the view—the traffic, the river across the street. When the food came, they spoke about *Cirque Écarlate*— the unforgettable sights, the tension, the erotic atmosphere that seemed to ooze from the lobby to the changing rooms.

The rest of the meal passed in silence. Addison figured B.A. was deciding how to start. B.A. hoped Addie would prove a genuine friend and receive what she was about to say.

After finishing, B.A. got up to refill her tea. Addison tidied the table, tossing wrappers and fetching a few napkins for the cookies. Talking over cookies couldn't be all bad.

When they were both seated again, B.A. unwrapped hers. "I have a confession to make, Addie. I hope you'll understand."

"B.A., whatever it is—without even knowing—I'll understand. I'm here for you. I'm in your corner, whatever it is."

"I'm glad to hear that. I... well, I'm not sure how to put this."

"Just say it, B.A. I'm open to being your confidant. There's no wrong here—just two friends who share a special bond. You have to admit, it's a unique connection."

B.A. drew a deep breath and let it out. "I knew who you were that day at *The Gilded Bean*. It wasn't a chance encounter. I hoped the book would catch your attention—to send the message of who I was, or rather, what I was wanting."

Addison sat quietly, listening.

B.A. continued, "Monty and I had been seeking a third for some time."

"Yes, he mentioned that at the farmhouse—the first night."

"Well, it was… a little more than that. But first, I want to preface it by saying Monty has no idea about the *why*."

"Oh, I see. And does your absence from the shopping excursion have anything to do with the backstory?"

"Yes. It's the reason—the reason for all of this."

"What *is* this?" Addison asked, keeping her voice even.

"I did my homework. I knew you were possibly the perfect fit for us—and, more importantly, the perfect fit for Monty. He's going to need someone to lean on when I leave."

The last three words canceled everything that came before them. Addison stayed composed—she knew it was the only way to let B.A. finish.

"You're leaving?"

"Yes. I'll be leaving…"

"Leaving temporarily—or permanently?" Addison asked, her tone measured.

"It's going to be permanent."

"Oh, I see."

After a pause: "And how do I fit into this permanent departure? I take it Monty isn't aware that his life is about to blow up?"

"Addie, please, don't get all righteous—"

"*Righteous!* B.A., this will destroy your husband. He adores you."

B.A. sipped through her straw, giving the comment a moment to settle. "Addie, this is where you come in."

"B.A., seriously? You think my presence will ease Monty's pain and devastation over your absence?"

"Yes…"

"You're delusional if you think this plan—or whatever it is —will stabilize my relationship with your husband, to the point of him waking up one morning, rolling over, and there I am!"

B.A. felt the conversation slipping away. She tried to regain control. "Addie, I'll support you and help you help him. It's not that complicated."

Addison leaned back in the tall chair, staring out the window at the street beyond the deli. She tried to absorb what her friend—her lover—was about to do, and what it would mean for her. Unsure she wanted to know, she decided to go with the flow.

"Okay, say I go along with this. How's it supposed to work? When will Monty be put in the loop about his *future?* And most importantly, where the fuck are you going, Missy?"

B.A. sucked chilled air through her straw and gave Addie a look—but her mind was smiling. She sensed Addie was coming around, even if through protest.

B.A. began the story—Kerns Corner, how she left, how she hadn't spoken to a single soul since boarding that bus.

Addison, captivated, nibbled her cookie slowly, her chewing giving B.A. the floor.

B.A. described the man she almost married—his odd sexual appetites, her gradual fascination, the leather ties and corsets, the European orders, the floggers, the whip. At first, she'd been nervous; later, she grew erotically empowered.

They took trips to New York—members-only boutiques, appointment-only clubs. Within a year, they were the exhibit. She described the thrill, the intoxicating sense of control, the kind of orgasm she couldn't explain.

Addison listened, remembering the farmhouse—B.A.'s intensity, her orgasm, the butt plug, the shared climax. She felt her cheeks warm as the memory replayed.

Sensing the tension building, B.A. moved to why she left Philadelphia.

"About a month before the wedding, he introduced breath play. I was against it, but he insisted. I let him control me that night until I used our safe word. He stopped—but I could tell he wasn't happy. About a week later, I finished early with a commercial client and came home sooner than expected."

"Oh, B.A....," Addison whispered, bracing for what she knew was coming.

"I could have accepted one person—but it was two. Two women. And him. In our bed. No flogger, no leather, no ties. Just him, naked, one woman on his face, the other riding his cock. It took the wind out of me. By then, I knew I was meant to be the one in control."

"What did you do?"

"I turned around, quietly, and left. Waited until my usual time, then came home."

Silence settled as they sipped their tea.

"When I got back, the bed was made, sheets in the dryer. That's when the floodgates opened. This had happened before—the dish on the stove, him freshly showered, the dryer running. I kept my routine: walked into the kitchen, kissed his cheek, asked about dinner, went to the bathroom, turned on the shower—and threw up."

"Did he notice a change in you?"

"No. Another realization—he'd been fucking around while I thought we were exploring a lifestyle together."

B.A. went on to explain how she told her boss the wedding was off—and surprisingly, why. He'd suggested she move to Northern Virginia, where a friend ran a booming commercial real-estate firm. She used their joint savings to secure an apartment, faked a female issue to avoid more sex, and waited for his business trip to Arizona. By the time he returned, the place was empty except for the bedroom set—and her engagement ring on the kitchen counter beside a handwritten note:

Now you can fuck anytime.

"I changed my number. Got my life together."

"B.A., I'm so sorry."

B.A. shrugged. "I seem to have a knack for walking away and regrouping. I tried to be normal"—she made air quotes—"but my true erotic satisfaction comes from being a dominatrix."

She told Addie about researching the BDSM world, reconnecting with New York friends who remembered her tenacity, and being invited to perform privately. One thing led to another—requests, sessions—and finally, an invitation to *The Marchmont Conservatory* in London.

"My entrance interview was the day of the shopping excursion," she said softly. "And I've been accepted."

Addison's eyes widened. She finally saw the full picture— how B.A. had found her, guided Monty, orchestrated it all.

"So who's idea was *Cirque Écarlate*?" Addison asked.

"The initial idea was mine, but Monty did all the planning and reconnaissance. Ken, the St. Regis... everything except the shopping. That was mine."

"Oh. Now I get why he was so upset—it was your idea, and then you—"

"I knew his anger would draw him closer to you. You two were already on that path. That solidified it."

"And the necklaces?"

"Those were a complete surprise. I had no idea."

They sat quietly, sipping what remained of their tea.

"What now, B.A.?"

After another sip, she explained that after the Florida trip she would tell Monty. She implored Addie to help—only she could soften the blow. This conservatory was her destiny, she said, and she was grabbing the golden ring it represented.

She made Addison promise to keep her confidence.

But Addison was firm. Once it was done, she would not deceive Monty into thinking she hadn't known.

"B.A., if you want your husband to recover, you'll *want* me to be honest. Saying I didn't know—and him finding out later that I did—that's not my style. I care about him. I can't lie about something that could hurt him more. Since you've included me in this plan of yours, this is how it's going to be—or I'm out now. I'll walk out of this deli and never speak to either of you again. I'm capable of disappearing, too. Just so you know."

B.A. drew a deep breath and agreed.

The women gathered their trash and belongings, embraced, and parted ways.

⁂

Looking out the window as the view drew closer, the flight attendant announced that trays should be returned to seat backs to prepare for landing. Another attendant walked the aisle collecting cups and trash as the plane descended.

Russell Tierney was exhilarated about his trip to Belhaven, Virginia—a new job in the works and, more importantly, the chance to spend time with Montaque Langford. As the metropolitan skyline came into view, the tall buildings of the business district rose like monoliths, their facades emblazoned with emblems of banks, financial institutions —some unfamiliar, one distinctly recognizable: **MLA&E —Montaque Langford Architects & Engineers, Associates**. The building where he would most likely work, once all the paperwork was out of the way.

As the aircraft passed over a large round building flanked by multilevel parking structures and a baseball field, Russell smiled to himself. He'd done his homework on the area—the professional basketball and baseball teams were the city's crown jewels. Along the river, another massive building loomed, with two cruise ships docked nearby. He was so filled with excitement, he nearly bounced in his seat like a twelve-year-old.

Crossing the interstate, the aircraft touched down and began its slow taxi toward the terminal as the flight attendant announced:

"Welcome, ladies and gentlemen, to Belhaven, Virginia. Please remain in your seats until the aircraft has reached the terminal and be cautious when opening the overhead bins, as items may have shifted..."

It was destiny, Russell thought. Seeing Monty that day at Lenox Mall had been monumental. It had been over ten years since he left Chicago. Monty looked like his old self again—smiling, that twinkle in his blue-gray eyes, clean-shaven, sharply dressed. Russell had feared he'd lost him forever after that bitch died. He'd done everything he could to snap Monty back, but all his effort and planning hadn't brought the results he'd wanted. Monty had lost his way— long hair, beard, jeans, tennis shoes, and that awful Bears jacket.

But now, Russell thought as the plane came to a stop, he'd been given another chance. Another chance to be with the man he loved.

"The man I love," he whispered aloud, the words startling even him.

The revelation made his body warm and his loins stir. *Calm down,* he scolded himself. *You've got two bitches to contend with. This time will require careful planning.*

He was confident he'd get what was his—Montaque Langford. His focus narrowed to that single thought, the only one that mattered: *Once he's been with me, those bitches will be a distant memory.*

Exiting the jetway, Russell followed the crowd to the luggage carousel, checking his phone for the Uber driver waiting at the curb. Snagging his suitcase, he rolled out into the blustery wind swirling leaves around the exit. Spotting his ride, he loaded his bag into the trunk. The car was moderately warm but comfortable.

Russell wasn't one for small talk; his preferences were clear. Off they went, navigating the maze of traffic circles that flowed without lights. Crossing a short bridge, they came to a signal where an enormous bird sculpture stood— seemingly made from airplane parts. *Clever,* Russell thought, before burying his head in his phone.

At the hotel, he tipped through the app as the driver unloaded his suitcase. "Thank you," Russell said with his practiced plastic smile—the one he used when he wasn't in the mood to be pleasant. He rolled his suitcase through the lobby, gave the valet the same smile, checked in, and headed to his room.

After unpacking, he decided to explore the business district. At the concierge desk, he asked about nearby restaurants. Exiting the lobby, he noticed a sign across the street: **The Gilded Bean.** Curious, he crossed and entered through the revolving door. The aroma of coffee was intoxicating.

To his delight, the menu offered light fare, teas, and desserts. He couldn't believe the variety of coffees from around the world—and the deli board was equally impressive.

Walking to the counter, greeted warmly, Russell actually gave a genuine smile. He placed his order—a pastrami on rye with gourmet slaw and a large hot green tea— peppering the barista with questions, which she answered patiently.

"Tapping his card, she handed him a table marker."

"Your order will be out shortly," the barista smiled.

Enamored with the place, Russell finally noticed the charm of the shop—browns and reds, wrought-iron chairs with plush red cushions, tables with glass tops gleaming under low-hanging lights. Oversized chairs in deep browns, sofas in lighter tones. The glossy medium-brown floor gave the place a luxe feel. *No drive-thru,* he noted approvingly.

He chose a two-chair table by the window. The sun was setting, traffic thickening—the rhythm of downtown life. A barista arrived with his tray: sandwich, slaw, tea under a mini cloche.

"Would there be anything else?" she asked.
"No, this is great, thank you," he said, smiling.
"Perfect. Enjoy your meal and tea!"

He removed the cloche. The steam was aromatic and inviting. The pastrami was delicious, the slaw tangy and unusual. He lingered over his meal, watching the stoplight change rhythmically a block away.

Before leaving, he studied the coffee board again, already planning tomorrow's order. Outside, the sun had vanished, the city lights glimmering like strings of stars. Wishing for a heavier jacket, he crossed the street, back to his hotel.

He would see Monty tomorrow. Maybe Monty could give him a tour. Maybe he could stir those old desires again— like in that men's room years ago. Maybe, just maybe, he could bring Monty to his knees.

Tantalizing thoughts filled his head as he stripped and stepped into the shower. The water was steamy, the gel slick in his hand. He began to stroke himself, slowly, deliberately—not a quick release. He imagined Monty's groans, his body moving beneath him, his mouth around Monty's cock. The fantasy pushed him to climax, knees weakening as he gripped the metal bar for balance.

Spent but relaxed, he finished his shower, slid into bed, and drifted off immediately.

Morning light flooded the room. Facing east, the sun warmed his skin. Russell opened his eyes feeling renewed. Today was his day—his day with Monty.

He shaved, styled his red hair, and dressed carefully: navy pinstripe suit, lavender shirt, navy-and-gray striped tie, navy Ferragamo loafers, and a light thermal shirt beneath for warmth.

Through the lobby, he checked his watch and asked the desk clerk for directions: two blocks down, right, then one block over. Plenty of time.

The morning chill met him, tempered by sunshine. He crossed in front of the hotel and again passed *The Gilded Bean*. In daylight, he noticed the red lettering against the brown facade, the matching awnings—a clever, eye-catching detail.

Inside, the air was thick with the scent of freshly ground beans. There was a line. He joined the shortest. Large windows on three sides filled the shop with natural light.

When it was his turn, the barista greeted him and asked for a name. Russell, taken aback, said, "You didn't ask last night."

The barista smiled. "Morning hours—no table service. Even if you're staying, we still need your name. Are you eating here or to go?"

"Am I what?" Russell asked, already irritated.
"Eating here or to go?"
"For here," he replied curtly.

Annoyance simmered. Where was the nice young woman from last night? He wanted to ask but didn't know her name.

"Would you like a minute to decide?" the barista asked, eyeing the growing line.

Russell turned and saw how many people were waiting—lines at every register. He quickly gave his order, pressed his card to the reader, and took his receipt.

He found a large armchair and waited. The café buzzed with suited professionals and women in dresses and sneakers. Conversations hummed softly; others stared at phones or through the windows at the opposite flow of traffic.

"Rusty! Order for Rusty!" a barista shouted.

Russell froze. Then, eyes blazing, he strode to the counter. "It's *Russell!* R-U-S-S-E-L-L. That does not spell *Rusty!*" He snatched his order and stomped away, incredulous.

At the condiment bar, he fixed his coffee and took a seat at a small table. The fruit, yogurt, and bagel were divine, especially with the house blend. He made a note to buy a bag once his movers arrived.

He smiled, remembering how quickly he'd packed his condo. Leasing it was the smart move—he could afford to keep both places. Monty had promised his salary would nearly double: management level, more responsibility. Russell was ready for anything—as long as it kept him close to Monty.

Finishing breakfast, he refilled his coffee and walked toward the MLA&E Tower—the way the desk clerk had described it. *A tower,* he mused. Monty had built an empire. And Russell would be part of it.

The lobby was minimalist—tall desk, two uniformed guards, escalators on either side. The guards were issuing passes. Russell approached, reading from his phone:

When you enter the lobby, stop at the desk for a pass. It's the only way to access the elevator. You're going to the twenty-fourth floor. You'll receive your permanent ID badge there.

The older guard nodded, entered something into the system, printed a badge, and clipped it to a metal holder.

"This is your pass, Mr. Tierney. You can use it only for the twenty-fourth floor. Once you leave, unless granted further access, it'll deactivate. You'll only be able to go down. The system's smart—remember, in and out."

Russell clipped the badge to his lapel and headed for the elevators.

There were sets marked 4–15, 16–25, and one for 26–30 with a key slot. His door opened, the light flashed green, and he rose nonstop to the twenty-fourth floor.

The doors opened to a reception desk.

"Good morning, Mr. Tierney. Welcome to MLA&E Associates. I trust you had a comfortable night at your hotel?" said the older Black woman behind the counter, her nameplate reading Phylis.

"Yes, very comfortable, thank you," Russell replied softly.

Phylis was the senior receptionist of six—managerial-level, long-tenured, and informed on everything happening in the tower. She walked around the marble counter, the firm's illuminated initials glowing behind her. Medium height, sneakers on, she noticed Russell's glance downward.

"Mr. Tierney, we occupy fifty-five percent of this tower. That's a lot of real estate. Practical is good—very good." She chuckled.

Russell smiled stiffly.

"Let me have that badge and have a seat. Margaret and her crew will be here shortly. Can I get you something?"

Before he could answer, she called out, "Sharonda, get Mr. Tierney a bottle of water."

Moments later, Sharonda handed him the water.

Seated in the plush high-backed chair, Russell noticed two more elevator doors on the wall behind him. It was dawning on him—this was an empire Monty had built. He smiled to himself, feeling entitled. Soon he'd be Monty's racquetball and golf partner, confidant, and lover. The wife wouldn't be a problem—not after what he'd seen in Atlanta.

His pleasant fantasy was interrupted by a group of four— three women and a man. The older woman extended her hand.

"Mr. Tierney, good morning. My apologies for keeping you waiting. I'm Margaret Flanagan, this is my team—Amy, Laurie, and Nigel. We're from Human Resources. By the end of today, you'll have a firm grasp of your position as

Manager of Concept & Project Models—the departments, vendors, teams, and the tower's schematics."

Russell shook each hand, noticing they were all smartly dressed—and all wearing sneakers. Amy caught him looking.

"Mr. Tierney, everyone wears tennis shoes unless there's a client meeting. We dress up, but comfort is key. You'll understand soon enough."

"Amen!" came Phylis's voice from the counter, and the group chuckled.

Russell didn't. He offered his polished fake smile, irritated to feel like the joke.

Margaret led them down the corridor. "First, we'll head to ID for your thumbprint, docu-sign forms—including your NDA—photo badge, and building diagram acknowledgment. Nigel will then give you a full tour. After that, Amy will introduce you to IT and show you your office."

Amy added, "That'll cover the week. You'll have time to review materials and explore the systems before your start date."

Nigel chimed in, "By Friday, you'll know the building and meet your team for a luncheon in the Gallery on twenty-five."

As they reached the double glass doors, Margaret paused. "Any questions this week, my assistant will contact me immediately. You're at my disposal, as are Nigel and Amy. When you return in two weeks to begin officially, Amy will assist you for four more weeks."

She smiled and turned into a set of solid wood doors labeled *Organizational Development*.

Laurie, holding open the glass doors, said, "Mr. Tierney, this way. Let's get started."

Russell followed. Nigel stayed close, narrating as they passed offices and departments until they reached a room of standing desks. Laurie motioned him forward for his photo, thumbprint, and digital signature. Handed a mini pad, Russell scrolled through the NDA and signed without reading.

Nigel handed him his new ID badge. Russell clipped it on, ready for the tour.

It was on his calendar. The week was about to end, and Monty still hadn't had the opportunity to see Russell.

One, Monty didn't want the staff to misinterpret his acquaintance with Russell. Two, Russell sometimes made him a little uncomfortable. Three, he needed to do something about it.

Monty decided to invite Russell to have dinner Friday evening with him and the ladies. Addison hadn't shown any contempt or dislike, as BA had occasionally vocalized.

Since the Atlanta trip, he had noticed his wife and Addison growing closer—lunches, coffee chats, sometimes even the subject of BA's own conversation. This change, he thought, might soothe his wife's unspoken need to dash from the marriage. He'd always known he cared more for her than she for him. The union was a paradox—an imbalance he hoped would be atoned through Addison's presence in their lives, sharing their bed and their marriage.

His wife's success as a commercial real estate broker gave her a spark—almost orgasmic.

After much consternation, Monty knew it would be better to set some parameters for Russell, and dinner with the ladies would be the perfect opportunity. He had no intention of ignoring their friendship; he enjoyed the competitive moments on the racquetball court, the golf, and the dinners and drinks afterward. They hadn't been particularly close when they worked together in Chicago, but this was different. Here, he was *the* company, and maintaining decorum among the staff mattered.

Now—how to extend the invitation? he thought. Better to have Ron, his personal office assistant, contact him.

Still hesitant, Monty procrastinated until the end of the day, mentioning it to Ron as an afterthought while heading to the parking garage. There'd been no chance to run into Russell, especially with his ongoing training sessions and familiarization of the building.

Once Monty stepped into the private elevator, he felt instantly more at ease. He pressed the button for **Garage**, which took him directly to the upper-level executive parking.

As he exited the elevator, his phone chimed. It was a text from Ron:

Invite accepted.
Reservations made for 4, Fri @ 6:30 — Oilo & Vino.

Monty responded once he settled into the wagon:

Italian is perfect. Thanks.

Russell and Nigel were in the model room, where several site models were scattered about the vast space. By the window stood the site model of MLE&A. The only difference was that the sidewalk trees were much larger now. Behind the tower sat a multi-story garage. From the main street entrance, you couldn't see it at all.

The sight made Russell long for his own household goods —and most of all, his car. *Soon,* he thought.

Nigel called his name. Russell turned to see him standing with another man, somewhat older than Nigel, perhaps closer to his own age. As Nigel approached, Russell quickly put on his plastic smile and extended his hand first.

"Hello, I'm Russell Tierney."

Ron gave him a firm handshake, introduced himself, and got straight to the point. Monty was inviting him to dinner the following evening. Russell accepted immediately, before Ron could continue.

"I'll text you the particulars in a few moments. May I have your cell number?" Ron asked, scrolling through a tablet he held close to his chest.

"Sure. You have my number?" Russell asked.

Ron repeated the number Monty had provided, and Russell nodded in approval. Before leaving, Ron paused to remind him that discretion was important to Mr. Langford.

"Of course. Always," Russell replied.

Ron walked through the glass doors and disappeared within seconds, leaving Russell a little red-faced. *How dare an errand boy lecture me on discretion.* He had known Monty long before Ron was ever an errand boy.

Nigel, seeing that Ron had gone, walked toward Russell. Russell pushed his irritation to the back of his mind and replaced it with that practiced plastic smile.

"All set?" Nigel asked, reaching for the door handle.

"Yes. Where to next?" Russell replied, carefully suppressing his temper.

As they headed to the final stop of the day, Russell's phone buzzed with a text:

Dinner Fri @ 6:30 – Oilo & Vino

He texted a brief confirmation to Ron while following Nigel to his new office.

The view from his desk was a distraction from the thoughts brewing inside him. Monty had sent a message through his errand boy when he could have simply found him, greeted him, and extended a quiet dinner invitation himself. *Of course I'll be discreet,* Russell thought bitterly. *I adore Monty. I'm where I belong—in his orbit.*

He pushed the disappointment aside. He and Monty would have a long, private discussion over dinner.

Nigel interrupted his thoughts. "Russell, tomorrow Amy will go over your office phone, connect your line to the mail system, and help you get familiar with your terminal. These are a few supplies. She'll help with anything else you need."

Russell walked to the window of his twenty-first-floor office. He had a partial view of the river and the concrete path winding alongside it. In the distance, a tall bridge arched across the water, ships beyond it gleaming white. To the far right was the parking garage, its top deck filled with cars.

He turned and saw Nigel fiddling with his phone.

"I'll give you a few minutes," Nigel said. "I'll be back to show you the best way to the garage…"

"But my car hasn't arrived," Russell interrupted bluntly.

"Yes, I know," Nigel replied.

"I'm in the hotel until Saturday. It would be counterproductive to show me something I don't require yet."

Taken aback by Russell's tone, Nigel decided against explaining the protocol. He would make time tomorrow during one of Russell's training breaks.

"Of course. I'll stop by tomorrow. Your training will be here in your office. When you're ready, I'll show you the elevator you'll use to come and go from the tower on foot. There's a separate route when you're using the garage."

The two men left the sunlit office. They walked in silence —Nigel scrolling on his phone, Russell memorizing the path to the elevators.

At the elevator, they exchanged a firm handshake. "Thanks for today's tour," Russell said with his polished smile, regretting his earlier tone. *I'll make it up tomorrow,* he thought as the elevator doors closed.

As it descended, he glanced at his wrist before remembering his watch was packed with the movers. He checked his phone instead. It was just before 4:30 p.m.

The doors opened to the quiet lobby. Only a few people rode the escalators. Four men stood behind the security counter—different faces from the morning shift—and one man in a jacket and polo shirt.

Badge clipped neatly to his lapel, Russell crossed toward the exit. One guard called, "Have a good evening."

Russell turned, gave his signature smile, and kept walking —his sense of belonging settling in. The thought of sitting across from Monty on Friday sent a rush of warmth through him, leaving him slightly aroused

⁎⁎⁎

Addison stopped by **The Gilded Bean** at Chesnut Walk on her way to BA and Monty's townhouse, located between the financial district and Kellum County's Municipal Center. Town Center, as the area was known, had a mix of upscale townhouses and high-rise condos with amenities for groceries, dry cleaners, barbers, salons, Pilates, Barre, and other eateries and boutiques—but no Gilded Bean. She'd always been on the fence about opening a location there, not wanting to dilute her brand. Willow Walk, although not walking distance from Town Center, was within easy reach of the financial district. She made her stop, bags in hand, then headed back to her SUV and drove to the Langfords'.

She had packed an overnight bag. Monty had tried to convince her to bring some things to keep at the townhouse, to make her future stays more convenient. Addison was aware of BA's future with her husband—the *throuple entente* would soon end. She wasn't sure how it would be without BA; she had to admit she did have feelings for Monty, though she hadn't yet allowed herself to define exactly what they were. *What would we be like without BA?* she'd been asking herself since that lunch with her. *Hell, how will I be tonight?* she wondered, carrying this bombshell, knowing what was coming.

She shrugged it off, telling herself to enjoy the moments—the sex and the fulfillment—something she had once fantasized about with Thayer before they decided to take the "let's make a baby" path. Then it had all been taken away by a hit-and-run taxi. She remembered the day her attorney called to inform her of the taxi company's settlement offer and how final it made Thayer's death feel. The police were unable to find the driver, and the taxi company couldn't provide a responsible party for an uncommissioned vehicle taken from their repair lot. Witnesses said they saw the cab but didn't remember the driver—just a ball cap and a beard, said the three people on the other side of the street. *As soon as he stepped from the curb,* they'd said. It always felt odd to her.

Pulling into the alleyway behind the townhouse, she parked in the driveway. The garage door was up; Monty walked out as she pulled in, instructing her to park behind BA's Jag—they would be taking his wagon.

The *throuple entente* were casually dressed; the mood was relaxed and upbeat. BA had gone back to wearing her short hair in its natural curl, paired with a low-cut sweater, pleated slacks, and heels that pleased Monty. Her softer look appealed to his sexual nature.

Addison, always appropriate in Monty's eyes, was more demure in an untucked olive silk blouse—several buttons undone to reveal lace in navy that matched her slacks—a navy Bottega Veneta knotted buckle belt, and kitten-heeled mules in navy suede. In contrast to BA's large Gucci slouch bag, Addison carried a Chanel pouch about the size of her cell phone. Both women wore their necklaces—BA with hoop earrings, Addison with her signature diamond studs.

Monty took in each woman's choice of fragrance. It was intoxicating. It made him firm as he thought about the after-dinner plans. They were ensconced in a solid relationship—BA expressing her satisfaction with his intimacy with Addie, as she called her. As the driver, he would wait to enjoy the after-dinner *throuple entente*.

He also wanted to observe Russell. Addison had mentioned a few things about him after meeting him at Lenox Mall and later at lunch at Houston's. He was curious about her observations and had purposely told Ron not to mention that dinner would be for four and not two. Could Addison be correct? Was he mildly attracted to him, in an obsessive way? Was it sexual—or just adoration?

Monty recalled the night at the awards banquet in the men's room. He'd become aroused when Russell was wiping the wine from his trousers but quickly dismissed the incident as intoxicated arousal.

The drive to Oilo & Vino was normally a short one from the townhouse, but not this evening. Traffic was backed up with fans heading to the arena for the basketball game. Sitting in traffic, Monty glanced into the rearview mirror and saw Addison in the back seat, looking out the window.

"Are you a basketball fan, Addison?" he asked.

"I like basketball—more so college basketball. The pros I prefer to watch on television. Football's my favorite, in person or on TV," replied Addison.

"I've tried to get into sports, just not my thing," interjected BA.

"I happened to date a quarterback in college—thus my interest in the sport," said Addison.

Monty, now moving the car forward, turned and said, "Dated a quarterback!"

"Yeah. It wasn't really serious, at least not for me. It was more about being cool—dating a star quarterback—than actually being in a relationship with one."

"Was he GIB?" asked BA.

"Oh, come on, BA! That's a little personal, don't you think?" Monty chided.

"It's okay, Monty," Addison said lightly.

"Well?" BA pressed. "Was he?"

"He was okay. Huge ego. Always wanted to be on top, always came quick, rolled off, and wanted to go again half an hour later. I'd wait for the second round and tell him to take care of me before he came again. He'd masturbate me to orgasm, then get back on top, come, roll off. It was more about social recognition than anything."

Monty pulled up to the restaurant valet and put the wagon in park. The *throuple entente* entered as the host greeted Mr. and Mrs. Langford. At the bar, Monty spotted Russell. He handed the ladies off to the host, who showed them to their booth, and made his way to Russell, who was engaged in conversation with another man a couple of stools away.

Monty walked up and placed a hand on Russell's back as he said his name, causing Russell to look over his shoulder. Russell lit up with a big smile, turning on the bar stool to take Monty's hand and shake it.

"Monty, old chap! You made it! I was beginning to wonder if you'd stood me up," Russell said, still holding Monty's hand.

"Traffic was heavy—the Bayhawks have a game tonight," Monty replied, with no hint of apology.

"Yes, I saw the arena the other evening when I took a walk around this area. I'm staying at a hotel a few blocks from here, just a short walk to the arena. Is that your design?"

"Yes, as a matter of fact, it is. One of four I've designed in the financial district. The arena was a major project for MLA&E. The planning council was so impressed with the tower they came to me. Zoning and permits were a walk in the park," Monty said, humbly boasting.

As Monty spoke about his firm, Russell gave him a look of sheer adoration—almost as if he wanted to kiss him. The man seated a couple of stools away noticed how Russell's demeanor changed in Monty's presence. The man—whose gaydar wasn't particularly alarmed—had to admit the stranger carried the confidence of Atlas, Apollo, and Dionysus, with the manliness of Ares. His thoughts were interrupted when Russell slid off his stool. He gave a polite "nice talking to you, have a nice life" tone before following the tall, handsome man.

Russell took short, quick steps to catch up with Monty's long, purposeful strides toward the rear of the restaurant, which delighted him. *Cozy, intimate dinner,* Russell thought. Before he could express his appreciation, they stopped in front of a booth where two women sat chatting —two women he immediately recognized.

"Oh, it's you two," Russell exclaimed, unable to hide his surprise.

BA spoke first. "Nice to see you again, Rusty!"

Monty interjected before Russell could respond. "Ah, Russell will be joining us tonight. He's new in town—his first Friday evening. I thought we could share a meal and some good conversation."

"Of course," BA chirped. "That's right, my love—you mentioned Rusty would be joining the company. Please, have a seat. We were just about to order appetizers for the table. Any allergies? Dislikes?"

Before Russell could answer, the waiter arrived, and BA promptly ordered in perfect Italian.

"Prosciutto e Melone Rivisitato, Arancini di Riso, Ostriche Gratinate, grazie. Una volta arrivati gli antipasti, ordineremo i secondi. Grazie."

Russell's head was still spinning. *This woman is fucking with me*, he thought, but he attempted to calm himself by inquiring—and perhaps flattering—Monty's sharp-tongued wife.

"Wow, I hope I'll like one of those. You're Italian, Mrs. Langford?"

BA turned from the waiter to him. "No."

Addison, sensing the tension in Russell and realizing BA was playing a head game, decided to intervene to keep the mood pleasant.

"BA's also versed in German and Swedish," Addison said smoothly. "She has a knack for languages. Monty and I are fluent in French. What about you, Rust... Russell? Any languages in your repertoire?"

Russell, unaware he was being soothed by an expert, relaxed and turned his attention to Addison, ignoring BA.

"I'm pretty good with Spanish. I went to high school in South Florida—it was swim or drown in the language vernacular," he replied sheepishly.

Addison, still keeping the tone easy, brought Monty back into the conversation.

"Monty, isn't your boat captain Spanish? Is he Castilian or Latino?"

"He's actually Brazilian," Monty replied. "They mainly speak Portuguese."

Monty was about to continue speaking when his phone rang. He removed it from his pocket, pausing the conversation.

"Oh, ladies—it's Caldwell. Excuse me, Russell." He slid out of the booth and walked away.

BA broke the silence. "That must be about the trip next weekend."

Russell, biting before he realized, asked, "Trip? Monty's going on a trip?"

"Yes, we're all going, along with our friend Perry," said Addison.

"That sounds like fun..."

While Russell was still speaking, Monty returned to the table with the phone to his ear, looking directly at him.

"Hold on a minute, Caldwell—let me check on something."

Settling back into the booth, Monty looked at the women. He wasn't worried about Addison—she was usually laid-back about most things—but his wife was a horse of a different color. He decided to go for it and hope for the best.

"Russell, your actual work schedule starts ten days from today, correct?"

The waiter returned with the appetizers and plates for the table, followed by another waiter carrying a dish. They placed everything in the center. Monty immediately told them to give the table a minute, and both walked away. The women began spooning items onto their plates, listening closely—both curious.

"Yes, a week from Monday," replied Russell.

"What about your household goods and vehicle?" Monty asked.

"They arrive tomorrow. They should have everything unpacked by nightfall."

"Excellent. How would you like to accompany us—and Caldwell—on a boat trip down the coast to North Florida on Tuesday?" Monty asked, glancing at both women's faces.

BA smiled. Addison remained expressionless. Monty didn't wait for Russell's reply; he put the phone back to his ear.

"Yes, we'll have enough for two golf carts. Sorry to hear about your friend having to back out. I have a friend here who'll join us for the trip down—he's a solid golfer, perfect for our outing at the Quay Island Golf Club. Let's plan to board and be ready for the ocean trek Wednesday around 4 a.m. You can stay at the townhouse Tuesday night. The boat will be at the marina by the cruise ship dock. I've arranged for a driver to take us from the townhouse to the marina."

As the implication became clear, Russell contained his excitement. He wanted to appear collected about spending time with Monty—even if *the bitches*, as he thought of them, were around, and some guy named Caldwell. He was going to spend time with Monty outside the office, and that was a good start.

Monty slipped the phone back into his jacket pocket and turned his attention to the women, who were immersed in tasting each appetizer. They didn't seem concerned that he'd just added Russell to their trip on the Hatteras.

The waiter returned, and each person ordered a different entrée. The wine flowed as conversation turned to the trip and Monty outlined the itinerary. The women watched Russell, gauging his reactions.

"We'll head down the coast to Quay Island Wednesday morning, departing by four," Monty said. "We can stop by your condo to pick you up if you like, Russell."

"Monty, you're too generous. I'll plan to Uber to the dock —just send me the address for the driver. What can I bring? What can I contribute to the trip?" Russell asked.

"Just bring yourself—we've got a set itinerary," replied Monty.

"There must be something…"

Monty interrupted. "We'll stop in Beaufort for a casual lunch, meander a bit, have takeout dinner onboard, hang out, play a game or two. Then we head to Charleston the next morning—should arrive by dinner. Overnight on board in Charleston, enjoy breakfast in town, pick up takeout before casting off late afternoon to arrive at Quay Island midmorning. I'll get you a room at the Ritz, where we're staying two nights. Our golf outing's all day Saturday. Nothing planned for that evening, but brunch Sunday before we depart."

"Sounds like a relaxing venture. I'll book my return flight from Florida later tonight. Thank you for the invitation— I'm looking forward to it. Best way to relax before I start on the project at the office," said Russell, graciously.

"How's that coming?" inquired BA.

"Oh, it's coming along great!" Russell responded, excitement in his tone.

Addison, quiet until now, asked, "What exactly are you doing at MLA&E?"

"I'm a senior-level project manager," Russell said, now looking at Addison and noticing her necklace—identical to Monty's wife's.

"Sounds like you landed well with the firm," Addison said, noticing his glance. "It's stunning, isn't it? A gift from BA."

"Yes, they're both stunning—the carats are amazing," Russell said.

BA and Monty sat silently, listening to the exchange. Monty was impressed by Addison's calm nature—how she could read people and defuse tension before it flared. Surprisingly, he allowed the exchange to stand. In that moment, he wanted to be a twin—to remain devoted to BA, but be with Addison as his mate. She was perfect for him—in life, in bed, in love.

He drifted off in thought until Russell's question pulled him back.

"Monty, tell me about your boat."

Before Monty could respond, the waiter arrived with their entrées. Dinner was served. Conversation shifted to comments about flavor and the authenticity of the Italian food, with intermittent talk about the week past—Addison quizzing Russell more about his position, Monty engaging with both of them.

BA was unusually quiet. Monty and Addison noticed she'd consumed nearly an entire bottle of wine when she asked the waiter for another bottle of Prosecco. Russell and Addison were drinking Cabernet Sauvignon. Monty, the designated driver, stuck with iced tea.

An hour and forty-five minutes after their arrival, the *throuple entente* said goodnight to Russell, who walked back toward his hotel. They waited for the valet to bring the wagon around. When it arrived, BA moved swiftly, heading Addison off. She opened the rear passenger door and got in, leaving Addison standing there, confused. The valet walked around to where she stood, opened the passenger door, and she climbed in slowly, still unsure.

"BA, are you okay?" asked Addison.

"Yes, I'm fine. I'd rather sit in the back. You two enjoy yourselves," she said, snuggling into the seat for a nap.

Monty and Addison locked eyes. He shrugged, uncertain. Pulling into traffic, he drove toward the townhouse. He glanced over—Addison was staring straight ahead. In the rearview mirror, his wife was asleep. The *entente* seemed somehow disconnected. He wondered if inviting Russell to dinner had unsettled her. They'd talked about being together after dinner, assuming they were all on the same page.

BA had seemed distant and then herself again over the weeks since Atlanta. Lost in thought, Monty had to admit— he wanted to be with Addison tonight. He wanted her all to himself. No need to be angry with BA for drinking too much; he'd talk with her before Monday. But tonight, he wanted to feel Addison—to be in her, to have her—to himself.

Addison stared out the side window, wondering how this would play out if BA was too intoxicated to join them. She'd had a couple of glasses of wine herself but wouldn't drive home. Maybe she'd call DJ to come get her and retrieve her SUV tomorrow. She felt disappointed; she'd looked forward to being with them.

With BA obviously out for the night, what would Monty want to do? The two of them, she thought. The idea aroused her. She decided on a nap, a cup of coffee, a splash of cold water on her face, and then the drive home later. She glanced at her watch—she could be home by 9:30, no later than ten. Maybe the yearning would ease by then.

Monty noticed Addison looking at her watch. He wanted to ask but was afraid of the answer. He continued driving, arriving at the townhouse and pressing the remote for the garage door. He parked, then turned toward her, lightly touching her hand.

His pulse raced as he said quietly, "I hope you'll stay."

Perry held a drink in one hand and his phone in the other. Sitting in his condo high above Dallas, he was on speakerphone with his daughter, who was complaining about having to pay her car insurance. He was calm and forever patient with his prima donna. He explained that it was part of adulthood and that to own and drive a car, insurance was a necessity.

Perry Caldwell Marchand loved his daughter and his stepdaughter, but that love was often tested when they failed to understand the nuances of adulthood. His patience waned, though he had sheltered them growing up—even through the failures of his marriages. He listened to her complain about everything wrong in her world while sipping Balvenie 21-Year-Old Portwood Scotch. He sat back in his leather recliner, kicked off his Ferragamo loafers, and relaxed as she ranted.

He drifted in and out with his usual *uh-huhs* and *mm-hmms*, offering small words of encouragement when she got wound up. His mind wandered instead to his recent conversation with Monty about their upcoming trip on *The Best Tide* to North Florida. Setting his crystal glass on the side table, he flipped to his notes app and began listing what he needed to pack—and what his assistant should pick up before wheels-up Monday evening to Belhaven.

He must have drifted too far—there hadn't been enough *uh-huhs*—because he suddenly heard his daughter yelling his name. In frustration, she gave him a quick, forced *goodbye* and hung up.

After ending the call, Perry scrolled through his recent texts. The last few were from Monty:

Caldwell, ol' chum! Lighten the load… will have my island attire delivered to the hotel by my plane crew day of check-in—especially the ladies!!

Two days later:

Cald… Mont here… found a bottle of Macallan Double Cask—25 years young.

Perry decided a duffel with jeans and polos would suffice for the boat, and a medium suitcase for his golf attire, jacket, slacks, and shirt for dinner on the island. He'd have his assistant make dinner reservations at the hotel restaurant for Friday night.

He was looking forward to the leisurely time with his friends. Relaxation had been an afterthought lately, buried under work demands. His family's development company and wells were profitable, but even success left him longing for the love of his life. Somehow, it had just never seemed the right time—or the best time—for them to gel.

He rose from his chair and headed to the bedroom to sort out his outfits.

Addison felt herself flutter when Monty touched her. A mix of emotions flooded her. Her mind told her to stick with the plan; her heart fluttered, telling her to say yes—no to a nap and coffee.

"Are you sure, Monty?"

"Of course I'm sure—one hundred percent." He raised his right hand as if he were under oath.

She smiled at the gesture. It was affirming—that he wanted her as much as she wanted him. Knowing BA's secret played havoc with her conscience. She wanted to tell him of her plans, but what would she say? *Your wife is planning to leave to attend a conservatory to become a high-end Dominatrix?* She wasn't sure when BA had planned to drop this bomb—or when she was leaving. For all Addison knew, she could change her mind. So what, she reasoned, could she possibly say to this man she had developed feelings for—no, she insisted, cared for—nothing more.

She agreed to stay, got out of the wagon, and walked back to her SUV. Pulling out her duffel bag, Monty immediately took it from her to carry inside. They almost forgot about BA, asleep in the back seat. Turning to look at each other, they both realized it at the same time, then moved to wake her.

BA, in a sleepwalking, hypnotic state, followed Monty's voice as he guided her through the garage into the kitchen. She stopped. Monty looked at her, then to Addison.

Addison guessed, "Water?"

Monty opened the fridge, took out a bottle of water, opened it, and handed it to BA, who poured the water into her mouth, streams running down her chin onto her chest, trailing into her cleavage. She held the bottle away from her. Addison, once again the mind reader, took the bottle as BA let go, then began walking back toward the garage door. Monty redirected her to the great room, toward the large sectional sofa filled with pillows. He held her close so she wouldn't bump into the table in her path. Once she stood at the sofa, he positioned her to sit.

Removing her top, Addison gazed at her round, perfect breasts supported by a full lace bra. Monty laid her back, swinging her legs onto the sofa. He removed her heels—which literally added three inches to her height—unzipped her slacks, and shimmied them down her legs, over her feet, and onto the floor. Her matching lace panties revealed a clean-shaven pubic area and taut abs. Monty stood over her, admiring his wife's physique. Addison, from the kitchen, admired too—with pangs of guilt. She was watching how BA's husband painstakingly cared for her in an inebriated state.

Monty turned to look at Addison and again shrugged—something she had learned he did when he was out of ideas about what was going on with his wife. This man, who ran a multi-million-dollar empire known worldwide, shrugging when it came to the person who was supposed to be closest to him. Addison felt her pulse quicken, her face flush, thinking about his life going forward after BA crashed his world around him.

Monty broke her thoughts. "Look in the first cabinet to the left of the sink—there's a bottle of acetaminophen and another bottle of water."

Addison followed his instructions, found the bottle, and grabbed an unopened bottle of water from the fridge. She placed both on a tray that sat on the ottoman closest to BA.

Monty had disappeared but returned with a small ornamental trash bin. He opened a trash bag, inserted it, and set it between the sofa and the ottoman. As a final touch, Monty laid a throw cover over her and turned off the lamp.

"That should do it," he said softly.

Addison nodded in agreement.

Monty grabbed Addison's duffel, took her hand, and led her upstairs toward his bedroom. She tugged her hand from his. He stopped. She shook her head—no. He turned and entered a guest room instead. The bed had high poles, decorated in gray and mauve—a mix of stripes and florals. An area rug encompassed the room, covering the white pine hardwoods. Plantation shutters were softened by floor-to-ceiling drape panels on each end of the double windows. The room was small, but the poles and panels added height, giving the illusion of space. A bifold door stood on one wall and another door opposite the windows.

Quietly, Monty closed the shutters, moved to the door, opened it, turned on a nightlight, and left the room without saying anything. Addison removed her jacket, slipped off her shoes, and sat on the bench at the foot of the bed—just as Monty returned with a glass of something brown, a glass of white wine, and two bottles of water. His shoes, jacket, and shirt were gone. His undershirt was untucked, and his belt undone. He sat beside her.

"I know this is unexpected—BA's condition. If you're uncomfortable—"

She interrupted. "That's your call, Monty. I'm here for you —for whatever you want or need. We can talk…"

"I want you," he said.

They sat quietly for a moment.

Taking her hand, he said softly, "Addison, I feel in limbo, but I can't explain it—why or what's the cause."

As she looked at him, she could see he was hesitant, but she could also feel the heat they obviously shared. She put her hand on his face, drew close, and kissed him gently on the lips. He moved in to meet her, wanting more. He took her head in his hands and kissed her deeply, probing his tongue into her mouth. He tasted of whiskey, his tongue slick and warm from the alcohol. She kissed him back. When he pulled away, he hugged her; she could feel his chest throbbing from his quickened pulse. He excused himself again and left the room.

Addison stood, removed her slacks, her shirt, and her bra. Leaving the lace teddy on and her French-cut lace panties, she removed the duvet from the bed and laid it on the bench. The bed had large matching shams, square pillows of all sizes, neck rolls, and sleeping pillows she left in place. She took her duffel into the bathroom, used the soft nightlight to remove a few toiletry items, returned the bag to the bedroom, and slid it under the bench. In the doorway stood Monty, watching her. He entered, sat on the bed, and took a sip from his glass.

He noticed she hadn't touched her wine.

"I'm good," she said, noticing his glance at the glass.

Intentional or not, they didn't speak after that. She climbed onto the bed, unbuttoned and unzipped his trousers, easing them down his legs and pushing him back against the pillows anchored by the headboard. She leaned over him, her touch deliberate, watching his response build beneath the fabric. He held his glass tightly as she lingered there, teasing through the barrier, her mouth following the shape of him, her fingers light and insistent. He set the glass aside, breath already uneven.

As she lowered the waistband, a single bead caught the light. She traced it with her tongue, drawing him further into the moment, then tugged the fabric away completely. He shifted to free himself, fully exposed now, his body unmistakably ready. She took her time, moving slowly, drawing him in and out of the sensation, alternating between mouth and hand, coaxing him higher. His moans rose and fell with her rhythm.

When he couldn't hold back any longer, he sat up, rolled her onto her back, and pulled away what remained between them. He moved over her, mouth and hands exploring with purpose, drawing soft cries from her as she opened wider to him, her fingers clutching at herself, pinching, urging, welcoming everything he gave.

He pushed her further, watching her react, her body arching, hips flexing, asking for more. He obliged, shifting his attention, letting his mouth travel, nipping lightly, teasing before returning to where she needed him most. The sight of her—eyes open now, watching him—only intensified his movements.

He slid into her decisively as she lifted her legs, taking him fully. Their sounds merged, breath and motion syncing as he braced himself above her, kissing her, feeling her pulse beneath him. Each movement pulled them closer to the edge.

He took her arms, lifting them above her head, holding her wrists there as his rhythm sharpened. Their eyes locked. The tension stretched, tightened, broke. He released her hands and she wrapped herself around him, drawing him closer until there was almost no space left between them.

A few final movements and they came together—raw, breathless, spent. He collapsed over her, kissed her forehead, then rolled to her side, the heat between them still humming in the quiet that followed.

Her chest heaved, breathless. He lay beside her, watching her flushed face. They stayed that way for several minutes before he got up, ran some water, and returned with a hot washcloth for her and himself. He laid back against the headboard; she rested partially on his chest and the pillows. He opened a bottle of water, took several swallows, and handed it to her. She finished it, giving him the empty bottle.

"More?" he asked.

She shook her head. He repositioned himself, pulled the sheet down; she got under it, and he pulled it up. They lay in silence for a moment.

"I love the way you make me feel," she spoke softly.

His pulse raced. He snuggled closer. He wanted to say so much but didn't know where to start.

"I know tonight wasn't what we had planned," he finally said. "I want you to know I'm okay with this. You please me in ways I've never known—which may sound corny coming from a grown man…"

"I'm also pleased we had this tonight," she said.

He reached over, turned off the light, and they spooned together among the pillows.

At dawn, BA—barefoot and quiet—looked through the opening of the door to see them both sound asleep, entangled in each other, breathing almost in sync. She closed the door, went to their bedroom, showered, dressed in sweats, and left the house to get morning croissants, bagels, and fruit. She wasn't sure what she was feeling— besides the hangover—whether she was happy or merely satisfied that they were becoming close. She knew he would need someone, but deep down there brewed a twang of jealousy. Something she did not want to admit—or would ever dare say aloud, especially to Addie.

△ ▽ ▽ △

The chill at 3:30 in the morning was brutal. Perry and B.A. scrambled back and forth, taking luggage and a few noteworthy supplies from the kitchen of the townhouse to the SUV. The driver, a smart guy, wore gloves and a wool hooded jacket. Perry, in a suede jacket, no socks, no cap, and deck shoes with jeans, was literally trembling. B.A., in a turtleneck under a sweatshirt and sweatpants, moved faster to generate heat. She instructed the driver not to turn the motor off and to crank up the heat inside the SUV—which he did.

"Why are there so many bags?" asked B.A.

"Most of this is last-minute stuff Monty and I picked up last night after he got me from the FBO," responded Perry.

"My goodness, isn't that what the crew was supposed to do?" she grumbled.

Upstairs in the primary suite, Monty was collecting notes he had made the day before regarding the upcoming series of meetings in Dallas with The Marchand Group after the trip. He'd already communicated with Ron from the office to send several files he planned to review while traveling from JAX FBO to Dallas. He was waiting for them to finish downloading before unplugging his laptop and putting it in his briefcase. There was an envelope—detoured and delivered to the townhouse by DHL yesterday—that wasn't in his case.

"What did I do with it?" he asked aloud.

He spotted the bright yellow envelope, barely visible between two books on the shelf. Pulling it free, it had been placed upside down, and the contents spilled out onto the floor. Baffled, Monty bent over and began gathering the items, noticing they weren't spreadsheets but envelopes—four of them, all unsealed.

The first, heavy cream stock, was light. He turned it over and read aloud, "Goldman Sachs International… London, United Kingdom."

Looking at the addressee: "Ms. Barbara A. Roberson."

He picked up the next envelope—much heavier—with the insignia UKVI, United Kingdom Visas & Immigration. The flap wasn't closed, and an American passport fell out, opening to a vignette sticker and a white folded letter as a bookmark. He opened the letter.

"…your application for a [Student visa] to enter the United Kingdom has been granted…"

Reading it aloud made him open the next: a gray, heavy-grain envelope with the silver insignia of MC, Marchmont Conservatory Office of Academic Affairs. The letter made him sit on the edge of the bed. It gave the admission date, the start date, and mentioned a realtor who would contact her about her flat. The letter went on to congratulate Ms. Roberson and expressed anticipation in crafting her skills as a high-ranking Dominatrix.

Beads of perspiration formed on Monty's forehead. His hand, holding the conservatory letter, trembled. He let it fall to the floor. The final envelope bore the branding of Virgin Atlantic. He reached for it, hesitated, then opened it.

"Virgin Atlantic Upper Class — One-way JFK to LHR," he read aloud from the itinerary.

Reading further, he discovered the trip was scheduled for three weeks after this one.

"Monty! We're waiting for you! The SUV is all loaded!" yelled B.A. from the kitchen.

Monty scrambled to gather the envelopes, stuffing everything back into the DHL pouch and shoving it into his case.

"Yes—yes! Be right there!" he shouted back.

He heard the door close downstairs. Monty sat back on the bed, opened his case, and realized his own DHL envelope was still tucked in a pocket. Carefully, he removed B.A.'s pouch, restored the letters and passport to their respective places, and this time set it in front of her pillow on her side of the bed. The reality hadn't fully sunk in, but he felt the universe shift—like it had when Ellen was found dead on their kitchen floor. He consoled himself: at least this wasn't as final.

In the bathroom, he wet a cloth and wiped his face. His eyes were red. He hadn't cried—or had he? Tears of disbelief, perhaps. His wife was going away to school, he reasoned. That wasn't so bad.

"A one-way ticket. Not even an open-ended return," he muttered to his reflection.

Was this really happening? He heard the door open and, before anyone could speak, said loudly, "I'm coming down now! Had to change my slacks—took longer than I anticipated."

Grabbing his laptop and shoving it into his briefcase, one jacket sleeve on and the other off, he hurried downstairs— only to see Addison standing in the kitchen.

"Addison."

"I got concerned—it's almost 4:20. You're never late, Mr. Monteque," she said with a smile, noticing his eyes but, in true Addison fashion, asking no questions.

"Well, let's go, Missy. We've got a trip down the coast to see unforgettable sunrises and sunsets."

She walked out first. Monty closed the kitchen door behind them and, once in the driveway, hit the button to close the garage. He saw DJ in the driver's seat of her Benz SUV, smiled cheerfully, and waved. Then he climbed into the front passenger seat of the SUV with B.A. and Perry inside —choosing not to sit in the back beside his wife.

The two vehicles pulled off, heading toward the dock on the riverfront.

Russell was already on board, holding a hot mug of coffee. His gear was tucked away in the cabin Addison had recommended. His second suitcase sat on the pier, ready to be added to the SUV and taken to the FBO for transport on Monty's plane to Quay Island and The Ritz.

The captain, hearing the group approaching the boat, instructed his two crewmen to get their things stowed quickly. He fired up the MTU twin engines, the rumble bringing *The Best Tide* to life. The group chattered about the cold, each wanting coffee—Perry even joking about a "coffee cocktail." Everyone stopped and looked at him quizzically until he flashed a grin and said, "Just kidding." Laughter followed.

The luggage—and the extra supplies Monty and Perry had picked up—was stowed away by the crew. Wrapped in blankets, the group gathered on the aft deck to enjoy the descent from river to bay to ocean. The predawn horizon glowed faintly with lights from houses along the shore. By the time *The Best Tide* reached the bay channel, the sky had begun to lighten.

Addison, wrapped in her blanket, sat beside Russell. B.A., bundled in two blankets, sat beside Perry, who sat between her and Monty. From her vantage point, Addison watched them all carefully. Something about the scene didn't feel right.

B.A. was unusually talkative. She had once told Addison she wasn't a fan of Perry—and during their trip to Atlanta, she'd confided she liked Russell even less. Yet here she sat, chatting away with Perry as if they were old friends. Perry, for his part, seemed to be enjoying the attention.

Addison's experience with Perry dated back to when Thayer was alive. Perry had always been a loner, his circle of friends small. She, Thayer, and Perry had shared many dinners together, and she remembered him as a man content to be alone. He never spoke of women, even after his second divorce. But something about Monty's presence changed him. Perry and Thayer had been close—like brothers—but around Monty, Perry was different.

Addison continued to observe until Russell excused himself to nap in the cabin. Monty walked over and asked if she was doing all right. She nodded and smiled. When he went to talk to the captain, Addison excused herself, Perry joining her as she moved away.

The sun was climbing now, scattering gold across the water. B.A. sat wrapped in three blankets, her back to the ladder leading to the captain's deck. Her view to port was the faint silhouette of trees along the shoreline. Warm and relaxed, she closed her eyes.

She wasn't sure how long he'd been sitting there when she opened them to find Monty in Perry's place, watching her, a steaming cup in his hand.

"Is that a coffee cocktail?" she asked, half teasing.

He sat silently for a moment before replying.
"No—and it sure isn't a one-way ticket to Heathrow."

B.A. flushed beneath the blankets. If this was coincidence, it was an unnerving one. She decided to play it off.
"That would definitely take more than one cup, wouldn't you say?" she said lightly.

Monty had had time to process his discovery while watching B.A. laugh and talk with Perry. He'd concluded that anger wouldn't serve him. Remembering what Addison had once told him— *"Calm brings out the truth faster than one can digest."*—he stayed composed.

"What would be your ideal coffee cocktail?" he asked evenly.

B.A. blinked, uncertain. "I suppose… rum."

"Which kind of rum?"

She looked toward the starboard side, away from him, thinking. Monty studied her closely, showing no emotion. It was a standoff of wills. She knew he must know something —but how much? Had Addison said something? He knew she could see that something was wrong, yet she avoided his eyes, as she often did when she wanted control of the room.

He wanted to blurt out what he'd found. She wanted to ask point blank if he knew—and whether Addison had broken her confidence.

After a long pause, she said, "For a special occasion, Ron Zacapa. But every day? Bacardi."

He appeared calm, but inside he was boiling. How could she just plan to leave? No conversation. No warning. Nothing. He'd known she had restless tendencies, but finding Addison was supposed to be the key—the thing that would bring balance. Then it hit him: *She* was the key. The key that would give B.A. someone to leave him for, so she could go without guilt.

He decided he wouldn't hold it in much longer. Letting her know what he knew would free him more than it would her. She'd made her plans. Now, he would make his.

Before B.A. could respond, the captain's nephew announced that brunch was served in the salon. Monty rose, leaving her wrapped in her blankets.

The salon was warm and fragrant. Food was set in the middle of the table, with a sideboard laid out with hot trays: breakfast breads, sweet rolls, bagels, hash brown potatoes, scrambled eggs, and sausages. The centerpiece was a platter of smoked salmon with onions and capers. Bowls of fruit, pitchers of orange and apple juice, a bottle of champagne, two insulated coffee carafes, cream, and sugar packets completed the spread.

Everyone was seated when B.A. entered. Two empty chairs —directly across from Monty—waited. She took a plate, served herself quietly, and sat without a word.

Monty had made sure those seats would be open. Perry, Russell, and Addison were engrossed in a lively game of trivia, laughing when someone got an answer right. Addison, though aware of the tension between the Langfords, stayed engaged, trying to keep things light. She suspected B.A. hadn't yet told Monty about her plan to move abroad, but perhaps he'd found out another way.

She kept the men occupied, tossing out playful questions. "What was the TV show about an alien named Mork who lived with a woman named Mindy?" she asked. "It was Margo and Klaus's favorite—those weird sounds used to get their attention for ten minutes straight."

The men were stumped, debating quietly. From behind her, Monty's calm voice cut through.
"Mork and Mindy."

The table fell silent for a beat until he repeated himself. Russell, unfamiliar with the show, looked to Addison.

Turning to him with a faint smile, she said, "Yes. He's actually correct."

Laughter followed, the name sounding absurdly funny to Russell and Perry, who had never seen it. Addison explained, but B.A. stayed quiet, pushing food around her plate without eating. Addison noticed but said nothing.

In her peripheral vision, she saw Monty watching B.A.—
not staring, but observant. Addison could feel his tension.
The men, still caught up in their game, hadn't noticed.

Russell challenged Perry to chess. The box of games sat
nearby: Monopoly, dominoes, decks of cards, and a
backgammon case. The two men retrieved the set, poured
more coffee, and settled into a serious match.

Addison remained seated, sipping her drink as she watched.
She joked to herself about the good old days when they
were a thriving, happy *throuple entente*. Pouring another
cup of coffee, she offered some to Monty, who accepted.
Then she gestured toward B.A., who declined, lifting her
orange juice laced with champagne instead.

Adding cream and stirring it in, Addison stood. "I'm going
to my cabin for a bit. I'll come back up later."

Before walking away, she turned to Monty. "What's our
ETA in Beaufort?"

Without looking up, he said, "Around sixteen hundred
hours."

Amused, she replied, "Aye aye, Admiral."

In that moment, Monty felt like a cad. He was ignoring the
beautiful woman who had brought joy back into his life.
Addison made him feel wanted—alive again. Her presence
had given him a happiness he didn't want to lose, even with
disappointment sitting across the table.

He looked up just in time to return her salute.

"Dismissed, sailor," he replied.

She smiled at him. He returned her smile. B.A. observed the exchange.

The captain's nephew entered from the galley, stacking plates onto a tray. Monty stood to help, but the young man insisted he had it handled. Monty thanked him and left the salon.

B.A. continued to sip her mimosa. The men, still immersed in their chess game, didn't notice she was the only one left at the table. Duarte, the nephew, moved back and forth between the salon and galley, clearing dishes and loading the dishwasher before disappearing into the crew quarters.

Several minutes later, B.A. rose and headed toward their stateroom. When she entered, she saw Monty lying on his side, eyes closed. Quietly, she climbed onto the bed and laid her head on the pillow with a soft sigh of relief.

"When were you planning to tell me about your move to the U.K.?" Monty's voice was low but firm.

B.A. froze. She hadn't wanted to get into it here—too close, too confined.
"Can we wait to talk about this?"

"Oh, please, B.A." His tone sharpened. "It's a simple, civilized question. One a husband might expect to ask a wife who has, quite painstakingly, secured a visa, entry to a prestigious conservatory, a flat—and a one-way ticket."

He knew.

"When were you planning to tell me about your move to the U.K.?" Monty repeated, his voice still low but colder now.

He turned, sitting up against the headboard. The shutters were closed, muting the light, casting the room in shifting shadows. She couldn't quite make out his face, but she could feel the weight of his stare.

"Look, I'm not going to beg you to stay. You don't have to worry about that," he said. "When were you going to tell me?"

The silence stretched until B.A. finally spoke. "Monty, I don't want us to argue. We have guests."

"Dammit, B.A.," he hissed through clenched teeth. "Answer the fucking question."

Quietly, she replied, "After the trip."

"Thank you," he said, turning his back to her as he lay down again.

She treaded carefully, her voice softer now. "I realize we have things to iron out. The prenup pretty much takes care of the Tower, the farmhouse, the holdings…"

Quietly, he interrupted. "I matched the funds you earned when you sold me the property where the Tower and the parking garage now stand. I invested them separately from my holdings. That was something I wanted you to have without encumbrance—had something happened to me.

"I saw that Sachs is handling your funds in the U.K. Give Ron your banker's name, and I'll have my guy transfer the stocks to your account. It's enough that you'll never have to worry about money, regardless of what you do—or decide not to do. The prenup stands. You'll get your share of the townhouse and those funds listed in the document."

B.A. was speechless. He was setting her up for life—generous, but final. She felt an emptiness in his tone, held back her tears, and listened as he continued.

"The Jag was a gift, yours to do with as you wish. Your jewelry—you may want a marine rider to protect them. Once you depart, I'll have them removed from the farmhouse policy. I'll maintain the life insurance, and of course, I'll rename a beneficiary for mine. I'll put the townhouse on a pocket listing. That should keep the news from spreading too quickly. With any luck, you'll be long gone before it's understood this is a permanent departure."

He paused. The room fell silent.

"You should keep the townhouse—you'll need somewhere to stay during the week," she said softly.

"Other than my clothes and office items, feel free to pack and ship whatever you want from the townhouse. As the prenup states, the farmhouse property is mine—as is the Tower and the other financial district properties owned by MLE&A."

He exhaled deeply, reached for the blanket at the foot of the bed, and pulled it around him. She sat half-propped against the headboard and pillows. The room went still for several minutes.

"The *Best Tide*, of course, isn't in the prenup—it remains my property, as does the art at the farmhouse," he said.

She wanted to protest the artwork—some of those pieces she had discovered during their travels—but she thought better of it. If this was the tone, she'd let it be. He was, after all, calm and generous. Financially, she'd never have to worry. Now, she had the means to purchase something in

South Kensington once her tenancy in Chelsea expired, giving her time to procure items suitable for a home in that area. She wasn't sure if she'd ship her belongings from the townhouse now, or pack and store them in America for later.

Monty had drifted off; she could tell by his breathing. *Was this over?* she wondered. *Had we gone through the worst? Would it stay this civilized?*

She tried to ease herself slowly off the bed, one foot on the floor—

"I realize you set me up," he said suddenly, startling her. "Actually, you set us both up. You knew that introducing us at *The Gilded Bean* that day, I'd be interested in her. That, B.A., feels like betrayal. I shared very private moments with you over the years. We experienced many swaps with other couples—St. Martin, Barbados, the conference in Panama, the resort in Thailand. Only two other single women during that time, and they disappeared without a word. How long did it take you to know she was the one?"

B.A. froze, moving back onto the bed. Her heart raced— because he was right. She *had* looked for someone like Addie—Addison.

"I wanted you to be happy, too, Monty," she said quietly.

"Does she know she was part of a plan?" he asked, his tone hard.

"No, she does not."

"This woman you found for me—who, I don't mind saying, is perfect. Bravo, B.A." He lightly clapped his hands together.

"Will you tell her?" B.A. asked.

"I'm not sure that's for me to tell, Miss Matchmaker. Do you?" he replied, turning onto his back.

"You…"

"No—stop there, B.A. I care about this woman—her beautiful spirit—and she's endured tremendous tragedy in her life. I'm not sure what to do at this point, but whatever I do, it won't involve my *former* wife. Do you understand?"

"Yes, of course," she said quickly.

It made her feel replaced. She knew he cared for her, but this sounded like he was *in love* with Addison now. She recalled the other night, when she'd found them asleep together, tangled in the sheets, breathing in sync. A twang of jealousy rose in her throat before she could swallow it down.

"She knows, Monty. She knows about the conservatory—the interview, my plan to live abroad. She's known for some time."

He closed his eyes tightly while she spoke. His chest heaved. His heart pounded. His head throbbed as her words sank in.

"In my defense," he asked, "she doesn't know you handpicked her to be our throuple?"

"No. She thinks we had a chance meeting at her coffee shop."

"Well," he said, voice low, "as I said, it's nothing for you to concern yourself with. You've got one foot across the pond, and soon it'll be planted firmly in the U.K."

He may have sounded sure and steady about his feelings for Addison, but hearing that she already knew made his eyes sting. He rolled back to his side and mumbled,

"I want everyone to enjoy this trip. If you don't think you can accomplish that, fake an illness, and I'll arrange for you to depart in Beaufort."

"No, I'll be the picture of happiness. We wouldn't want Addison to feel uncomfortable with you three men onboard —even though Russell would be ecstatic to see me go, not realizing he'd then have to contend with Addison *and* your attention to her."

With that, she slid off the bed and quietly left the room.

When he heard the door shut, he threw the blanket off and sat up in bed, gripping a bottle of water. He drained it in one long pull. He knew he had a lot to face after this trip. The deal with Caldwell's family business would be a long-term one—developing a mixed-use district in the heart of Texas. Travel would be constant. Night meetings. Endless hours.

How would Addison handle that kind of environment? She had before, with her late husband in high finance—but was she still built for that? She seemed so settled now. Or so he thought.

He knew she'd spent those two weeks after their first time at the farmhouse at home, not with relatives as she'd implied. His investigator had reported that she kept a steady routine with her dogs and rarely left her gated community except to walk them. Something he'd never mentioned to B.A.—and now, he was thankful he hadn't.

Still, her demeanor in Atlanta—the way she looked at him, how she always seemed to know what he was thinking before he spoke—lingered in his mind. He was glad she'd picked that piece of jewelry; he'd wanted to give her something personal. Something that wasn't tied to *them* as a throuple entente, but to her alone.

Walking into the ensuite, he splashed cold water on his face and looked at himself in the mirror. His eyes were pink. He leaned closer, studying the stubble on his jaw, the silver threading his temples. After brushing his teeth and rinsing with mouthwash, he stayed there, gripping the counter.

"Do you want her? Can you make her happy? Can you be happy—just the two of you? No more frolicking. Travel, yes, but just that?" he asked his reflection.

He grabbed his shaving kit from his duffel, pulled out a comb, and ran it through his hair. Looking back in the mirror, he said aloud,

"Yes. Yes. Hell, yes. Absolutely."

He knew it—he'd already fallen for her. But had she for him? He wanted to court her, the old-fashioned way, the way his father had courted his mother. He would weather this storm—this B.A. storm—before he began his pursuit of that beautiful spirit, that extraordinary woman, Addison.

Monty stepped out of his stateroom. The group was gathered around, munching on veggies dipped in dressing. B.A. sipped a cocktail. Addison, one hand in a small bag of chips, was playing backgammon with Russell. Perry stood on the aft deck, enjoying the view.

They all turned when Monty appeared.

"What?" he asked.

Russell and Addison spoke in unison. "We thought you got lost."

"Just a nap. I'm good now."

He moved to the sideboard where the veggies and chips were laid out and began to munch.

The second mate came in to announce that they were entering the channel to Beaufort, having passed the first channel marker.

They looked up at once, clearing the game and putting things away. B.A. gathered the tray and basket, taking them to the galley. The others headed to their cabins to shower and change for dinner.

Monty let B.A. go first, then climbed to the captain's deck to make a few calls. He radiated a quiet energy—an air of renewed excitement, no longer feeling melancholy.

The first mate was stationed on the bow. The captain stood at the wheel, the chart plotter and depth sounder active. *The Best Tide* had passed the red-and-white buoy marker, and Captain Duarte was aligning the yacht with the lit range markers onshore.

He didn't acknowledge Monty when he arrived, and Monty knew not to distract him during their passage into the channel. Moving to the opposite side of the bridge, Monty searched for a signal to place a call. When his phone finally showed life, he spoke quietly—barely audible to the captain.

As Duarte throttled down to a steady eight knots, Monty braced himself. The captain spoke into his two-way radio to his first mate.

"Red buoys to starboard. Copy."

"Copy."

The captain made small, deliberate adjustments to counteract the tide—no crosswind. Passing the jetty tips, he checked the depth sounder and GPS to stay mid-channel. Farther into the inlet, the first mate scanned diligently for crab pots and small craft ahead of the yacht, reducing speed to five knots as they encountered calmer water. Staying within the marked channel, Duarte eased into the turning basin toward Beaufort's docks.

Monty stood quietly behind him as the captain completed the docking at their designated slip. The first mate and Duarte's nephew threw lines to the dock crew and set the fenders. *The Best Tide* idled for a moment before the captain cut the engines.

"As always, my friend—perfect!" exclaimed Monty.

"Thank you, Monty. It's my pleasure."

Monty went over the itinerary for the evening, giving Duarte and his crew the night to themselves. They reviewed the morning's departure and arrival into Charleston. Monty double-checked that the captain had the card he used for provisions and crew meals. With that settled, he wished him a good evening and headed below to shower and change—hoping B.A. was dressed and gone from the stateroom when he got there.

Showered and refreshed, Monty stepped out wearing khaki slacks, a hunter-blue polo, and navy leather drivers. His hair was still damp, comb marks accentuating the silver at his temples.

The men were gathered in the salon; Addison sat on the aft deck, her back to them, phone in hand, checking in with DJ —as she often did when away. Russell slid open the glass door to the deck just as she ended the call.

"Are we all set, Mr. Tierney?" she asked as she stood.

"Yes, we are, Miss Addison," Russell replied with a smile.

He had to admit—she was growing on him. Much nicer than *that wife*, he thought, though he reminded himself she could also be competition for Monty's attention. He walked toward the ramp leading to the pier, spotting B.A. farther down, phone on speaker. He couldn't make out what she was saying. He would give anything for her to be the first to go—and Addison, a close second.

No, this trip wasn't the right moment to make a move. He needed to get settled at the office first—then plan an invitation for Monty to dinner. Private. Relaxed. Somewhere unexposed. The men's room in Chicago, the shower at the club—those had been mistakes. If he was going to *rock Monty's world* with his "mad skills," he needed him open, comfortable, and unguarded.

He could feel his groin heating, his body responding as he imagined their first time together.

Perry and Monty came out on deck. Monty looked around, puzzled.

"She's on the phone down the pier, waiting for us," Addison said.

Monty didn't respond. He walked to Russell. "Well, man, let's be on."

Russell and Monty stepped onto the pier. Perry followed, turning back to extend his hand to Addison as she stepped off.

B.A. walked up just as Addison joined them.

"Are we ready?" she asked.

Monty passed her without a glance, still talking with Russell. Addison noticed. B.A. noticed, too—especially the starry-eyed look on Rusty's face—and muttered something nearly under her breath.

"Did you say something, B.A.?" asked Perry.

She shook her head and slipped her arm through his, deliberately guiding him forward, leaving Addison walking behind them alone. Perry glanced back briefly but said nothing.

When B.A. and Perry caught up with Monty, she asked, "Where might we be headed, master of tour arrangements?"

"Moonrakers—just a couple of blocks from here," Monty said.

"It's a lovely evening for a walk. It'll be even nicer on the way back. We can indulge in some Southern cuisine," said Addison, as she walked past the group to take the lead.

Russell was quick to agree, though he stayed close to Monty's side. B.A. remained entwined with Perry's arm, as if staking her place in front of Monty.

"Are you familiar with the restaurant?" asked Monty.

"No, not really. How difficult can it be to walk until I see the name?" she retorted, without looking back, increasing her pace to move farther ahead.

Deep down, Russell was taking it all in—bursting with delight. There was discord between the women, and that tension was spilling over between Addison and Monty. He felt thrilled, his face flushed. Walking beside Monty, he had to fight the urge to take his hand. *I know he cares,* he thought. *He's walking with me, not either one of those bitches.*

Monty looked back at the group, a couple of steps behind him and Russell.

"Caldwell, you're awfully quiet."

"Just taking in the salt air and enjoying the company," Perry replied with a smile, glancing down at B.A.

Monty looked briefly at his wife and decided to correct his own attitude. If he wanted her to be civil, he had to show he wasn't angry—even though he was. Dropping back to B.A.'s other side, he took her hand.

Russell's blood boiled. He could barely contain himself.

"Oh, seems I've been replaced!" he exclaimed.

He stopped walking. Perry, passing by, looped his arm through Russell's and guided him forward, forcing him to keep pace with the group. Addison turned, catching the spectacle.

"Hmm. What do we have here?" she said, too far away for them to hear.

"Come join us, Addie!" B.A. called.

Addison stopped—not to join them, but because she was standing in front of the restaurant. She entered as Monty gave the host his name. The timing was perfect; they were seated immediately. Monty ordered two bottles of wine— one white, one red. The waiter scurried off.

Monty looked at his wife. "No Prosecco for you, young lady."

B.A., seated between Monty and Perry, looked bewildered. Addison was between Perry and Russell—who, of course, had made sure to sit next to Monty. Everyone but Addison turned to look at B.A.

"What?" she asked.

The waiter appeared with help, carrying glasses, two bottles, and a chiller for the white. After uncorking both,

Monty said he'd pour, ordering appetizers for the table before sending the waiter off again.

Warm plates soon arrived—calamari, flatbread, jerk wings, roasted portobello—crowding the table alongside small plates and extra forks. They passed dishes around and placed their entrée orders.

Russell opened the conversation, asking about the next day's itinerary. Perry answered, explaining that they'd head for Charleston in the morning. Monty nodded in confirmation, his mouth full of mushrooms.

B.A. asked Russell if he'd ever been to Charleston.

"No," he said.

Perry leaned in, taking the opportunity for a brief history lesson.

"When we reach Charleston, you'll see—the city's defined by its harbor. The Ashley and Cooper Rivers meet there, forming the gateway to the Atlantic. It's where the first shots of the Civil War were fired at Fort Sumter. The old quarter's intact—Georgian homes, cobbled streets, church spires—a living museum, if you will. There's also the Low country culture—shrimp, rice, and bourbon on every table."

Monty added, "We'll dock at the waterfront and make our way inland to Queen Street, I believe."

"Yes, Monty, that's correct. Queen Street—Poogan's Porch. It's an institution of Southern cuisine, the backbone of Charleston," Perry concluded.

"Am I the only person who hasn't experienced Charleston?" Russell asked.

Monty looked to Addison, who was chewing a piece of flatbread.

Perry helped her out. "Lady A was born and educated in the South. She may not possess that drawl we all expect, but she's a Southerner—a Southern lady."

"That's interesting, Addison. I'd have never guessed you were from the South," Russell said, sounding intrigued.

"That explains her calm, demure demeanor," added B.A.

"I agree—she has this way, this sense of knowing when something's brewing," added Monty.

Having swallowed her food, Addison replied, "My demeanor has nothing to do with being Southern. Least y'all forget, I have a couple of degrees in psychology." She paused, then with a playful drawl added, "But the *lady* part —that's very much my Southern upbringing, my taste for beautiful surroundings."

Monty was captivated again by this woman who took pride in hiding herself, yet commanded attention just by being in the room. He felt himself stirring, wanting her—wanting to be with her again, as they were last Friday. His head swam; he reeled himself back into the table's conversation.

"That's some drawl, Addison," said Russell.

"I've perfected the King's English and its pronunciation after years of living in Yankee country," she said lightly. "Working in New York had its challenges, but my accent was a constant topic of conversation. My late husband teased me when I complained that it surfaced whenever I was tired—like a comforting blanket." Her diction was flawless, not a trace of the drawl she'd just used.

The waiter appeared again with two assistants. One cleared the small plates and used silverware, replacing what was needed with clean settings. The other balanced a tray loaded with entrées while the main waiter placed each dish in front of its owner. When all were served, she stepped back and asked Monty if there was anything else.

Monty looked around the table. Everyone was focused on their plates. "No, thank you," he said, and she hurried off.

"How is everything?" he asked, holding up a forkful of the chef's fresh catch of the day.

Murmurs of approval rippled around the table, mouths too full for conversation.

As the meal wound down, talk circled back to Charleston. Addison shared that she'd spent a lot of time there during college, and as an undergrad, quite a bit in Myrtle Beach. Russell was fascinated by the South—its preserved architecture, its complicated history.

"Painful as it is," he said, "it's still a pivotal part of American history."

The table nodded in agreement. Even B.A. joined in, though she found it shocking to see Russell behaving like a civilized human being. To her, he was still the same little snot—barely able to hide his admiration for her husband. *My soon-to-be former husband*, she thought. *And if Russell has his way, his soon-to-be lover.*

Everyone agreed to take dessert and doggie bags back to the yacht. Coffee would be better on board, and the men had already decided on poker. Each carrying a small bag, they walked toward the dock and *The Best Tide*. The night air was cool, the waterfront alive with faint music from nearby restaurants. Addison, the only one who'd thought to bring a sweater, drew teasing glances from the others.

"Come on, guys—it's only a sweater," she said, laughing.

Lagging behind, Monty took it all in. Perry and Russell seemed to connect on a historical level. B.A. was keeping her word, behaving herself. And Addison—always proper, elegant, confident. He slowed to watch her walking ahead, then realized she'd noticed he'd fallen behind.

When she turned, he waved her off with a small shake of his head. She raised her eyebrows, silently mouthing *shhh, okay*. He smiled. He was smitten with this belle who'd surprised him from the start. He quickened his pace to rejoin the group.

Once aboard, everyone disappeared into their cabins to change, reemerging in sweats and soft flannel pajamas. Russell wore black flannel bottoms with a hoodie; Perry, a matching sweatshirt and pants; B.A., a robe monogrammed with her initials; Monty, collegiate sweats; and Addison, Duke blue top and bottoms.

The men settled around the table in the salon—Russell shuffling cards, Perry stacking chips, Monty counting out stacks for Russell. Addison disappeared into the galley. With the crew still ashore, she brewed a pot of decaf from her own blend, preheated the carafe, and arranged a tray with cream, sugar, and the pies and cakes they'd brought back. Balancing the tray, she nudged the galley door open with her hip and slipped through.

Monty jumped up to help, taking the tray from her and setting it on the sideboard.

"There's beer in the fridge if anyone wants one," Addison said, catching her breath.

"I have something better," Monty replied, opening the cabinet door.

From it, he pulled out a green felt bag and withdrew a tall bottle sealed in gold wax, its white label marked with a green ribbon: **The Macallan Highland Single Malt Scotch Whisky**.

"This, gentlemen," Monty announced, "is poker-drinking Scotch."

He retrieved four crystal glasses, each wrapped in clear plastic.

"Miss Lady Addison, may I offer you a glass?" he asked, unwrapping them.

"Why yes, kind sir," she replied, her tone softly Southern. "I think just a finger will do."

Monty poured two fingers each for Russell and Perry, setting their glasses by their cards. For Addison, he poured a modest splash—barely covering the bottom—and handed it to her before serving himself a short pour.

Not seeing B.A., Addison slid open the salon door and stepped out to the aft deck. The view was quiet and moonlit. She climbed the ladder to the flybridge, cradling her drink carefully, and settled onto a cushioned bench near the captain's deck.

The air was cooler now. She tucked her hands inside her sleeves, holding the glass for warmth. Her mind drifted to that morning—to Monty, his eyes red, his smile to DJ oddly strained. She wondered if he'd been crying or simply overtired. Then her thoughts shifted to B.A.—so quiet today, so unlike herself. Was it Russell's presence? Or Perry's?

Then came the obvious question: *Will they be together on this trip?*

She doubted it. B.A. would have to make the first move, especially after last Friday's twosome. Maybe she'd been drunk on purpose, Addison thought. Maybe this was her way of setting up her exit. Keeping a secret from a husband while sharing a bed with both him and his wife felt wrong.

She sighed, finishing the last sip of Scotch. *I'll talk to her about it,* she decided. Setting the empty glass beside her, Addison leaned back against the bench, the soft hum of the marina in her ears.

Within minutes, she was asleep.

She woke to the sound of a rowdy group walking down the pier to another boat. She had taken her watch off when she changed. She had no idea what time it was, but she noticed the boat traffic around the marina had disappeared. Her legs were stiff when she stood. She stretched, placed the empty glass in the pocket of her sweats, and climbed down to the aft deck.

The salon was dark. The men were gone. No sign of BA. She slid the salon door open slowly, moved through to the sideboard, and placed her empty glass on the tray. The bottles of water that were there earlier were gone.

Moving deeper into the salon, she saw that the door to the main stateroom was closed. Her door was closed. Moving down the hall toward the galley to get a bottle of water, she saw a dim glimmer of light and heard a noise. She paused, listened. A man breathing, she asked herself.

Moving more slowly, she noticed that Russell's door was ajar—barely open, but unmistakably so. Inside, kneeling on a pillow at the foot of the bed, Perry's head moved in a steady rhythm at Russell's waist. Russell, facing her, had his head tipped back, lost in the moment, one hand holding Perry in place as he murmured,

"Yes, Perry, it feels so good. Don't stop. Make me come."

Perry looked up briefly. "You've done this to me. I want to finish, too."

Addison stepped back from the narrow opening, retreating into the darkness of the hall.

They shifted toward the bed. Russell reached for protection and lubricant, handing them to Perry.

Perry paused. "Are you sure? Once I take you, I won't be gentle."

Addison couldn't see Russell's expression, but his voice was clear and unhesitating.

"Well then, Perry Marchand—do it right, and make it worth it."

Before Perry prepared himself, Russell leaned in again, drawing him closer, his hands firm and knowing. Perry responded, pushing forward until Russell pulled back, took control, and finished preparing him. Russell coated his hands, steadying himself, then turned away, bracing.

Perry followed, spreading lubricant with deliberate care, taking his time before moving closer, testing boundaries, then pressing in fully. Russell's response was immediate, his voice rough, urging him on.

"Yes. I know you want this. Take it. It's yours."

Leaning forward, gripping the edge of the bed, Russell began to move with him. Their rhythm built together, rough and unguarded, their sounds merging into something shared and private.

"I'm close—" Perry muttered.

Russell lost control first, his release spilling onto the cabin floor as Perry's movements grew frantic. They collapsed together moments later, breathless, spent.

Addison slipped past quickly to the galley, grabbed a bottle of water, and carefully moved down the hall to her room. In the dark, she pulled back the covers, undressed, and reached into her cosmetic bag on the side table, finding her familiar comfort.

She let her thoughts drift—Monty, the memory of his touch—enough to carry her over the edge quickly. She rolled onto her side and fell asleep almost at once.

The sound of the twin MTU outboard motors roaring to life brought the group to life. Perry had stayed with Russell, giving him a go at him later that night. He had left Monty on the top bunk of his cabin, fast asleep, having lost at poker and had one too many glasses of scotch.

Monty had confided in Perry about BA's departure—her move across the pond. When he began sobbing, it baffled Perry. He spoke as if it was all good that BA was leaving. Monty had fallen asleep before he could finish his story. When he did, Perry knocked on Russell's door to hand him a bottle of water. Perry neglected to tell Russell that Monty was not with BA that night—or that he was asleep in the top bunk of his cabin.

Perry returned to his cabin to shower and change; Monty had left. They would talk further while on the golf course at Quay Island, he thought. BA leaving the marriage was unexpected, yet intriguing. And his new friend made this news all the more exciting.

By the time everyone showered and dressed, *The Best Tide* was well on its way to Charleston.

The group sat on the aft deck during the journey to Charleston, playing trivia and word games. During intervals, one of the group would disappear to their cabin— likely for a nap—and return with fresh trivia and lively conversation.

When Addison disappeared, Monty had gone up to the captain's bridge. When he returned to the deck and noted she was gone, he asked if anyone wanted anything from the galley, and everyone did. He grabbed the tray from the sideboard in the salon and headed back toward the cabins. He stopped and knocked on Addison's door. No answer. He stood for a few minutes, knocked once more. No answer.

As he turned to walk farther down the hall, he discovered her in the galley, speaking Portuguese with the captain's nephew. She looked up when he walked in.

"There you are," he said.

"Yes, I am here." She smiled.

Feeling awkward, he reached into the fridge to retrieve water bottles. The nephew, busy cutting fruit into a bowl, turned from Addison back to the bowl.

"Everything okay?" he asked her.

"Everything is fine. Are you okay?" she responded.

"A little hung over from last night, but otherwise okay," he said sheepishly.

Addison turned to Duarte. *"Espero que você consiga entrar na escola. Parece uma oportunidade maravilhosa."*

Duarte smiled at Addison. "*Obrigado. Estou ansioso pela minha oportunidade.*"

"Can I help with any of that, Monty?" Addison asked as she turned to leave the galley.

"No, I've got everything. Duarte, you'll bring the fruit?"

By the time he maneuvered the bottles and a couple of bags of snacks, Addison had gone to her cabin. Monty walked with a feeling of defeated dread. He had looked for her last night, hoping to stay with her, having announced to BA that she could have the room to herself.

Leaving the stateroom, he stopped at Addison's door, knocked several times, and got no response. He stood there waiting, hoping she would come to the door. In his inebriated state, he went to Perry's cabin because it had bunk beds. He'd spilled his guts about him and BA, and he thought he'd told Perry how he felt about BA leaving because of his feelings for Addison.

Was she avoiding me? he asked himself.

As *The Best Tide* approached the sea buoy, the sky was overcast, and the winds changed to the north with choppy seas. The captain slowed to eight knots, letting the active stabilizers counter the vessel's roll in the chop as they proceeded through the channel to Charleston's resort marina.

They had made good time to Charleston. The group dispersed to their cabins to change for their next shore adventure.

Monty had thought of everything. As the group piled onto the pier—the ladies dressed in jeans, tennis shoes, long-sleeve tops, and sweaters; the men in long-sleeve polo shirts, jeans, tennis shoes, and jackets in hand—Russell remarked:

"I guess we all learned our lesson in Beaufort. Jackets—and BA with a sweater."

In the parking lot of the pier sat an Escalade ESV. The driver stood on the passenger side of the SUV as the group arrived. Once in, Perry, who sat in the front, announced:

"Let the abbreviated tour begin."

The SUV eased out of the resort at Patriots Point, passing the USS *Yorktown* and the Naval & Maritime Museum next door. Crossing the Arthur Ravenel Jr. Bridge over the Cooper River to downtown Charleston along East Bay Street, the waterfront opened up to Joe Riley Park, where the Pineapple Fountain cascaded water as a welcome to Charleston.

Russell, on the driver's side, had a picturesque view of the water and fountain. The others were silent while Russell oohed and aahed. BA stifled a laugh listening to him. Monty, sitting in between them, looked at his wife and shook his head.

Addison, in the back row, observed Monty's body language when he looked at his wife. She wondered, almost speaking aloud but instead whispering to herself, that Monty knew BA was leaving. Running it back in her mind, she attempted to pinpoint when. Nothing came to mind. Around the group he was the same, but there was something about him when he looked at her. She recalled their encounter in the galley.

"Just strange," she whispered.

BA turned to look at her. "Did you say something, Addie?"

"No, not really—just admiring the view."

The view changed as they continued south on East Bay. Pastel townhouses lined the street, and farther down, as they trailed past The Battery and White Point Garden, the live oaks and harbor came into view. A bit of traffic slowed the driver as they passed St. Michael's Church. Heading east into the French Quarter along Church Street, they saw St. Philip's Church and the French Huguenot Church. Russell was impressed by the color—pink—for a church. Then came the first building in America built as a theater: Dock Street Theater.

The driver turned onto Queen Street toward Poogan's Porch, where they had reservations.

Monty looked at his Piaget. "Here we are, just in time for our reservation."

Everyone got out, mingled for a moment, and thanked Perry for the tour. They headed into the restaurant for another evening of food and conversation.

"Guys, that was amazing!" exclaimed Russell.

Addison chimed in, "The splendor never gets old, even after seeing it many times. You are correct, Russell — amazing is apropos."

Monty, first behind the host, followed to a round table. Determined to spend quality conversation time with Addison, he attempted to jockey a position to sit next to her. Addison, straggling at the back of the others, watched as BA sat in the chair next to where Monty was standing. There was one seat vacant next to him and one on the opposite side of the table.

Perry walked over. "Thanks, Monty. Maybe we can chat about a couple things regarding the project." Perry pulled out the chair to sit.

Addison, seeing the once-vacant chair, takes a seat on the opposite side of the table between Russell and BA. Monty sits and runs his hand over his hair, trying to hide his disappointment.

Adjusting her chair to the table, Addison notices Monty's motion and body language. *Odd,* she thinks. *Is that something new, or have I just not noticed before?* Everyone is talking but her; she's lost in thought about him. Wondering what will happen once BA leaves. Will they remain friends? Will he want them to engage in more threesome connections?

The thought gives her pause. *Would I want that?*

She's so far in her head she doesn't hear Perry calling her name. He finally says:

"Lady A. Earth to Lady A. Where are you?"

She returns from the far reaches of her mind back to the table. She looks at Monty—he's looking at her. She looks away because she feels a flutter. *Oh my gawd,* she screams silently to herself, *what the fuck was that?*

She quickly picks up the menu and begins to read it as if it were the last written thing on earth. Burying her head to cover her eyes, she mouths to herself:

What am I doing? Why am I setting myself up for...

She couldn't quite figure out *what for.* She looks over her menu at him again—and her stomach flutters once more.

When the waiter comes to take their order, Addison is the first to speak, skipping their tradition of appetizers and drinks.

BA asks, looking quizzical, "Hungry, Addie?"

The Escalade was waiting for them when they left the restaurant. No doggie bags; everyone was ready to retreat to the boat.

On their ride back, Monty reminded them: breakfast at the Harbor's Resort on the marina, be ready by 7:45—he wanted to shove off by 9:30 for their final destination, Quay Island.

They arrived at the marina. Everyone headed to their cabins; Monty and BA went to their stateroom. BA turned to see Addison heading into her room. She held the door open, catching Addison's attention.

Addison, looking up, quietly said, "No, I'm a bit tired. Have a good night."

BA shrugged her shoulders and closed the door. Addison, still standing in her doorway, heard the lock click.

Confused by her emotions, Addison entered her room, fell across the bed, and slept through the night on top of the covers, clothes still on.

Still dark out, Addison awoke, realized she was still dressed, and looked at the clock. It was almost time to get up for breakfast. She headed to the ensuite bathroom, looked at her face in the mirror—her eyes were swollen. Had she been crying? She hadn't drunk last night. Why were her eyes puffy?

She wet a hand towel with cold water, returned to the bed, lay on her back, and placed the cool towel across her eyes. Baffled, she spoke aloud to herself:

"What on earth are you doing? He's going to be pining for his wife. You cannot expect this man to be yours overnight —if ever. This thing we have is only because of the erotic fulfillment of being with his wife *and* me. Men like that kind of stuff—women together getting it on. It's hot shit. It's the best of both worlds. This thing is not a thing at all.

Get your head out of your head, girl, and be real. All that in Atlanta was erotic sense."

Then she thought about last Friday at the townhouse. *There was something between us. I'm not making this up,* she thought. Then she realized they hadn't been around each other alone since. Was that on purpose? Was he pulling back, not wanting to get too deep?

She understood why her eyes were puffy as tears streamed from the corners of her eyes.

"I cannot believe this. I'm emotionally in upheaval over someone else's husband. His damn wife is about to drop an 'I'm leaving you' bomb, and I am wanting second dibs. What the fuck, Addison Hollace, are you doing?!"

The sound of her own words made the tears flow harder. Knowing sleep was impossible, with almost two hours before meet time, she got up, stripped her clothes, and walked into the shower—hair and all—standing under the hot water, where she cried some more.

Addison, now in a ball cap and sunglasses, got a cup of coffee from the carafe on the sideboard and went out to the aft deck. The sky, still dark, was beginning to show shadows in the predawn. She loved predawn—everything was pure and hopeful before the light of day made reality clear. Deep down, she hoped Monty would be the first out. She just wanted to see him, though she wasn't sure what she'd say.

The deck door opened. Turning to look, she saw Perry walk out with a cup of coffee.

She and Perry were on their second cup when Russell and BA walked onto the deck, and behind them, Monty. They left the boat and headed to breakfast. The place was full, causing the group to split up.

By this time, her doubt was so heavy that she walked to a two-top, resigned to eat alone. Perry and Russell, who seemed to be hitting it off fantastically, sat at another two-top across from her. Monty and BA sat in a booth on the other side of the room.

Russell, still enamored with yesterday's tour, led the conversation before, during, and after breakfast, with Addison and Perry mostly listening. In a strange sense, she felt relief that the husband and wife were sitting away from them.

The three waved to the couple and headed back to the boat.

"Russell and Perry have hit it off," said BA after the waitress took their order.

"Yeah, kinda surprised me too," replied Monty.

"At the risk of creating a scene—are you still very upset, mildly upset, or not upset?"

Monty looked over his coffee cup at her. "I've got nothing else to say. I've told you the legal standpoint—the prenup. I'm giving you a sizable amount of an investment portfolio I had for you. You're out. I don't want anyone with me if they're not *with* me."

"So, does that mean *she's* in?"

"Aww, come on, BA. You don't get to ask me shit like that anymore. You're out because you chose to be out. You can't have your cake and eat it too."

"Seems like that's what you've had these last few weeks."

Monty put his coffee down. "Fuck, BA—you baked the goddamn cake and served it up to me! Now you want to play jealous wife? What about all the other wives and husbands you found for us to swap with?"

"You could have turned them away. No one made you."

Monty picked up his coffee and began to take slow sips. Without much effort, he could see Addison sitting alone. He was tempted to take his coffee, get up, walk over, and just sit down—tell her how much she meant to him. That he had a lot on his plate, but he wanted to make time for *them*. Time for dates. Dinner dates, movie dates, walks in the park. And most of all, he wanted to tell her he'd fallen in love with her the first day he met her at *The Gilded Bean*.

Just saying it to himself made him feel lighter.

BA continued talking. "I kept my promise. I haven't said one word to her. But I hope you remember that I was forthright when I told you she knows. She knew that I was leaving. That's your honey pot keeping secrets from you."

Monty chose to ignore her. She was trying to get him to react, and he wasn't falling for it—not this time, and never again.

He wanted to focus his thoughts on the new MLA&E project with Perry's family. He wanted to be excited about the footprint he could leave in Texas. He wanted to be excited about the hopeful prospect of a future with Addison.

The food arrived; they ate in silence.

The guys and Addison left the restaurant. Once he and BA finished, they walked back in silence. Monty knew he had to have his head together before boarding the boat.

They were all on the aft deck, enjoying the view as *The Best Tide* departed Charleston Harbor for the open sea. After there was nothing left to see, Addison quietly got up, went to her cabin, took off her clothes, and got into bed. She fell asleep.

The hum of the two large motors drowned out Monty's light knocks on her door. He didn't want to knock too loudly since everyone had retired to their cabins. He stood there, waited, tried the knob—it was locked. He turned, went to the salon, and fell asleep, semi-stretched out on the sofa.

The first mate gently brought Monty from his nap. He wanted him to know the captain was approaching the sea buoy—they should be dockside in about an hour. Two SUVs would be waiting to transport everyone to the hotel.

Monty thanked him, stood, and headed to his stateroom. He couldn't help thinking this would be the last time he'd see BA in his stateroom. Maybe—hopefully—he thought, as he turned the handle to enter, he'd soon be opening this door to see someone he had come to love.

That thought made him stop.

BA looked up from her suitcase on the bed as she was packing her things.
"Are we almost there?" she asked.

"Yes, within the hour, most likely."

Then he paused.

"What?" she asked, as she liked to do.

"Nothing," he quickly responded.

He'd just had a brilliant idea: send her flowers. *Flowers,* he thought. But where to?

He went into the room, pulled his duffle, and began putting his things inside. Moving around BA without so much as a word, as if she weren't there. He was so deep in thought about when and what to send, he'd blocked her out entirely.

BA was not pleased with this display. She knew for certain he and Addison had been together during the trip down. She was convinced it was the night in Beaufort when he didn't stay in the stateroom—and Addison's refusal of BA's invitation to join them was further proof.

BA sat on the bench, watching him pack his duffle and take it, closing the door behind him.

Monty made an announcement down the hall, knocking on the other three cabin doors, announcing they'd be in harbor within the hour. He heard Addison yell back, "Okay, I'll be ready." It made him wonder why she hadn't answered his knock earlier. He was determined not to be dismayed. He just kept thinking—flowers.

An hour later, as the sun faded, *The Best Tide* pulled into Quay Island Marina. Two men dressed in hunter-green polo shirts and khaki pants waited at the dock. Once the yacht was tied and the fenders lowered, Monty was the first to get off.

"Mr. Langford?"

"Yes."

"I'm John, this is Tim. We'll be your drivers during your stay on the island. Welcome to Quay Island, sir. If there's anything you need at any time, let Tim or me know. I believe the office has provided you with our cell numbers?"

Monty shook each man's hand with the firm poise of a successful business magnate—confident but never portentous, comfortable and kind-mannered.

"Yes. As a matter of fact, I do have a request. Let's talk over here—it's personal and confidential."

John followed Monty away from the yacht as Tim made his introductions to the others, who were now disembarking with suitcases and duffels. The first mate handed them off to Tim, who carried them up the pier to where the SUVs sat idling.

For whatever reason, the four hopped into Tim's SUV, leaving Monty to ride with John. Once they were in the vehicle, Tim led the way out of the marina, across the bridge to Quay Island Parkway, and on to the Ritz-Carlton.

Pulling onto the property, the valets opened the doors so the four could get out. Behind them was Monty, taking his leather pouch with him into the building. At the front desk, the group waited in the entrance lobby.

"Mr. Langford, welcome back to the Ritz-Carlton. We have everything arranged and taken care of just as you requested. Everyone is on the Club Floor; their luggage arrived this morning and is already in their respective rooms. I had the chef prepare a special meal for you all, knowing you might be a little exhausted from your travel.

"I've also arranged two separate spa treatments for Mrs. Langford and Ms. Hollace. Your tee time and carts are confirmed for tomorrow morning. If there's nothing else, here are your spa times and key cards for each guest. Please let them know that this card also serves as elevator access to the Club Floor. The concierge has all the same information upstairs."

She handed him the key cards, each clearly marked: *Perry Marchand, Russell Tierney, Addison Hollace, BA Langford,*and the last, *MLA&E.*

Monty walked over to the group and handed out the key cards, gave the men their tee time, and told them the chef had prepared something waiting on the Club Floor—but, for obvious reasons, he didn't mention the elevator access.

Only BA asked, "Is the luggage in our room?"

Without explaining that *her* luggage was in *her* room, Monty simply responded, "Yes, BA."

He also gave her the spa card.

Walking over to Addison, who had wandered off to look out the window at the surf, Monty cleared his throat to get her attention.

"Ms. Hollace—your key card and your spa card. I hope a spa day will brighten your spirit."

She looked at him, taking the cards. "Thank you, Mr. Langford. I hope your golf day brings you birdies."

He smiled. She had a way of doing that—here he was, concerned about her, and she cheered him with clever golf vernacular. He wanted so badly—he could feel it deep in his loins—to take her in his arms, hold her, kiss her, and tell her, *Whatever it is, I'll make it go away.*

He took a step toward her when, from behind, he heard:

"Are we ready to head up, shower, and enjoy a nice meal?"

Perry, taking his arm as if to keep him from making a public spectacle.

"Yes, yes, of course," Monty responded, motioning for Addison to go ahead of them.

BA and Russell were standing at the elevators. When Perry disappeared, the door opened and BA stepped inside. Russell hesitated.

"Aren't we going to wait for the others?" he asked.

When BA swiped the key card to access the Club Floor, Russell hopped on just as the doors were closing. Standing there facing the rear, seeing himself—red from the sun, hair windblown—he realized that throughout the trip he and BA hadn't engaged in any one-on-one conversation.

She stood there with her oversized handbag of fine leather. He decided to dive in.

"I've admired your bag since the start of the trip. Don't tell me—Chanel? Gucci? No…"

"Bottega Veneta," she said dryly.

"That was going to be my next guess."

"And yours?" she asked.

"Tumi," he replied proudly.

BA gave him a quick smile and looked up to gauge the elevator's ascent.

"That leather envelope Monty carries—it's exquisite. Who is that?"

"Who is *that*?"

"You know—who makes it?"

"Oh, it's custom. He knows a tailor who does leather clothing as well as men's suits. If you look closely, you'll see his initials embossed by the zip."

Before Russell could say anything else, the bell chimed. The door opened, and she was off down the hall.

He looked at the room numbers on the wall, noticed his room was in the same direction, but decided not to try to catch up with her. He studied her from behind: medium height, narrow hips—not particularly shapely as women go, but with plenty of cleavage. Russell complimented her silently on knowing how to use her assets.

Her curly brown hair with caramel highlights was becoming, he thought. She must have heard him walking behind her; she turned to look at him. He quickly looked toward the room numbers and noticed he was about to pass his room.

"Oh, this is me!" he chirped.

"See you in a bit," she said without turning back again.

When she heard his door shut, she took a deep breath and let it out, nearly walking past her own room number. *This can't be right,* she thought. *We normally get one of the suites down the hall with the full ocean view.*

She stopped, hesitated, then swiped her key card. The light blinked green, and the latch clicked. She pressed down on the door lever and the door opened.

"What the fuck, Montaque!"

She walked into the room, past the bathroom, deeper inside. The king bed, upholstered settee, and coffee table all faced a view of the houses lining the shore. It was dark out; only the lights were visible.

She walked back to the luggage rack, where her suitcase sat —her initials clearly there. There had been a mistake. Did they think this was Addie's suitcase? Were the key cards labeled incorrectly? Were her things down in *my* room— with her husband's?

Someone needed to rectify this—now.

She marched over to the phone, looked for the front-desk number, and pressed it. A man's voice answered—

"Front desk, Carl speaking. How may I service you?"

She went in hard and hot. Carl put her on hold. She became incredulous but stood there in her bare feet, waiting. *Monty will be very upset at this mistake,* she thought.

Downstairs, Monty stopped to ask the bellman a question. Perry and Addison had already taken the elevator up together. As he walked toward the desk, the young woman who'd checked him in and Carl were huddled together. Carl looked up.

"Mr. Langford, we seem to have a slight problem."

"Yes," agreed the female clerk beside him.

"What might that be?" Monty asked, now walking closer.

"I may have given the incorrect key card to Mrs. Langford."

"She's holding on the phone now," said Carl.

Monty—always calm, a man who waited to get all the answers—handed the female clerk his key card. She ran it through a reader and looked at Carl.

"What seems to be the mix-up? Is that the key card for the oceanfront suite?" Monty asked.

"Yes, Mr. Langford, it is. But Mrs. Langford is calling from one of the other rooms, not the suite," Carl said in a hushed tone.

"Is it a room with a view?"

"Yes," stated Carl.

"Does it have a king bed and a seating area?"

"Yes, Mr. Langford, it does indeed," Carl replied.

"Well, then there's been no mistake. I'm in the suite, and she has her own room. Is that right?"

The two clerks looked at each other, baffled—each thinking, *Who's going to tell the woman on the phone?*

Monty, without hesitation: "Tell her I'm on my way up. I'll handle this. What's the room number?"

They spoke the number in unison. Carl picked up the receiver and clicked the blinking line. Before BA could speak, Carl announced that Mr. Langford was on his way. Cordially thanking her, he hung up.

BA, holding the receiver, stared at it. "That snot hung up on me. Oh, Monty is going to have a field day with this."

She slipped on her shoes and wondered if Monty would wheel her suitcase down to the suite—or if a bellman was coming to help. A few minutes later there was a knock at the door. She peeped through and saw Monty standing there.

Opening the door in a huff, she began, "Can you believe these people? I tell you, Monty, service everywhere in America has just fallen to mediocre—"

He quietly, calmly interrupted her rant. "BA, it's not a mistake. This is your room."

Knowing this would be a tussle, he dropped his leather envelope on the table, slipped his key card into his pocket, and sat in the chair nearest the sliding-glass window, looking out into the darkness.

"Mistake? You *mean* a mistake!"

"No. I said what I meant."

"Monty, darling, you said *not* a mistake. Is the bellman on the way?"

"No, a bellman is not required."

"Why not? You're going to transport my luggage?"

"No. Your luggage isn't going anywhere—at least not until you check out."

"Why is that, Monty?"

"Oh, come on, BA. Don't play your freaking mind games. I'm not playing them anymore. You're smart enough to understand—"

"Understand what?"

"BA."

"No, Monty, say it! I've watched you pine for the last two days. You've moved that bitch into my room! Say it!"

Hearing her call Addison a *bitch* infuriated him, but he was determined to remain calm.

"No. Addison is not moving into your room—which is *here*. Nor is she moving into my suite."

"Oh, but you're having a nice big room to yourself where you can fuck her at your pleasure! I keep telling you, Monty, she knew all along about my plans. She knew about the interview in Atlanta."

"All that to say what, BA?"

"That she's not on your side in this. I found her—"

Monty interrupted. "Just stop there, *Miss I'm-moving-to-London-to-be-a-Dominatrix*. You may have found her, but now *I* have found her. And just so we're transparent—"

She tried to interrupt.

"Let me finish, or I'll get up and walk out to *my* suite."

Feeling the throes of defeat, BA took off her shoes and plopped on the bed, facing him.

"BA, let me remind you—this is over because *you* decided it was over. No discussion, no 'let's see if we can do this,' no compromise. Honestly, I don't know how I would have reacted if you'd talked about it first—but you didn't, and that's a slap in the face. Especially after all the unconventional things we've done as husband and wife. You didn't give me a chance. You wrote me—"

BA tried to cut in again. "Monty, it's not too late—"

"Oh, hell yes it is!"

"I love you, Monty."

"A little too late now, I'd say."

That fired BA up again.

"Oh, I get it! You've got little Miss Southern Girl to keep your dick wet—"

He stood, picking up his envelope. "Stop right there, BA. I'm tired of your bashing and blaming, whatever you call yourself doing, about someone who did *not*—I repeat, did *not*—have any bearing on your choice to pursue your next life across the pond. As *you* so proudly announced to me several weeks ago, you'd found 'the perfect woman.'"

He walked to the door.

"Well, Mr. Know-Everything—just so you'll know, your red-haired Irishman has the hots for you. Maybe you can add him into your *throuple entente*. I'm sure Miss-Love-to-Fuck-Someone-Else's-Husband won't be around long after you're single. What's the thrill in that?"

"Yes, BA—get your last and final dig in."

He put his hand on the lever to open the door but stopped, standing still, facing it. Then he turned around to look at her—sitting on the bed in a lotus pose, her shins stacked close to her body. Her eyes sparkled from tears, her curly hair wild, her cheeks flushed red.

He took a seat at the foot of the bed, exhaled deeply, and extended an arm toward her. She sat stoic and silent.

In a hushed tone, he said, "I want you to understand, BA. This is nothing like the future I saw for us. Yes, Addison is a wonderful third for us, but I now realize she was just a distraction you created to help you walk away from this marriage guilt-free."

"But, Monty, I understand the error of my ways and I am ready to—"

"No, BA. You don't get to rewrite the script again. You're not in your domain chamber, in control. Not anymore. I'm resigned, and I am letting you go. Everything I said on the yacht will be yours. My attorney has drawn up the papers for you to sign on Monday. Ron will coordinate everything you need once you land in Belhaven. But I'm out.

"My things have been moved from the townhouse—you'll have it all to yourself to prepare for your new life. Unfortunately, we'll be in matrimony limbo for twelve months according to the Commonwealth. And to be transparent, yes, I am going to pursue a life with the woman you found for us—and now for me. In some weird way, I thank you for that.

"As for Russell—he and Perry, surprisingly, seem to have hit it off. But you yourself know that was just something I experimented with. Well… not him, but *us*—and the other couples. I want you to be happy, and I hope, somewhere down the road, you'll want me to be happy. I get that you can't see that now."

She sat, legs still crossed, tears streaming down her face. He reached farther toward her, patted her exposed leg, then picked up his envelope, stood, and walked out the door— composed and calm.

When the latch clicked, tears were already staining her top. She fell back onto the bed, realizing she had lost him forever.

"This will strengthen my resolve as I go forth in my new life," she said aloud.

She reached for her purse, pulled out her phone, and texted Addie:

Hey, not feeling well. I'm going to pick up some food and eat in the room. How 'bout late lunch after spa?

She threw the phone on the bed, grabbed her key card and a handful of tissues, and hurried down to where the chef's food awaited. Grabbing a little bit of everything and a bottle of water, the attendant asked if he could help her take her food. She agreed that a tray would be more useful.

She piled a couple more small plates with food, added two bottles of Stella, and they scurried down the hall—she determined not to see anyone, especially Addison.

It seemed everyone but Perry and Russell decided to eat in their rooms. Russell was disappointed that Monty wouldn't be joining him and Perry. He felt more optimistic now about a relationship with Monty, especially since Perry had taken a liking to him. *Monty can't overlook me much longer,* he thought. *And if Monty is as good as Perry, the anticipation alone...* He felt it tighten in his pants.

The two sat enjoying steamed shrimp, broiled scallops, smoked salmon, Brussels sprouts with tomatoes, and cucumber salad. Perry picked the onions out of his salad, glancing at Russell, who smiled.

"Already ahead of you," said Russell, pointing with his fork at the pile of onions he'd moved to the side of his plate.

To anyone watching, they acted like a long-term couple—comfortable, teasing, in sync. Perry rose to fetch them each another bottle of Stella. He opened both and lifted his to toast.

"To new and old friendships. May they mesh well."

Russell was giddy at the thought that one day the three might be together. He looked at Perry adoringly; Perry gave him a wink. They finished their meal, taking their beers with them. As they drew closer to Russell's room, Perry told him he'd be there shortly—something to take care of in his own room. They parted briefly. By the time Perry knocked, Russell was standing in the doorway naked, a bottle of lubricant in hand.

"Come on in, handsome. I've been waiting for you."

Morning breakfast found the group scattered. Perry left Russell's room just before dawn, heading down to the lounge for coffee and a bagel to take back to his suite. He was tired from the previous night's activities. No sign of BA, but Addison caught a glimpse of Perry going into his room. Cup and bagel in hand, she had no idea he and Russell had spent the night together. She poured herself a cup to take along the beach.

As the elevator doors closed, Monty was approaching the lounge to get his oatmeal, banana, and coffee. Seeing no one, he decided to eat there in hopes of catching Addison. After finishing his oatmeal and a third cup of coffee, he filled a to-go cup and headed back to his room.

Russell, showered and dressed for the golf course, came out just as Monty was walking by.

"Good morning, Monty. Did you have a good night?"

"Russell, good morning. Yes, I slept well. How about you? A good night's sleep?"

With a bashful chuckle: "It was a *very* good night."

"Great. I'll see you downstairs shortly," said Monty as he walked toward his room.

"Okay, see you shortly."

Russell's excitement gave him the look of a Cheshire cat—grinning from ear to ear, chatting up anyone who made eye contact for more than two seconds. It was obvious he was heading for the golf course—and a very friendly morning.

The men met in the lobby and were transported by a large golf cart to the Quay Island Golf Club's pro shop. Their clubs had been dropped off the previous day by Monty's pilot when he brought the luggage. At the shop, they met Ben, Kyle, and Dyson—retired residents of Quay Island.

The men paired off, two to a cart, for Florida Best Ball—skins game and beer. Perry and Russell, Dyson and Ben, Kyle and Monty. Russell used his charm to fit in with the older men. Monty seemed more relaxed during the outing, something Perry quietly observed.

Monty tried to push Addison out of his mind—with complete failure. *Tomorrow,* he told himself. *After the group lunch.*

Addison had walked about two and a half miles from the hotel—five miles round trip. By the time she returned, the men had already left. She sat at a table, finally responding to BA's text:

Yes, sure. Say 2 in the café shop in the lobby area.

Grabbing a croissant, some fruit, and her coffee, she sat to eat and read her emails. The one she'd been hoping for had come in at 7 a.m. She opened it first. Great news—her last-minute request was confirmed. The arrangements were finalized. The message lifted her spirits, and she was ready for a full spa day before lunch with BA.

She headed back to her room to change and go down to the spa.

BA, meanwhile, had slept fitfully. Monty had left her wounded, though she'd never let him know it. *Did I make a mistake by not talking to him first? Maybe he was blowing smoke about agreeing to my change in lifestyle. Maybe he wasn't.*

The thoughts turned her from one side to the other through the night. *Would he take Addie as his new mate? Was that more smoke? Why do I care?* The questions chased her into dawn. By first light, BA was hovering between incredulous and sad. She had a black coffee and juice, then headed down to the spa. The entire day she wouldn't see Addie.

After her spa treatments, Addison felt refreshed and ready for lunch with BA. She chose her denim shirt-dress that buttoned down the front, navy leather closed-toe mules, her hair caught in a bear claw, and a crossbody phone case with *AH* embossed on the flap in oxblood. She texted BA to confirm the time:

We still good for 2?

Dressed and ready, she looked at her watch and decided to head down to the café. At 1:55, Addison walked into the coffee shop and was seated at a table with a view of the ocean and the people coming and going. She ordered hot tea—English Breakfast.

The waiter brought her a heated cup and a small carafe of hot water with two tea bags. She told him she was waiting for someone.

"No problem. Let me know when I can get you some more hot water."

She thanked him, poured the hot water over her tea bag, and covered the cup to let it steep. Going back to her phone, she began reading emails. Uncovering her cup, she sipped slowly and checked her watch again—it was 2:15. No text response. No BA.

She waved to her waiter, who came over immediately.

"Yes, miss—more water?"

Looking at the menu, Addison replied, "No, I'd like to order. My lunch guest is delayed."

As she began to read from the menu, BA arrived in a huff, just as Addison was ordering.

"I'll have a glass of Prosecco."

Addison continued her order without looking up. BA plopped her large handbag in the extra chair at the table. The waiter nodded politely. "I'll be right back," he said, then left the table.

"Well, is he going to bring my drink or what?"

"I'm sure he will, BA."

"How long have you been here? I saw your text, but I was getting ready and figured you'd see me when I got here."

"Apparently," Addison said dryly.

"What's wrong with you? How were your spa treatments?"

"There's nothing wrong. My treatments were very relaxing, and I'd like to remain in that energy."

"Whoa, what the fuck, Addie! I just asked—"

"No," Addison interrupted. "No, you rush in late and it's all about you—ordering wine while I'm ordering lunch."

"Well, Miss Lady, I didn't realize he was taking an order, I —"

Addison interrupted again. "No, apparently you didn't. Did you think he was standing here waiting for you to show up to get your drink order?"

Before BA could respond, the waiter returned with her glass of Prosecco. She didn't want to order food yet and rudely told him she'd let him know. The women sat in silence while BA drank her wine and Addison sipped her tea. When Addison picked up her phone, BA asked,

"You're not going to talk to me?"

"Yes, I can talk to you. How were your spa treatments?"

"They were good."

"What treatments did you have?"

"The salt scrub, the deep-cleanse facial, and the full massage."

"Your face is glowing, BA. It looks great."

"Thanks, Addie. Your face always has a glow. Did you have a facial too?"

"Yes. I did the ice bath, then the steam room, a facial, and then a massage."

BA took another sip as the waiter brought Addison's Caesar salad with grilled scallops, along with another carafe of hot water and a saucer of tea bags. He took BA's food order—a fish sandwich, plain, with tartar sauce on the side.

"That looks good, Addie."

Addison, chewing, took a moment before replying. She looked at BA, who seemed like she wanted to say something.

"Something on your mind, BA?"

"Well, sorta." BA took another sip of wine.

Addison decided not to prompt her further. If BA had something to say, she could just spit it out. Addison continued to fork her lettuce and eat. BA sat there as if waiting for Addison to pry it out of her. Addison chewed slowly. When she finished, she took a sip of tea, then added a fresh bag and poured hot water over it, covering it again to steep. She looked up at BA as she gathered more lettuce onto her fork.

Unbelieving that Addie wasn't going to pry, BA blurted out, "Did Monty spend the night with you the first night on the boat?"

Addison, mouth full, chewed deliberately, swallowed, uncovered her tea, and took a sip.

"No."

"No?"

"No."

"Well, he wasn't with me that night. I assumed he was with you!"

"He wasn't with me. But I do have a question."

"What's that?"

"When do you plan to let him know you're moving abroad?"

"I thought *you* told him! He—"

"Wait, what? *I* told him?"

"Yes, you! Didn't you tell him? I didn't tell him—he told me he knew. I assumed you had broken your promise."

"Oh, fuck, BA. Seriously? Just like that, you assumed—"

"No one else knew. You were the logical assumption."

"No, I haven't said that—or much of anything else—to him. It was a heavy burden—"

"Oh please, Miss Southern Girl, spare me the theatrics."

"No theatrics here, BA. And I won't say what my opinion of all this is."

"Hey, speak your piece, Miss Addie. I'm all ears."

Before Addison could answer, the waiter returned with BA's sandwich. She decided not to take the bait—not to say what she thought of BA's plan to leave, and especially not what she felt for Monty. The water was already muddy enough after that night—BA getting drunk, passing out after dinner, Addison sleeping with Monty, then sharing the same bed.

She'd felt something. Even knowing BA was leaving the marriage, it made her uneasy. A three-way with a husband and wife was one thing, but her feelings—allowing that night to happen—had changed everything. The water was muddy.

"Well, what do you have to say, Addie?"

"Actually, BA, I got nothing."

"Interesting."

"What's that supposed to mean?"

"You sleep with him and you've got nothing?"

"Oh, give me a fucking break, Miss Dom Puppeteer. Do you think I didn't figure out this whole throuple thing was your master plan? I figured it out in Atlanta—the way you threw us together, then conveniently took off to do your thing."

"I had to make sure he liked you. Of course, I knew he would—and like you, he did. That first day he met you at your coffee shop, he beamed. He gets that look when he's enchanted."

They fell silent, BA chewing her sandwich, Addison her salad.

"I mean, he *has*—had—it for me. I suppose now that we're divorcing, he no longer has it for me."

"So it's come to that? Divorce?" asked Addison.

"Yes. However he found out, he's started the ball rolling in pure Montaque style—as he does."

"I'm sorry to hear that, BA."

"But are you?"

"Yes, BA, I am! It's always sad when two people separate —divorce, break up. Feelings and emotions run high. There's confusion, trepidation."

"Oh, I get it. From a clinical standpoint."

"Don't be a bitch, BA. I didn't grease the tracks for this train—you did. You plotted and planned. But the one thing you didn't consider was human emotion. And if I *can* be clinical, since you brought it up, that's the one thing you don't seem to have a handle on—emotions."

"Oh, here we go—the psychological profile."

"I'm serious, BA. I care about you. We've been intimate, and I think of you as a friend. And as someone who cares about you—I think your life, as a girl, lacked love. A warm kind of love, the kind that allows girls to feel secure. I believe you love Monty, and he loves you. It takes a strong couple to do the things you two have experienced. Honestly, I don't know if I could."

"Well, Addie, let me clue you in—that's who he is. And if you plan to be with him, that's what life's going to look like. He's already told me as much."

That took Addison aback. A lump rose in her throat, and she couldn't speak. She sat there looking at BA—and then it hit her. Another ploy.

Finding her voice, Addison said, "Well, I'm not much on the throuple thing anymore. You've cured me of that. So I guess if that's who Monty is, I'll bow out gracefully."

The look on BA's face told Addison she was right. BA had changed her mind. She no longer wanted Addison and Monty together. Addison wondered, seeing the pleased look on BA's face, *What has she told him? Is that why he's been off around me? Why we haven't connected on the yacht?*

And if he wasn't with BA that first night, who *was* he with?

That, Addison decided, she would find out on her own. BA clearly had her own agenda. Addison was glad she'd made her own plans—and even gladder she hadn't mentioned them. She relaxed, sitting across from the Dom.

Addison smiled. "Well, BA, it was a lot of fun—our throuple. I loved our time together. But it's no fun if you're not going to be there, so I should move on."

"Oh, I concur, Addie. You and I will move on. Monty will be on his own when we leave."

And there it was, Addison thought. *He'll be alone.*

When lunch was over, they rose from the table and walked out to the lobby. Addison made an excuse—there was something she wanted to get for her guys from one of the shops. She and BA hugged; Addison kissed her on both cheeks.

"BA, I wish you safe travel and wonderful things in your new adventure."

"I wish you well, too, Addie. Sorry you and Monty aren't going to work out. I tried."

Addison, annoyed, rolled her eyes as she hugged BA—for what she knew would be the last time. Turning, she walked in the opposite direction, feeling a quiet dread that she'd have to sit across from her again at lunch tomorrow.

Strolling past the shops, she spotted Russell.

Monty had put a lot of thought into today's lunch. He felt hopeful—his plan would bring the results he wanted. A lot of minefields on the table; he would have to be strategic with BA in the mix. Today would be the last day he'd see her. His lawyer and Ron could handle things after lunch—something he intended to reiterate.

Canceling the jet ride back to Belhaven would have been awkward with Addison traveling alongside her. Keeping those plans in place would serve as his final gesture. Once BA landed, she'd be handed the separation papers—everything legal and tidy. With him in Dallas, he'd avoid the fallout from her protest.

The farmhouse was secure; a new system was being installed today—new codes, additional cameras. His clothes and work drawings were already settled in a condo on the other side of town by Willows Walk—cluster homes with garages and one connecting wall. The photos Ron had sent made it appealing enough to buy sight unseen. It would be sparse for a while, especially with the Dallas project demanding so much of his time, but it was distance from the townhouse he and BA had shared for almost ten years.

He said it out loud:

"Ten years, almost. A decade."

Sitting on the balcony of his suite, the salted air swirled around him. He wished she were with him right now—in this moment—talking and laughing. Yet doubts lingered, thanks to BA's comments. Would he really want to continue that lifestyle—the sharing, the swapping, the pretense of excitement? He was ready for *normal*.

Then he thought of Ellen—how normal their life had been, and how normal it could have remained, especially now with his success. He wondered if she hadn't been killed, would he have felt that same relentless drive? To leave Chicago, start his own firm, sink everything into building the Tower?

He sighed, facing the unknown again—ending a marriage in an instant while daring to imagine a future with a bright, intelligent, beautiful woman. They shared tragedy. Could they build from that?

So many questions.

He stood, heading inside to shower and dress for lunch. It would all be in motion soon enough.

✲
✲✲

It was a private room used for smaller events. Just off the lobby, it offered a view of the dunes in the distance and the Atlantic Ocean as a backdrop. The table was long, with plenty of space between seats and a floral arrangement centered in the middle. One chair sat at the head of the table, two on each side. At the far end, an oblong table held two carafes of coffee—regular and decaf—alongside two tubs of ice, one with beer, the other with wine. Coffee cups, wine glasses, and beer mugs were neatly arranged with folded napkins. On the wall near the entrance, a smaller square table held four swag bags. All three tables were covered in crisp white linen. Soft music threaded through the room from the sound system.

Monty arrived first. The hostess appeared as he walked through the door.

"Mr. Langford, I hope everything looks satisfactory."

"Yes, this is outstanding. And I see the bags arrived."

"Yes, sir. They're labeled exactly as you requested, per the items inside."

"Great."

"I'll begin service whenever you're ready—just let me know."

"Yes, I will. Thank you."

"My pleasure, Mr. Langford."

Monty poured himself a glass of Sauvignon Blanc, took a sip, and walked over to the window to enjoy the view. Perry and Russell entered a few minutes later, chatting easily. Then BA walked in—her hair slicked back, wearing a black V-neck dress with long sleeves, patent leather Louboutins, a ruby pendant on a gold chain, gold hoop earrings, and a small patent clutch. Perry crossed over to greet her, sensing an awkward pause from Monty, the ever-gracious host.

BA greeted Perry warmly. He kissed her cheeks, complimented her outfit, recalling their night poolside at the farmhouse. He knew she was soon to be the former Mrs. Langford. They all did—including Russell. Though Perry hadn't spoken privately with Lady A, he assumed she knew as BA's friend. Still, he planned to keep Monty occupied with his family's company's big Texas project— less time for Addison once BA was gone.

As he stood with BA, Addison walked in.

"My apologies for the delay," she said softly as she entered.

She wore a cream crew-neck knit sweater with the Polo Bear embroidered on the front, sleeves pushed up, paired with jeans and navy suede TOD's drivers. A Louis Vuitton drawstring sac hung crossbody from her shoulder, her hair pulled into a high ponytail.

She took Monty's breath away. Russell was in awe of her grace and confidence. He tried not to like her—especially since she stood in his way of having Monty to himself.

Monty hesitated, torn between wanting to rush over and remembering BA's sharp eyes on him. He paused, letting Perry greet her instead.

Addison requested iced tea with lemon. Hearing that, Monty disappeared to find the hostess. While he was out of sight, Perry insisted everyone take their seats. He sat to Monty's right, BA across from him, Russell beside her, and Addison next to Russell. They were chatting when Monty returned. Seeing them already seated, his heart sank— Addison wasn't beside him.

The hostess entered with Addison's tea, followed by three more waiters carrying trays. They placed plates in front of each guest, set cold dishes in the center, and moved the floral arrangement to the table holding the swag bags.

As Monty sat, he noticed the arrangement being set by the bags. *All was not lost.* Each bag was clearly labeled; he'd make sure the right one reached the right person. He smiled.

"Enjoy," he said warmly.

The hostess looked around. "Will there be anything else?"

Monty scanned the table. No one spoke. "No, nothing else at the moment."

It was a twist on Southern seafood: steamed shrimp, crab cakes, broiled scallops, string beans, potato salad, coleslaw, and cornbread. Bowls of sides were passed around, followed by a basket of warm cornbread.

"A toast to us," said Perry.

"Cheers!" the group echoed.

"A toast to our host—"

"And hostess," interrupted Russell.

"Yes, host and hostess," Perry repeated.

Glasses clinked, but the voices were subdued.

"It's been a pleasure—*my* pleasure," Monty said. "Thank you for accepting my... er, *our* invitation to voyage on *The Best Tide*. I hope you three enjoyed it as much as I... er, *we* did."

BA lifted her glass to his speech but said nothing. The reality of tomorrow pressed on her—would it be the last time she saw Monty? Her mind raced. He said he'd moved out, but had he really? Wouldn't there be a proper goodbye? They *were* married. Her thoughts were interrupted by Monty's light touch on her arm.

"Are you feeling okay, BA? You haven't touched your food."

Looking down at her plate, fork in hand: "Yes, I'm fine."

Monty returned to his meal.

Leaning closer, BA whispered, "Will we have a chance to talk tomorrow before your wheels up?"

He set his fork down, motioned for her to stand. As she did, the conversation at the table fell silent.

"Excuse us a moment," Monty said cheerfully. "We'll be right back."

The others resumed their talk—Addison explaining the art of crabbing with a string. Perry and Russell were fascinated by her description of the old-school method, hand-lining, and soon forgot Monty and BA entirely.

Outside in the lobby, Monty closed the door behind them. He knew after all he'd said to her, he'd have to be gentle this time.

"BA, you look lovely today."

"Thank you."

"About tomorrow..." he began. "Today will, in all likelihood, be the last time we see each other for some time —unless circumstances change."

"Today? You're not leaving until tomorrow. Perry told me that. You're on his jet, so I think—"

"BA," he said softly. "Listen to me, please. Let's make this a positive experience—a clean break. I wish you only the best, and I've already set everything in motion, just as I promised."

"Well, you're clearing the way for someone who doesn't want you—unless you stay the course and get a third," she snapped.

Monty, tired of her mind games, ignored the jab. "BA, what I do from today forward isn't your concern. You're walking away with some heavy assets."

Her daunt faded. *Maybe I was wrong,* she thought. *I haven't seen them together—Addie didn't say anything at lunch. Maybe I misjudged.*

"So this is it?" she asked. "Goodbye to my husband?"

"Yes. You're a free woman. You have my blessing, and I mean that. I want nothing but happiness for you. Apparently, it wasn't meant for us."

Monty stepped forward, held out his arms, and embraced her. She wrapped herself around him tightly; he gently pulled away.

"It wasn't all bad," she said, looking up at him. "We had some great times, didn't we?"

"Yes. A lot of good memories," he said, turning to open the door.

Inside, Addison was still describing hand-lining when she saw them return. She caught the tension in BA's face, the calm in Monty's, and knew—instinctively—that he'd just said goodbye to his wife.

The two rejoined the table and finished their meal.

The hostess appeared to clear plates. A waiter followed, setting dessert plates and fresh flatware, removing the bowls from the center. The hostess reappeared with a Key Lime pie, already sliced, and reminded them which carafe held decaf and which was regular coffee.

The pie was cut into five pieces. Addison rose to pour herself a cup of regular coffee, offering to pour for anyone else.

"Look at you," laughed Perry, "being the coffee hostess you are."

"Coffee hostess?" asked Russell.

"There are several coffee shops in Belhaven called *The Gilded Bean,*" said Monty.

"Yes, I've been to a couple," said Russell. "There's one a block from my hotel—very nice. Another by that pedestrian mall heading toward the northern river area with all the chestnut trees. That one's lovely, especially the covered outdoor space."

"Those belong to Addison," said Perry.

"You!?" said a stunned Russell.

Before Addison could reply, Monty took the moment to say what he felt for her—indirectly, of course.

"Addison is quite the businesswoman. She not only owns *The Bean,* as it's affectionately called by us locals, but she was instrumental in developing Chestnut Walk. It was a collection of older houses that had gone from residential to business—not very well maintained, I'm afraid. When the Board of Commissioners of Kellum County wanted to raze the area and turn it into a thru-way, Addison and her team of lawyers, along with investors—some local, most from out of state—presented the county with an alternative that provided a real-estate tax base, retail, entrepreneurs, employment, and sales revenue.

"The structures were spared demolition and refurbished under strict guidelines to blend architecturally. The street was closed to traffic, rerouted toward the freeway, and reopened to pedestrians. According to the planning commissioner, the deal-sealer was the parking plan—spaces behind the buildings with valet on both sides of the shops."

Addison could only sit and absorb that Monty knew so much about what she'd built with Chestnut Walk—*The Bean* being its centerpiece. Thayer's associates at the hedge-fund firm had been pivotal in helping her bring it to life, and they'd been well rewarded. She couldn't help wondering what else Monty knew about her.

"It's a benefit to the county," Addison said quietly.

"Yes, it is," Monty replied. "The shops range from modest to high-end, and the restaurants scattered throughout add charm—for those after-dinner strolls. What inspired such a wonderful idea?" asked Russell.

"Like I said—it benefited the county to add something with charm. With the retail mall near the municipal center and the sparkle of the financial district's towers, something quieter and more intimate just fit," Addison said, rising to pour another cup of coffee.

Returning to her seat, she noticed BA idly scraping her fork through her pie, barely eating. She also noticed Monty watching the same thing. Their eyes met—the familiar silent exchange. He arched his brows; she gave a quick, knowing smile.

Monty stood and announced that he had something for everyone, asking them not to open their bags until they returned to their rooms. He walked to the side table and selected Russell's first.

"Russell, my friend—great golfing yesterday. I'm glad you joined us on this trip. I hope we'll do it again. And I hope your joining MLA&E brings you much success and happiness."

Returning to the table, he picked up two more bags— Perry's and BA's—and placed them before them.

"My partner and my friend—a new venture awaits the three of us. I wish us all the success and positive energy we can muster. Good luck to you both."

"Thank you, friend. My family and I look forward to working with MLA&E on this project. The next four years, we'll create and build an icon of mixed-use development," Perry replied.

Standing beside Addison now, Monty hesitated. He wanted to kneel—to be closer to her—but resisted, careful not to overplay his hand in front of BA. He set her bag on the table and returned to his seat.

"Addison, I hope you continue to have enormous success. Thank you for joining BA and me on these great adventures. We love having you in our lives. You're dear to us both. I... hope you like the bag."

Monty could feel sweat forming at his collar; his mouth had gone dry. *I hope you like the bag.* Ridiculous. He took a long drink of water.

"Well, folks, I guess this is it. Russell, what time's your flight?"

Russell looked at Addison. Monty frowned, confused, just as Addison began to speak.

"Russell is catching a ride back with me."

"With you?" BA broke in.

"Yes—if you'd let me finish, please," Addison said, glaring at her.

"I... I don't understand," Monty said.

Taking a brief pause, she continued, "Russell is flying back to Belhaven with me today. The car's likely out front, our bags already loaded. The jet will depart when we arrive."

Monty was stunned. BA was speechless. Only Perry spoke.

"Oh, Lady A—give me a hug. I hate to see you leave. It's been great spending time with you after all these years, since my days with you and Thayer. Godspeed." He stood and embraced her.

"Right now?" was all Monty could manage.

She walked up to him, gave a proper European kiss on each cheek, then embraced him. As he held her, he whispered,

"Addison, no. I've looked forward to talking with you after this lunch—there's so much I want to say."

She looked back at Russell. "Give me a minute? Would you let the valet know I'm on my way, please?"

"Sure, Addison." Russell hugged Perry. "I'll text when I get back to my condo, and we can talk. Sound good?"

Addison hooked her arm through Monty's and led him toward the window, the ocean framed behind them. She turned and looked up at him. The distress on his face was clear.

"Addison..."

"Monty, this is for the best. You've got a lot going on—with BA, with the new project in Texas. You need time to settle. I'm asking you to take the time to know what you want your future to look like. Please. That's not too much to ask."

"No—and you're right. There's so much happening, not just BA. This project is life-changing, not only for me but for the firm. So much good... so much gain."

She nodded. "Then do that. And at the risk of being forward—you know where I'll be, if you think there's something for me to wait for."

Before she could finish, he drew her into his arms and kissed her—long, unhurried, full of everything unsaid.

When he pulled back, the room was empty; the others had gone. He kissed her again, and this time she wrapped her arms around his neck, leaning into him, and he felt himself harden against her.

"I've been trying to talk to you for five days," he murmured. "You've been avoiding me. I was beginning to think you were—"

She stopped him, placing two fingers gently over his lips. Then another kiss—slow, final.

Stepping back, Addison said softly, "It's been confusing, and I know why. I don't want to make what you're going through any harder. Let's talk when you get back to Belhaven. How does that sound?"

"Do I have to wait that long? I'm not sure how long this first trip to Texas will be. BA leaves in three weeks—can we at least text when I get a minute? Make plans for when I return?"

She nodded, stepped forward for one last kiss—just as the door opened and Perry appeared.

"Hey, Addison—they're waiting for you."

She smiled faintly, touched Monty's cheek with her fingertips, and whispered, "Safe travels, Monty."

He watched her leave, sunlight catching her ponytail as the door closed behind her.

∗
∗∗

△ ▽ ▽ △

BA could not believe how the weeks had flown by.
Deciding what items from the townhouse she wanted
shipped to the UK—and what to do with those furnishings
she didn't—took more time than expected. Having resigned
from the real estate firm before the trip, she threw herself
into packing personally rather than using professional
packers. It was therapeutic: wake up, work out, organize,
pack, repeat.

Finding a shop that accepted furnishings was a task in
itself. She finally found a consignment company in the next
county but had to arrange for movers to transport the pieces
to their location. When the final week arrived, she was
ready to take flight.

No word from Monty. His attorney had a messenger deliver
the divorce papers, the prenup final payout, and the
documents that had been forwarded to Sachs International.
She was more than ready to dive into Marchmont
Conservatory's curriculum.

A week after arriving home, she texted Addie:

Hey stranger… haven't heard from you. All's well?

Not hearing back, she texted again a couple of days later:

If you don't talk to me, how will I ever be able to apologize?

Two days later, Addison responded:

I'm in New York on business. Nothing to apologize for.

Then—nothing.

BA's conscience was bothering her. Trying to dissuade Addie from a relationship with Monty had been low. Even lower, feeding false information to Monty. BA truly wanted to move on. If Addie was who Monty turned to after she left, well—good for *me*, she thought, *because I put it together.* No longer angry, BA took pride in her plans not to leave her husband empty-handed. She would look for Addie and hope to find her, to have that last conversation of remorse.

BA hired a driver for her last three days in the States. Having sold her Jag, she wanted to make a few stops—to say good-bye, something she had never done during previous departures. Lunch at her favorite deli, a large gratuity in the tip jar. Her dry cleaner, her salon stylist one last time. Finally, she had the driver take her out to Chestnut Walk. She went in hoping to see Addison at *The Gilded Bean*—no luck. She bought a tea to go and headed home to an empty space, letting the real-estate broker worry about the bed in the living room.

On the next-to-last day, she had the driver take her back to Chestnut Walk. As he pulled into the parking lot, there sat the Benz SUV she recognized as Addison's. Her pulse quickened, her mouth went dry. She got out—dressed in a plain sweatshirt, jeans, and Gucci clogs, her freshly trimmed curls framing her face—and walked inside.

Looking around, she didn't see Addison. She went to the counter to order a hot tea, hesitated to ask, then as an afterthought said, "Hey, is Addie around? That's her SUV, right?"

"Yes, she's outside."

"Thanks, I'll just give her a quick hello."

Stopping to doctor her tea with honey, BA headed to the patio door, casually opening it and looking around. Addison sat near one of the heaters, her three dogs lying at her feet, working on her laptop. She didn't notice BA until Scout stood and gave a yawn. Addison looked up just as BA froze, watching Scout stretch.

"It's okay, boy," Addison said. "Come over here, let the lady have this chair."

The other two dogs lifted their heads to check out the visitor. Addison told them, "It's okay, guys—lay down." They did, but kept an eye on BA.

Addison began, "Surprised to see you, BA."

"Well, Addie, I didn't want to jump the pond without saying good-bye."

Addison let silence fall for a moment.

"That's considerate of you, BA. And there's nothing to apologize for."

"I do feel I need to apologize for my behavior during the trip. Is that why you left early? Didn't want to fly back with me?"

"No, BA. I was ready to leave. I had work piling up," Addison lied.

"Oh. Okay. I'm glad to hear I didn't run you away."

"Nope."

The dogs took turns sneaking sniffs beneath the table—Margo getting a whiff of BA's shoes, Klaus swishing in with Scout for a closer look. Bold Scout circled the table entirely.

Addison smiled softly. "You guys are the slickest."

By then they'd settled again, each giving a heavy sigh and pretending to sleep.

"When do you leave?" Addison asked.

"Tomorrow, late morning. Heading to New York for an evening flight to Heathrow."

"Safe travels."

"Thanks, Addie. You've been a good friend—to me and Monty."

Addison ignored the mention of Monty. She and he were on a good trajectory, and she didn't want to give BA any window in.

"Well, this is where it all started, huh?"

"Yes—with a book with no dust jacket. You did your homework, I'll give you that. And that's all I have to say on that subject."

Addison pushed her chair back; the dogs stood. She gave them the *down, stay* command. They obeyed but remained alert. Addison stood, and BA took the hint, rising too. Addison stepped forward and embraced her lightly.

"You stay safe and be well, BA. Thanks for stopping by."

Addison sat back down, looking up at BA's stunned expression as she walked off without another word. Then Addison returned to her laptop, and the dogs went back to snoozing.

The next morning, the driver arrived, took BA's suitcases, and loaded them into the SUV. BA got in; the driver closed her door and walked around to the wheel.

"Will there be anything else, Mrs. Langford?"

"Yes. It's *Ms. Roberson*. To the airport, please."

The last three weeks had been a circus of meetings, drafts, redrafts, and conference calls with his staff in Belhaven. His engineers kept him fed with finite element analysis, shear and torsion data, dynamic loads, live loads, static loads, and tolerances. There was also the time difference— but the team adjusted, and things were finally coming together. Monty could see a small light: the point where he'd finally be able to head back to Belhaven and take a night to have a proper date with his lady.

She had accepted his request—the note he'd slipped into her swag bag asking permission to court her. They had texted intermittently over the past three weeks. He'd even sent his jet to fly her to and from New York.

Why rent a jet, Addison? he'd texted when she told him of her trip to her editor's office.

She had resisted until his next message arrived:

Too late. Jet is on its way to Belhaven—here for the duration. Let me do this for you, please.

She had to admit—it made the quick turnaround easier than flying commercial. There were flowers on the jet and a handwritten note from him. His texts always brightened her day—or night—when he wished her goodnight.

He'd once complained that Perry was being hypervigilant about him waiting until the divorce was final. She reasoned with him that Perry was just being a mother hen, something he was prone to do. Then Perry had texted her:

Lady A, don't be a rebound. The ink isn't dry on the divorce. Take some time. Monty is preoccupied with our work at hand.

It struck her as strange—especially since all Russell could talk about on the flight from Quay Island was how wonderful Perry was. She recalled witnessing how *wonderful* Perry had been that night on the yacht. Still, there was a sense of unease with his text.

If he's engaging in romance, why deprive Monty of happiness? she thought.

At night, lying in bed, she would search her memory of Perry back when he'd been around her and Thayer. He was always calm and collected, even when being otherwise was justified. A nice guy—she had always thought of Perry that way. But lately, there seemed to be something else: a passive-aggressiveness bubbling at the surface.

"A rebound?" she muttered aloud one morning while walking the dogs.

Was she a rebound? The thought swirled in her head for days, until she finally decided to ignore Perry's passive-aggressive tone. She'd have a few words for him next time she saw him.

That same afternoon—when BA had visited *The Bean*—Addison, running errands, stopped in at the financial district location just to check in, as she often did. She ran into Russell. Curious about his and Perry's relationship, she invited him to sit and have coffee and a snack—on the house.

"If you have time, that is."

He did. And he was no different than on the jet ride home—chatty, eager, glowing about Perry and the attention he was getting, even though Perry was "slammed in Texas."

"The tower is jumping since the project began. It's got several teams, including mine—which you can imagine I'm thrilled about, working with *my guy*."

Addison sat back, sipped her English Breakfast tea, and listened to Russell go on about the plans he and Perry were making. She encouraged him with small nods and soft murmurs, letting him talk.

"Oh, will you look at the time! I need to head back. Just needed a break, some fresh air—and thank you for the coffee and snack. It was so nice running into you, Addison. I love *The Gilded Bean*. It's one of my favorite places in Belhaven. I can't wait for Perry and me to sit, relax over tea. He likes tea, you know. I love coffee, but as they say— opposites attract. Don't you agree?"

"Yes, Russell, I would agree with you on that."

They embraced, and Russell scurried out the door, back to the Tower. Addison sat for a moment, pondering the conversation.

"Is Perry serious about Russell?" she asked herself aloud.

A couple of days later, Addison received another text from Perry:

Hi there, my lovely friend. Russell told me about you all's chat at your store. Let's chat soon.

Addison responded right away:

Yes, of course. Call anytime.

Buried in work, she didn't give the text another thought. It had been almost four weeks since she and Monty were standing in the room where the group had lunched. She was beginning to long for him—especially at night. She wondered if he was longing for her, too.

That night, tossing and turning, Addison reached for familiar comfort. As release overtook her, she thought of Monty—his body over hers, the weight, the warmth—and how much she wanted him now.She picked up her phone. It wasn't too late in Texas.

I am missing you.

She backspaced—deleted.

I just had an orgasm thinking about us together. Guess I'm horny.

Backspaced—deleted.

Lying there, staring into the dark of her bedroom, she didn't notice when the three bubbles appeared.

Thinking about you too. Sitting in this meeting—can't wait to see you.

It startled her. She dropped her phone; it bounced off the bed onto the floor, waking the dogs. Before she could reach it, Scout stepped on it—causing the phone to dial Monty's number.

"Oh shit. Oh shit, shit," she exclaimed, scrambling to end the call.

She had fallen off the bed flat on the floor, Scout sniffing at the phone, she quickly texted:

Oops—butt dial. Sorry.

Now all three dogs hovered around her. Assuring them she was fine, she climbed back into bed, heart racing and cheeks warm, when her phone buzzed again:

You can butt-dial me anytime

She smiled, tapped a heart-eyes emoji over his text, plugged in her phone, and fell asleep.

Perry witnessed the exchange, unaware that Monty had seen the three bubbles indicating that Addison was about to text him. He was annoyed that neither of them seemed to be listening. Turning his attention back to the presentation, he tried to refocus.

When the meeting ended, it was late—even for Dallas time. He walked over to Monty, who was placing items into his leather satchel.

"Let's make time for a leisurely breakfast tomorrow. What do you say?" Perry asked.

"Yes, I think that's a great idea. What time are you thinking?"

***

Perry decided to skip his usual morning routine of meditation and coffee. He showered, dressed in a polo shirt, slacks, and loafers, and left the house without drying his hair—a subtle homage to BA, maybe even a way to get a rise out of Monty and gauge where things actually stood with his wife. He needed accurate updates before moving to the next part of his plan.

They had agreed to meet for breakfast at Monty's hotel, the Fairmont Dallas. Perry arrived first and ordered coffee and juice. A few minutes later, Monty walked in and ordered coffee as well.

"You look tired, my friend. Are you sleeping okay?" Perry asked.

Monty took a sip of his coffee. "As soon as my head hits the pillow, I'm out."

Perry sipped his own coffee. Silence fell between them as the waiter came to take their order.

"Where does it stand with BA? Has she left for Merchant?"

"Marchmont," Monty corrected. "Yes, probably a week now."

"Where does that leave you? Are you still married—divorced? Limbo is nowhere to be, with so much tactical business rolling through. But the good news is, you're unencumbered. You can give the business twenty-four-seven. No one to call and explain why you won't be home for dinner."

Monty took a few more sips of coffee before responding. "Well actually, Caldwell, I'm hoping not to make those kinds of calls. I'd rather be calling to say, 'Let's get a late dinner,' or, 'Hope you're still up—can I drop by?' That sort of thing."

Perry's expression stayed neutral, though he felt a twinge of disappointment. He played it cool. "Montaque, that's the best news. Have you chosen the lucky person?"

Monty gave him a quizzical look and set his cup down. "Caldwell, Addison, of course. We talked about this on the trip—the night on the boat when I sank into that scotch-induced depression about finding the woman I know is best for me and fearing rejection. You don't remember?"

"Yes, I remember," Perry said slowly. "But really, Montaque, do you think that's wise? Especially how she came into your life. What if that's what she wants for the two of you? You said you wanted to leave that lifestyle behind once BA sailed away."

"Yes, I did—and I meant it."

"My friend, I think the world of Addison, but the way she became your intimate partner... talk about unorthodox."

"Look, Caldwell, I appreciate your concern. I value your opinion, but you're far off the mark when it comes to my relationship with her."

"So you're the cause of BA leaving?"

"No. Absolutely not."

"Not trying to upset you, Monty, just trying to understand where your life is headed. I want to be there for you."

"I understand that, Caldwell. So listen when I tell you— you're off the mark about who she is to me and what we are... our potential for a future."

"I hear that, Monty. Just don't be a bullet train. Slow it down. Take some time to be sure."

"I am, Caldwell..."

The waiter brought their breakfast and refilled their coffee cups.

"Montaque, I'm just thinking about how you went into that shell when Ellen died..."

"Fuck, Caldwell! What's that got to do with Ellen? She didn't just die—she was murdered in our home! Why or what does Addison have to do with that? Agreed, it was a dark time. Losing a wife is traumatic, but having things— personal things—missing was unnerving. Like some sociopath was stalking me and she... fuck, I don't know. Still haven't figured it out. Neither have the police."

Perry chewed thoughtfully before speaking. "Not my intention to upset you. I want you to be happy, and having the right person in your life permanently is something you deserve."

Monty ate quietly, sipping his coffee, glancing at his watch, wondering what Addison might be doing right now.

The two finished their meal mostly in silence, except to ask the waiter for more coffee.

"We've got about another ten days of preliminary work," Monty said finally. "My engineers should have final drafts by the end of the year. I'm going to head back to Belhaven."

Perry nearly choked. "No, not yet. There are several things that need ironing out—and should be done in person. Things get cloudy over teleconference. Monty, please wait at least a couple more weeks."

"Caldwell, I haven't been home to Belhaven since we left for the yacht trip to Quay Island. I'm ready to head back. So much is unsettled—my personal position, the new condo, the sale of the townhouse..."

"The townhouse? I was under the impression BA was in possession and handling the sale."

"That was the original plan, but she realized the difficulty of managing that from London with a six-hour time difference. She relented. The townhouse is mine to deal with. Ron's already juggling enough with this project. Besides, I may decide to keep it."

"Keep it? Why would you do that? I thought you had a new place."

"Yes, I do. But I haven't seen it. I may not like it. And if I need something professionally decorated, it might as well be something familiar."

"I'll admit, it's a very nice space in a convenient area near your office. You've got security all set up, garage codes—everything. That's something else you'd have to redo, I imagine."

"Yes, it would be."

"Do you still use your birthday backward for your numeric codes? I think that's just ingenious. You've got this way with numbers—guess that's part of your engineer's astuteness."

Monty chuckled at Perry's observation. He'd always found Perry meticulous about the smallest things. "Yes, for as precise as I am in my structures, I like things inverted when it comes to remembering codes."

"So, heading back to Belhaven in ten days?" Perry said. "Okay, I get it."

"Yes, that's the plan. I'll return just before the holidays—before we take the holiday break, not the New Year."

"Okay, my friend. I'm here. Just talk to me—let me be there for you. Can you promise me that?"

"Of course, Caldwell. You and I—beyond this project—we're close friends."

Perry smiled as he took the check from the table. They left the restaurant together, Perry heading to the valet, Monty back up to his room to retrieve his leather envelope.

⁂

In his car, Perry dialed a number. It rang three times before Russell picked up.

"Hey, you! Got a second to chat? I have news."

"Of course. Give me a second—let me walk into the hall."

Perry could tell there were people around Russell; then, the background chatter faded.

"What's up, lover? Please tell me you're finally heading this way. I'm missing you bad! I'm masturbating every day just to keep calm."

"Mmm, I love when you talk dirty to me."

"Honey, that ain't dirty—that's self-preservation!"

"Well, you're going to love my news. I'll be there in six days."

Perry heard Russell squeal.

"That's the best news! I'll plan to—"

"No, lover. It's a quick trip, but I'm carving out some time for us. Mum's the word. Just be hot and ready to be bothered when I get there."

"You mean I can't boast about my man coming to take care of business?"

"No, not this trip. But definitely next time—after you've made the trip out here to Dallas for the holidays."

Perry heard another squeal through the phone.

"Oh my gosh, my heart is pounding and my cock is throbbing," Russell whispered.

"Let's do simple takeout and spend the night in bed. I'll probably fly out the next day."

"Aww, I'm sad it's a short visit—but happy to see you," Russell whispered back.

Perry disconnected and immediately dialed another number.

By the end of the week, he had managed to keep Monty off balance—causing him not to call or text Addison about his plan to return home soon. With all the confusion Perry kept stirring, Monty didn't want to risk canceling or postponing.

By Thursday, Perry told him at the last minute about a design change to one of the buildings and said they needed to head to the site for clarification. He'd meet Monty there Friday morning.

Monty rented an SUV, giving his driver the weekend off. Relying on GPS to guide him to the site—just outside Honey Grove, near Caddo National Grassland, about a two-hour drive—he set out early, leaving Perry a quick voicemail before hitting the road.

⁂

Addison and the dogs were on their after-dinner walk. Deep into late fall, approaching early winter, the sun was setting earlier each day.

Inside the house, Celeste answered the gate guard's call on the house phone, authorizing entry into the neighborhood. She stood at the front door, chilled by the evening air, as a delivery van pulled into the driveway and stopped with its engine running. The driver stepped out, holding a bouquet of flowers in a short glass vase.

"Ms. Hollace?" he asked.

"No, but I'll accept them for her. She's not here at the moment."

He handed her the arrangement, and she slipped him a ten-dollar bill. "Thank you," he said before getting back into his van and driving away.

Celeste noticed the card attached to the bouquet, took it into the kitchen, and set it on the island counter.

A few minutes later, the familiar commotion of Scout, Klaus, Margo, and Addison filled the kitchen as they entered from the garage.

"Wow! What do we have here?" Addison asked.

The trio gathered close, but their focus wasn't on the flowers. Addison plucked the card from the arrangement, then noticed their hopeful faces.

"All right, all right—yes, your after-walk treats. How silly of me to forget those first."

She reached into the ceramic cookie jar shaped like a dog's head, took out three treats, and handed them out. Satisfied, they trotted back to their pillows in the corner of the kitchen to enjoy them.

Feeling the chill of the evening, Addison put a kettle on the stovetop and dropped a tea bag into her favorite oversized mug. While waiting for the water to boil, she slipped off her jacket, shoes, and ball cap.

When the kettle began to whistle, she poured the water over the tea bag, dunked it several times, and tossed it into the sink. She sat at the counter, cradling her tea, and opened the card.

Addison,
I am taking a day to see you—no one knows I'm leaving here.
A quick trip. I miss you.
Meet me at the townhouse Thursday, 5:00 PM.
Monty

She sipped her tea, reading and rereading the note. Something about it felt off, but she couldn't quite pinpoint what. *The townhouse?* she thought. Other than it being the last place they were together, why there?

She set the note on the counter, took another sip, and decided not to overthink it. *Don't be a negative Nellie,* she told herself. *He's taking the time to see you. Appreciate the effort—the gesture.*

When she looked down, three pairs of eyes were staring up at her expectantly.

"No more cookies, guys."

All three dogs sighed and plopped back down in unison. Addison smiled, shaking her head at their theatrics. Picking up the card again, she read it once more—and felt her pulse quicken at the thought of seeing him.

Monty had tried calling Perry a couple of times, but only reached voicemail. Figuring Perry was already at the site, he focused on the highway and the GPS.

When he arrived, the site was bustling. Survey stakes marked the perimeter, orange ribbons fluttered in the wind, and trenching had begun for the utilities infrastructure.

Excavators, bulldozers, scrapers, backhoes, dump trucks, and a caravan of water trucks lined the access road, waiting their turn. The dust was tremendous—workers wore masks and goggles to shield themselves.

Monty stepped out of his SUV into a puff of dust, donned his hard hat, goggles, and mask, and set off to find Perry. With so many machines rumbling across the property, it was easy to miss a vehicle or a person. After walking a quarter of the site's perimeter, he decided to head toward the group of four trailers serving as the site offices.

As he entered one, a man inside looked up. "Can I help you?"

"Yes, thank you," Monty said. "I'm here to check on the situation regarding one of the building placements in relation to the infrastructure. I'm the engineer from MLA&E."

"Oh, Mr. Langford! Didn't recognize you with the mask and goggles. Let's step inside—cooler in here, and less noise and dust."

The man led him into the quieter, air-conditioned space of an inner office. He sat down and motioned for Monty to do the same.

Removing his hat, mask, and goggles, Monty nodded.

"Mr. Langford, I'm Walter Barge, the site foreman. We met at the big meeting a few weeks back."

"Yes, I remember. I was wondering if you've seen or spoken with Caldwell Marchand today?" Monty asked, pushing his goggles to his forehead.

"Ah, no, sir. I usually let my assistants handle day-to-day communications so I can focus on the site. I can radio one of them to check—"

"No, that won't be necessary. Just tell me—what's the issue with the building location in relation to the infrastructure?"

The foreman scratched his head, then wiped it with a handkerchief. "Mr. Langford, there isn't one. Everything's spot-on. Your company's done a damn fine job. We're just following the site plans, confirming and installing."

Monty kept his composure. "I see."

"Well, sir, if you'd like to look at the site plans, I can take you next door to—"

"That's not necessary. Sounds like a mix-up in communication. I won't take any more of your time. If you happen to see or speak to Caldwell, let him know I was here."

"Yes, sir. Will do."

Monty shook his hand, replaced his mask and hard hat, and left the trailer. As he walked back toward his SUV, he took in the vastness of the site—the movement, the rhythm of progress—and wondered why Perry had sent him on a wild goose chase.

Back in the SUV, he dialed Perry's number again. Voicemail. He started the engine and pulled onto the main road back toward Dallas, giving two more attempts to reach him but leaving no additional messages.

When he called Perry's office, the secretary informed him that Perry had flown to San Francisco for an unexpected meeting and would return tomorrow. That explained the radio silence. Monty told her to let Perry know he'd been trying to reach him.

His next call was to his pilot.

"Andy, how soon can you have us wheels up?"

"What's our destination?"

"Home."

"Give me a couple of hours. Hopefully less, but count on two hours max."

"Okay, make it happen."

"Got it. See you shortly."

Traffic had picked up as he got closer to Dallas. He considered texting Addison to let her know he was coming home but decided against it. *No*, he thought. *Surprise her.*

"Yes, take something nice and surprise her," he said aloud.

He called his jeweler in Belhaven. "Something small," he said. "A token. A gesture."

"I'll have Ron pick it up," Monty added. "Text me when it's ready."

He hung up, then dictated a message to Ron:

Heading home in a few hours. Need pickup from Oscar's. Will text when ready for pickup.

Then another to his pilot:

Wheels up?

Several minutes later, the pilot replied:

Short delay — aircraft maintenance check.

Monty cursed under his breath.

Is it major?

After a pause, the reply came:

To be 100 percent safe, I'll text in an hour.

Well past lunch, Monty decided to pack his things, check out, and have a late meal. It would be evening by the time he landed in Belhaven. He figured he'd call Addison once he got to Corporate Aviation at DFW.

In all his planning, he didn't notice that Perry still hadn't returned a single message.

⁎⁎⁎

Perry landed at Suffolk County Executive Airport, the next county west of Kellum. From there, it was a twenty-minute drive to Russell's condo on the river, just south of Belhaven's financial district.

Calling in a favor from his cousin—a man with a history of poor judgment involving a girlfriend and the law—Perry had arranged the details discreetly. He'd kept the secret from the cousin's wife and the rest of the family. The cousin rented an Embraer Phenom 100 for the two-hour flight from Dallas Executive Airport to Suffolk Executive and made sure a car was waiting upon arrival.

Using his phone for navigation, Perry followed the quiet route into Belhaven and parked on the street instead of in the building's garage. *No cameras,* he reminded himself. Pulling a trucker's cap low on his forehead, he entered through the side street entrance and pressed the call box for Russell's unit.

Russell's voice, bright and eager, came through the speaker. "Come on up!"

Perry avoided looking into the lobby camera as the door buzzed open. When he reached the unit, the door was already ajar.

Russell stood waiting in a red silk robe, holding two glasses of wine.

"Don't move," Perry said softly as he closed the door behind him. "Let me look at you—I want to take it all in."

"Oh, baby, look who's happy to see you," Russell purred, glancing down at the swelling under his robe.

He handed Perry a glass and took a gulp from his own. Perry accepted it but set it on the counter untouched.

"Aren't you drinking, my love?"

"Yes," Perry said easily, "just let me wash my hands first. Where's the bathroom?"

"Right through there," Russell said with a grin. "But you might as well stay in there—I want some of you before we eat."

Perry leaned in for a slow, deep kiss, then slipped into the bathroom. When he came out, he'd removed his polo and shoes, folding them neatly on the valet stand in the bedroom corner.

"I've missed you," he said, unfastening his trousers. "I'm done with self-preservation. I want you."

Russell drained his glass. Moments later, the two men were tangled together in the sheets. Perry checked his watch before removing it and setting it aside.

What followed was raw, urgent, and unrestrained. As Russell basked in the intensity, Perry encouraged him to drink more—refilling his glass, topping it off again, each time pouring a little heavier.

When the bottle was nearly empty, Perry got up, retrieved it, and quietly opened his small duffel. From it, he took a tiny vial, tapping fine white powder into the remaining wine. He swirled the bottle until the powder dissolved.

Returning to the bed, where Russell now lay flushed and drowsy, Perry poured two glasses and handed one to him.

"To us," Perry said. "To the love I discovered on a yacht."

Russell sat up, clinked glasses, and took several gulps, never noticing Perry hadn't taken a sip.

Perry refilled his glass, and Russell raised another toast, words slurring.

"To the man who rescued me from a hopeless dream—for someone unattainable. I love you, Perry Marchand. Thank you for loving me."

He swallowed more wine, his speech nearly gone.

"I'll take a quick rinse before we eat," Perry said smoothly, stepping into the bathroom.

"Sure, babe… I'll heat the food. Chinese… it's good…" Russell mumbled, his head nodding.

"Yes, lover. Anything you chose is fine by me."

Before Perry finished the sentence, Russell was out cold—sprawled across the bed, naked, breathing heavy. The mix of wine and sedative had done its job.

Perry collected the glasses, washed them thoroughly with hot soapy water, and set them upside down to dry. He poured the remaining wine down the drain, shoved the cork back into the bottle, and tucked it into his duffel.

Back in the bedroom, Russell hadn't stirred. Perry showered quickly, leaving the hot water running after he stepped out.

In the closet, he dressed in Russell's clothes: jeans, a "Cowboy Carnival" T-shirt with a bull-rider graphic, a ball cap, and a black zip hoodie. From the mirror, Russell stared back at him.

He checked his watch. *4:15*.

Back in the kitchen, the glasses were dry. He placed them neatly among their matching set, left the bagged Chinese takeout on the counter, and made a final sweep of the condo.

From his duffel, he removed a large ziplock bag, carried it to the closet, and pulled out a crisp white dress shirt—one embroidered *ML* on the cuff. Hanging it prominently among Russell's dress shirts, he turned the initials outward.

One last detail—the condoms. He gathered them from the nightstand, sealed them in the bag, and zipped it into his duffel.

He glanced at his watch again. *4:21.*

Everything was in place.

Perry used the coat sleeve of his hoodie to pull Russell's condo door shut behind him, careful not to leave prints. He moved quickly down the hall toward the stairs—no cameras, no eyes. In the lobby, he paused, peeking around the corner to make sure it was empty before slipping out into the late afternoon air. His car was parked a half block away. Once inside, he checked his watch. *4:26.*

Traffic was light as he merged onto the main road, humming softly to himself. Everything was unfolding exactly as planned.

⁂

Addison decided on something simple—jeans, flats, and a striped shirt with a wool blazer. *Should I bring an overnight bag?* she wondered. She packed a small duffel just in case and left it in the back of the SUV. Thoughts circled: *Would the furnishings still be there? What would he say?* Mostly, she felt a rush of excitement. *He's a separated man now, and I'm single. Maybe this time, we get it right.*

The familiar scent of her Jo Malone Wood Sage & Sea Salt perfume filled the air, luring the dogs into the room, noses twitching as they investigated. Scout sniffed her shoes, gave a short howl, and was quickly joined by Klaus and Margo, who were all over her jeans and feet.

"Look, guys, a girl's got to have a social life. It can't be all about you," she teased, ruffling their heads.

As she walked from the closet into the bedroom, they followed in a tight pack. When she reached the kitchen, Margo stopped in front of the counter, staring pointedly at the dog-faced cookie jar. Klaus joined her, tail wagging. Scout, as usual, stuck to Addison's side.

"Look, Scout, how about a treat before I go?"

She slid the cookie jar toward the counter's edge to get his attention, pulled out three biscuits, and handed one to each dog. They trotted off to their pillows to chew happily—her perfect window for a clean getaway.

She grabbed her purse, slipped through the garage door, and got into the Benz. Backing out, she checked the dashboard clock. *4:20.*

Normally, it would be a quick drive, but an accident on the expressway slowed traffic to a crawl. She considered calling to say she'd be late but decided against it when traffic began to clear. Once past the wreck, the lanes opened, and she made up lost time.

By the time she exited, the digital clock read *4:57.*

Zipping through the quiet neighborhood, trying not to speed, she turned into the familiar alley behind the townhouse. Her heart thumped. *Why am I nervous?* she thought, pressing her palms against the steering wheel.

The garage door was open—but the bay was empty. Odd.

She parked to one side, thinking maybe he'd stepped out for something. Getting out, she wiped her palms on her jeans and checked her watch. *5:04.*

Monty had finished his early dinner and decided not to wait for his pilot's update—it had been nearly two hours since their last call. The bellman loaded his luggage into an SUV with a new driver.

"Corporate Aviation at DFW?" Monty asked as he got in.

"Yes, sir," the driver replied.

Moments later, Monty's phone rang—Andy, his pilot.

"We're set," Andy said. "It was a small issue, but you know me—I don't taxi unless it's perfect. We'll be ready to roll as soon as you arrive."

"I'm on my way. Hold on."

Monty leaned forward. "How long to Corporate Aviation?"

The driver checked the mirror. "Fifteen minutes, sir. Traffic's light."

Back on the phone: "Andy, I'll be there in ten. Be ready."

"Got it."

Monty glanced at his watch—*4:18.* Time to call Addison. It would be after eight by the time he landed in Belhaven. He'd already texted Ron to hold the jewelry pickup until they met. Still no word from Perry. *Something must have come up in San Francisco,* he reasoned, though it nagged at him that Perry hadn't checked in.

As the SUV turned through the airport gate, he dialed Addison's number. Voicemail. Tried again. Straight to voicemail.

"What the—" he muttered as Andy opened the door.

Monty climbed out, handed off his briefcase and leather envelope to one of the crew, and started up the steps. "What's the runway wait?" he asked.

"Three minutes tops," Andy replied.

"No, hold on. I need to make a call first."

Standing in the doorway of the jet, the engines from nearby runways roaring in the distance, Monty tried Addison again —twice. Straight to voicemail. He scrolled his contacts and found *Darnell Jefferson (DJ)*.

"DJ," he said when the call connected.

"Yeah, Monty—sorry, it went to voicemail before I could grab it. What's up?"

"I've been trying to reach Addison for twenty minutes. Straight to voicemail. Is she okay?"

"I thought she was with you."

"With me? DJ, I'm still in Dallas. About to take off for Belhaven. I wanted to surprise her. Why would you think she's with me?"

"Hold on," DJ said. Monty heard shuffling and muffled voices. Then static.

"DJ?"

"Yeah. According to Celeste, she got flowers with a note saying to meet you at the townhouse at five."

"What?"

"Yeah. Celeste says she left about an hour ago."

"DJ, what the hell is going on? Why would someone—"

"Monty, board your jet. I'll look into it right now."

"I'll call you as soon as I land."

Monty hung up, relayed the situation to Andy, and took his seat. The co-pilot sealed the cabin door. The ground crew waved them forward as Andy radioed the tower.

Monty stared out the window, heart pounding. His thoughts blurred with fear and disbelief.

What could be happening?

And somewhere in the back of his mind, he felt the cold, familiar echo of another night—Ellen.

The light over the range was illuminated. There was another light in the distance—not very bright—but Addison ventured into the townhouse. As she entered the great room, a light turned on.

"Hello, Lady A. Welcome. I thought you were going to stand me up," Perry said in a calm monotone.

"Perry?"

"Have a seat. Give me your phone."

"My phone? Why would I give you my—"

Perry pulled out a .32-caliber revolver. "Your phone, Addie!"

Addison took her phone out of its case and handed it to Perry, noticing he was wearing black cloth gloves. His hoodie was unzipped, showing some obscure print in rainbow colors.

"Perry, what the fuck—"

Perry interrupted her. "Don't get in a tizzy. I'll give you all the information you'll need before you leave this—"

Addison cut him off. "What are you even doing here? I'm here to meet Monty!"

"Yes, I know, princess. I sent the flowers and the note."

"You?"

"Yes, me. And if you would sit the fuck down and shut the fuck up and stop interrupting me!"

His raised voice—and the way he motioned with the gun— got Addison's attention. She stepped over to the chair and sat, arms crossed in front of her, defiant. She studied him now. He seemed too calm. *Dare I think manic?* She was trying to figure out how to get to her phone—or dash out of the room, maybe knock over the lamp. *Did I close the kitchen door to the garage? That could be—*

Perry interrupted her thoughts. "Don't think you're leaving this townhouse the way you walked in, princess. I've planned this. And I have to tell you, I'm very good at planning. People see me as some poor guy—no wife, always in the background. But once I get away with this one, too, I'll have my prize."

"For the sake of conversation, Perry, what are we talking about?" she said, calmer now, watching him closely.

He smiled at her, holding the gun with both hands. "What are we talking about? Princess, you know I've called you that for a very long time. I practiced in the mirror, just how I would tell you my story."

"Okay, Perry. Tell me your story. I'm here. I'm a captive audience—tell me everything."

His face twisted. "Hmm, princess, I'm not sure you can handle everything."

Addison took a deep sigh, feigning impatience. "It's your show, Perry. Give it all to me. But before you do, I have a question—if I'm allowed one."

"Yes, princess. I'll give you one. What's your question?"

"Whose clothes are you wearing? Clearly they're a bit too small."

Perry gave a laugh. Once he started, it became a deep, uncontrollable belly laugh. Addison sat still, arms folded, trying to figure out how to divert him. He finally stopped.

"One thing I've always given you credit for—you're smart, princess. But not smart enough."

"So, no on answering my question?" she asked.

"Of course I'll answer, but I'll answer when I get to it—in my story."

"Perry, is this some kind of game?" she asked, starting to rise from the chair.

"Sit down, Addison!"

"Perry—"

"Sit! I mean it!"

She sat back but didn't cross her arms this time.

"Addison, I've wanted him... well, it seems like forever now. I almost had him, then he met Ellen—fell head over heels in love with her. I couldn't stand the thought of him in bed with her every night. It became physically unbearable for me. Then that little redhead shit started buzzing around like a honey-starved bee."

"Russell? Are you talking about Russell? What does Ellen —"

"I'm speaking. Let me talk, Addison. Use your therapy voice."

"Oh, I see. You're using me for therapy. Okay, I'll be quiet. Continue, Perry. Let it release—you'll feel better."

"Thank you, I will." He rolled his eyes at her like a twelve-year-old.

She saw the beads of perspiration forming on his forehead but stayed silent as he continued.

"Don't you remember the story, Addie? I told you the whole thing—well, some of it. Ellen was not going to have him. He knew me first. We were getting very close—close to me showing him how I felt. Then boom—it was all he could talk about: Ellen. So I got rid of her, just like I told you. I have the souvenirs to prove it. Well, minus one now."

Addison, now nervous, remembered him telling her the story. "You didn't tell me you were the one who got rid of her. You left that part out."

"Yes, I did. I wasn't sure if you were going to get in my way, too. Ol' Barbara Ann took herself out of the game—lucky her. She would've been my third obstacle," Perry said, his tone calm but confident now.

"Third? Who's the second? Monty's only had two wives, Perry. Are you counting me?"

"Well, yes, princess—but you're four. There was a mishap between the first and second."

"Aww, a mishap," she repeated, trying to egg him on.

"Well, you see, I was so distraught when he shut himself off from everyone after Ellen was out of the picture—"

"You mean murdered Ellen, don't you, Perry?"

"Now, princess, it's not like you to be rude. So I'll just rip the old band-aid off, since you're being mean."

"Let her rip, Perry!"

He paused and smiled at her. She could only stare back, realizing the depth of his psychosis.

Taking a deep breath, Perry blurted out, "I had no choice. Believe me when I tell you—it almost broke my soul. I had no choice."

"Yes, I believe you, Perry. No choice."

"I loved him like a brother. We were so close growing up."

"Who—"

"I was the driver of the cab that hit and killed Thayer."

For a long pause, the room was silent. Addison was processing what she had just heard.

"I made the awful mistake of confiding in him about what I'd done to Ellen. He loved you so much, I just knew he'd understand. He got so angry that day I told him. He threatened to go to the police—to tell them about me. I couldn't let him do that, Addison. I just couldn't. I would lose Montaque forever if I went to jail."

"Lose him?" she yelled.

Perry continued. "He told me that day I had until the next morning to turn myself in. He didn't care if I did it in Illinois or New York. I had to—or he would. Then, as an afterthought, he offered to go with me. Well, I was just outdone by my childhood friend. Some kind of friend he was. So I stole a cab from the maintenance shop, waited for him to leave the building, followed a couple of blocks, and when he crossed the street... I did what I needed to do to keep me safe. As anyone would."

Addison sat there, trying not to hear, but hanging onto every word—remembering the waiter, the phone call, the waiting room, the words: *he was gone.* Tears streamed uncontrollably as her hands gripped the sides of the chair. She was in shock all over again. The hit-and-run driver—Thayer's best friend—was sitting in front of her. She wanted to lunge at him, but she sat frozen in time.

"I didn't want to, Addison. I really didn't. I had no choice. Then he met Barbara Ann. I was even sadder because I'd lost my best friend."

She could say nothing; her words were trapped. All she could manage was a glare of pure contempt.

"Now I have another chance to make Montaque a happy man. No more bitches. And to answer your question, princess—these are Russell's clothes. Russell's gun. He's going to take the fall, and I'll be the only one left to help Montaque with his grief and disbelief. You know—your death, and Russell being convicted of murdering you. Isn't that great planning?"

A noise made Perry glance beyond Addison. Seeing him distracted, she began to rise.

A neighbor out walking his corgis was passing by the Langfords' door when two loud bangs rang out. He ducked and ran for cover. Two other neighbors across the street stopped, crouched behind a parked car. All three pulled out their phones and dialed 911.

6:42.

△ ▽ ▽ △

EPILOGUE

Buried on page four, below the fold, in the *Belhaven Journal*, was a five-to-six-inch article about the gunshots in the upscale townhouse neighborhood just outside the financial district. Neighbors described hearing two gunshots. No comment was given by police, who were present shortly after the shots were reported. One neighbor, who asked to remain anonymous, said two ambulances and several squad cars arrived. Another, also requesting anonymity, said the house's residents had moved several weeks earlier and thought it to be empty. Further inquiry into city records indicated the townhouse was owned by an LLC located in Millbrook, New York.

The Belhaven PD wrapped its investigation two weeks after the incident. Detective Archibald Greene, a ten-year veteran and former Army Ranger (retired), was cleared of any wrongdoing in discharging his backup weapon while off duty. Detective Greene had come to the scene when a former Ranger and friend called to ask him to check on a possible situation at the townhouse. Entering through the rear—finding an open garage and interior door—he heard the confession of Mr. Caldwell Perry Marchand of Dallas, Texas. The detective was able to record the confession on his cell phone while observing what was clearly a hostage situation.

As reported by Detective Greene, a gust of wind caused the kitchen door to close, prompting the hostage, Ms. Addison Hollace, to attempt to run—being shot by Mr. Marchand, who was then fatally shot by Detective Greene. The subsequent investigation revealed the drugging of Mr. Russell Tierney by Marchand, an attempt to frame him for the attempted murder of Ms. Hollace. Further investigation, based on the recorded confession, cleared two other murders: one in Illinois, twelve miles north of Chicago near the campus of Northwestern University (a fatal stabbing), and another in Manhattan, New York (a hit-and-run)—both committed by the deceased Marchand.

Addison returned home from the hospital three days after surgery to remove the bullet from her left arm. Her arm remained in a sling, and a butterfly bandage covered her forehead from her fall after being shot—a flesh wound and a mild concussion, the doctor told DJ, Celeste, and Monty, who had paced frantically during emergency surgery.

"She'll be fine. She's still heavily sedated. Keep the visits to a minimum. We'll let her go home in a couple of days," the surgeon advised.

The weather forecast carried severe snow-storm warnings for all of Kellum County and surrounding areas. Detective Greene had just left after giving Addison, DJ, and Celeste the news that the investigation had been concluded and closed. Addison's arm was still in a sling, the scar on her forehead healing.

Get-well floral arrangements were scattered throughout the living room—and one special arrangement on the kitchen counter, which had arrived with a familiar box from a jeweler in Atlanta. Inside was a pendant of two brilliant diamonds resembling asterisks. A note attached to the bag read:

A symbol of our fresh start.
M

She had Celeste put it on her. Two weeks later, she was still wearing it when Monty came to visit.

DJ showed him in, calling the dogs to go with him to meet some new friends. Addison looked quizzically at them both.

"I'll let Monty explain," said DJ, ushering the dogs out back.

Monty was speechless seeing her. He'd wanted to get all the business in Dallas under control before walking back into her life—knowing that once he did, he wouldn't want to leave. She sat, legs crossed, her eyes searching his. He finally sat on the sofa—a pillow apart. More silence.

"Thank you for the necklace. I think a fresh start would be wonderful."

The words touched him—her saying it first. He reached out, laid his hand on hers. She intertwined her fingers with his. They spoke quietly about grief, about learning their spouses' fates at the hands of someone they had both once considered a friend. It seemed to bond them.

The commotion from out back shifted the moment. Monty's new wards—two Labrador retrievers, brothers who had belonged to his recently deceased security manager—were making themselves known. Monty had adopted them. He'd moved into the house he had purchased sight unseen during the yacht trip. They were good company and helped him move on from all that had happened.

"Dogs have a way of soothing the soul. They're beautiful, Monty," she said, standing at the door overlooking the backyard.

He stood, walked beside her. She leaned against him. He put his arm around her waist.

Still looking out the window, Monty said softly, "I fell in love with you the first day I saw you. I didn't realize how much until I saw you lying in that hospital bed."

She looked up at him. He gently kissed her.

"When you're better, we're going to have a proper date," he said.

The barking was loud enough to pull their attention. The five dogs gathered at the door, wondering why it hadn't been opened. Addison opened it, and they rushed in.

"Ahhh, I think we have a circus. These guys are hitting it off, and we're gonna be outnumbered," she laughed.

"Alright, boys, it's time to go. We've got errands to run before the big storm."

"We'll walk you out," Addison said.

She grabbed the throw blanket from the chair, struggling to wrap it around her immobilized arm. Monty helped her drape it over her shoulders as they walked out the front door.

The air was heavy, the sky gray.

He walked to the wagon and let the dogs climb in. By the time he came back toward her, Scout had taken his position on her flank, Margo stood next to Scout, and Klaus stood on Addison's other side.

"Am I allowed to hug you?" he asked.

"Yes. They're still feeling the vibe of my injury."

He stepped closer, tugged the blanket tighter around her, drawing her nearer.

"I will never leave you. I am exclusively yours. Forever," he said.

"Yes. That's what I want, Monty. Just us—and the circus."

He gently kissed her again, then returned to the wagon, rolling the window down for the dogs. Backing out of the driveway, he looked over; she stood watching him drive off.

Standing there, the first flakes began to fall.

"All right, guys," she said, smiling faintly. "Let's get inside and batten down the hatches. We're in for a lot of snow."

**